NIGHT GATE

Also by
Isobelle Carmody

THE OBERNEWTYN CHRONICLES

Obernewtyn

The Farseekers

Ashling

The Keeping Place

Book One

THE GATEWAY TRILOGY

NIGHT GATE

ISOBELLE CARMODY

RANDOM HOUSE 🏠 NEW YORK

www.randomhouse.com/kids
www.randomhouse.com/teens

Library of Congress Cataloging-in-Publication Data
Carmody, Isobelle.
Night gate / Isobelle Carmody. — 1st U.S. ed.
p.   cm. — (The gateway trilogy ; bk. 1)
SUMMARY: Seeking a cure for her sick mother, Courage "Rage" Winnoway
and her dogs pass through a magical gateway to a strange land known as Valley
where they must find, before the sand in an enchanted hourglass runs out, the
powerful wizard noted for his healing magic.
ISBN 0-375-83016-2 (trade) — ISBN 0-375-93016-7 (lib. bdg.) —
ISBN 0-375-83017-0 (pbk.)
[1. Magic—Fiction.   2. Wizards—Fiction.
3. Mothers and daughters—Fiction.   4. Dogs—Fiction.   5. Fantasy.]
I. Title.   II. Series: Carmody, Isobelle. Gateway trilogy ; bk. 1.
PZ7.C2176Ni 2005   [Fic]—dc22   2004006453

Printed in the United States of America
10 9 8 7 6 5 4 3 2 1

*This book is for my mother,
because all children, out of love,
try to save their mothers.*

If human lives be,
for their very brevity, sweet,
then beast lives are sweeter still. . . .

1

Rage Winnoway sat under the big, untidy shrub that grew beneath the window of the next-door neighbor's kitchen. Mr. Walker was curled on her lap, asleep, and Bear lay alongside her. From time to time Rage caught sight of Elle and Billy through the leaves as they romped together. The shrub was a round shape, with gaps where she could hide. Sometimes she pretended that it was a giant tree in the depths of a dark, greenish forest filled with wet, mossy smells. She imagined the whisper of raindrops falling around her, blotting out the babble of thoughts in her mind.

Today, however, she did not imagine rain. Instead, Rage felt so tense and heavy that a storm might have been gathering in the sky overhead, all boiling gray and churning purple fury.

Bear gave a snuffling sigh, lifted her misshapen head, and rested the weight of it on Rage's leg. The huge, loose mouth and pushed-in nose gave the old dog a ferociously ugly appearance, but to Rage she always looked wise and sad, as if she knew too much.

Elle pushed the branches aside and dropped a soggy

1

green tennis ball at Rage's feet. Rage reached over Bear to pat the bull terrier. "Poor wooden dog. You don't think enough about anything to be sad, do you?" That was what her mother had called the sleek tan-and-white dog when she brought her home from the pound: the wooden dog. Elle was so stiff-legged that it seemed she must be made of wood. Sometimes Rage wondered if Elle's head were made of wood, too. She was terribly brave but not very smart. Most people were afraid of her because bull terriers had been bred to fight one another in pits while men watched and made bets on the winner. Mam always said the men who trained the dogs to fight were the real beasts.

Rage threw the ball and watched Elle hurtle after it. There was nothing vicious in her nature, despite her long, sharp teeth and hoarse cough of a bark. She wasn't even the boss of the dogs. Bear was. For all Mr. Walker's yapping and nipping, Bear had only to look his way to silence him.

On summer nights Rage and her mother often sat on the back step and watched the dogs, the way other people watched television. They didn't have a television set. Mam said it was chewing gum for the eyes. She wasn't like other mothers. She was much younger than most of them and, being very small, looked even younger. Her black hair was short and spiky like a schoolboy's. She never used makeup, wore her own homemade perfume, and only dressed in black, moss green, and purplish crimson. People seeing Rage and her mam together couldn't believe they were mother and daughter. "Night and day," Mam always laughed, and told people that Rage took after her grandmother Reny, who had also been a cream-skinned blonde. The only thing Rage and Mam had in common was their amber eyes. Mam said all the Winnoways had eyes that color, even Grandmother Reny, because she had been a distant cousin to Grandfather. Not that anyone saw Mam's eyes much, since she always wore dark glasses.

Rage thought of her mother lying still in a hospital bed, her soul hidden behind her closed eyes all these weeks. But it was only an imaginary picture. Everyone agreed it was better that she didn't see Mam.

Water gurgled down the pipe behind the shrub, which meant the tap at the kitchen sink had been turned on.

At the same instant, down at the far end of the yard, Rage saw a flash of color—orange and molten red, like the embers that glow underneath burning wood in a campfire. Rage squinted and saw it again, this time in the orchard, flying over the ground. Not fire after all, but some kind of animal. Maybe a fox?

Now it was streaking up the side of a tree. A cat?

Mr. Walker woke as Rage leaned forward to see better, and gave a suspicious growl. That was enough to set Elle off. She abandoned the ball and began barking wildly, racing down to the end of the yard. Above Rage the kitchen window slid open with a protesting rasp.

"Now you quiet down, you dogs," Mrs. Johnson cried in a tremulous voice. "I can't hear myself think in all that noise!"

Elle was earnestly sniffing the wind, lifting her head up high to catch hold of any smells that might try to slip by her. She turned toward the orchard, shivering with excitement. Mrs. Johnson's goat had scaled the brick wall and was trying to reach the upper branches of a fruit tree. Elle put her front paws up on the wall and barked at the goat.

"Oh, those dogs," Mrs. Johnson sighed through the window.

Rage patted the tan Chihuahua in her lap until Mr. Walker settled back to sleep, tucking his little dark snout under his feathery tail.

"You're too old for all of this, Rose," said a younger, sharper voice.

Rage grimaced. It was Mrs. Somersby from the town. Mrs. Busybody, Rage's mother called her.

"We're neighbors," Mrs. Johnson was saying.

Mrs. Somersby made a snorting noise. "Where is the girl now?"

"Out somewhere by herself, sitting and brooding, I suppose," Mrs. Johnson answered with another sigh. "She's been like this ever since the accident, poor little mite."

"You mustn't indulge her. Youngsters should not be allowed to wallow."

"Surely it's natural for her to be upset," Mrs. Johnson said reproachfully.

"That girl is slow. I always said so."

"Not slow . . ."

"But what else can you expect, with the upbringing she's had? A flighty, irresponsible mother and no father to speak of."

"A lot of children have only one parent. I read in a newspaper article that it's far better to be the child of one good single parent than of two parents who hate one another."

"What a child needs is a strong parent. You can

hardly call Mary Winnoway that. Look at the way she ran off when she was just fifteen and came crawling back with a child."

"Hardly crawling. She came back to nurse her sick father, which is a credit to her, given what he was like. If you ask me, Mary ran away as much to find her brother as to escape her father."

"Well, she found *someone*," Mrs. Somersby said nastily. "A girl has no business running away like that. It's different for boys. And what did she have to run away from, anyway? A bit of discipline never hurt anyone. It wasn't as though her father hit her."

"He did worse than hit. He crushed her and everyone around him, though I don't like to speak ill of the dead. I knew Mary's mother when she was a girl, and she was like a bright little bird. Adam Winnoway married her, and she lived in his shadow for the rest of her short life. I always feel as though she faded rather than died. After I married my Henry I came to live here, and I just watched her get paler and quieter every year."

Rage shivered. She had no memory of Grandmother Reny, who had died before she was born, but it was a cold thing to imagine a person fading like a blot of disappearing ink.

"Fanciful rubbish!" Mrs. Somersby snapped. "Reny Winnoway was weak-minded, and so were her children. Rage is the same. She has no idea how to fit in with people. Do you know that she has no friends at school? Not a single one!"

I do have friends, Rage thought. *I have old Bear and Elle and Mr. Walker. I have Billy Thunder. It's not friends I want. It's Mam.* Her eyes filled with tears.

"She's right, Rose." Mr. Johnson's crackly voice broke

in. "All she has are those damn dogs. Four of them, for heaven's sake. It's ridiculous. It was mad, bringing home abandoned strays the way she did. They could turn on you at any time."

"Now Henry, you know those dogs are as sweet as pie with Rage."

"That mean old dog of her granddaddy's growls at me every time I walk in my own yard!"

"I don't suppose the poor thing had much kindness in its life, with him keeping it chained from daylight till dark. Besides, Bear's old, and that makes some folk mighty cranky," Mrs. Johnson said pointedly. "There's no harm in the dog except for someone who would hurt Rage. All of them are devoted to her, especially that pup of Bear's. That Billy Thunder."

When Mrs. Somersby spoke again, her voice was sulky. "All I'm saying is that the child might just as well be told that her mother is unlikely to wake up and come home. Knowing a hard truth is better than bearing false hope."

"Where there is life, there is hope," Mrs. Johnson said firmly.

"My sister's a nurse at the hospital. She said Mary Winnoway will die if she doesn't snap out of this state and exert some will to heal."

Snap, Rage thought, turning the word around in her mind and feeling sick with dreaminess. *Snap, crackle, and pop.*

"We've done our neighborly best," Mr. Johnson said piously.

Rage looked down the yard to where Elle and Billy Thunder were playing. They were barking, but the wind was carrying the noise away from the house now. It was like watching the television with the sound turned down.

"They'll have to go, of course," Mrs. Somersby said.

"It will break her heart," Mrs. Johnson sighed.

"If you ask me, we might as well get rid of them right now and be done with it," Mr. Johnson said briskly.

"Maybe we could advertise them in the paper, but I don't know what good it will do. Someone might take the little dog, and maybe even Billy. For all his size, he's not much more than a pup, and I never saw a sweeter-natured animal in all my born days. But I don't know about Bear or Elle. Bear's too bad-tempered for anyone to want, and Elle is so strong and so aggressively friendly."

"If the police find that brother of Mary's, he can take them," Mr. Johnson said.

Rage took a deep, shaking breath. What she had overheard told her what she had already sensed. If they were talking about getting rid of the dogs, time must be running out for her mother. Rage was sure Mam would get better, if only she could find a way to see her. But when she had asked, her words had been brushed aside as if they were a bit of spilled flour.

Don't ask, whispered an urgent little voice into Rage's ear. *Just go.*

Rage shook her head automatically. She couldn't just sneak away without telling anyone and make her way alone through the hills to the hospital in Hopeton. It would take days, and she'd certainly be caught before she got there. She would get into terrible strife. Mam always said to make sure she didn't cause anyone any trouble.

But she can't say anything, the little voice urged. *She needs you.*

The thought that her mother could need her scared Rage—that was not how it was supposed to be. But she could not get the urgent voice out of her mind. *She needs you.* A picture of Mam smiling flashed into her mind, and something in Rage's chest twisted hard and seemed to tear free.

She gave a gasp and suddenly felt half suffocated by the shrub, the dogs, the voices inside and outside of her. She pushed Mr. Walker to make him get up and crawled out from under the branches.

Rage found herself heading for the gate in the fence that led to Winnoway Farm. Mr. Walker ran down the yard to join the other dogs, but Bear followed Rage as she went into her own front yard and up the back step. Fortunately, the homesteads on both properties were close to the fence line that divided them, so it was a short walk. Her hands shook as she used the spare key under the mat to get inside, and they shook harder as she opened the hall cupboard to get her good long coat and her hiking shoes with the rippled soles. She dared not think about what she was doing. It was too frightening. Who would have thought that being bad would feel so dangerous?

Once she had changed, she went to her bedroom and took her mother's pink-gold locket out of her jewelry box. She hardly knew why, except Mam cherished it above everything they owned. It had been the last present given to her by her own mother.

Opening the locket, Rage gazed at the photographs inside. There was one of Grandmother Reny looking sweet and vague, and one of Uncle Samuel, taken not long before he had run away. He had been only a few years older than Rage was now. He had dark, unruly hair like Mam's and a wild, hurt look on his unsmiling face. Had he been thinking of leaving when the picture was taken? Everyone always said it was different for boys. Perhaps that was why Mam had come back to Winnoway, while Uncle Samuel had never returned. He had written a single letter to Mam, which she kept in her handbag.

Rage wondered if the precious letter had been burned up in the car crash or if it had been rescued along with the locket. Pushing the locket deep into her coat pocket for safety, she went out the front door and closed it quietly behind her.

"Maybe they'll let her keep one of the dogs, though how she'll choose which, I don't know." Mrs. Johnson's voice floated on the air as Rage and Bear walked down to where the other dogs were playing.

The dogs stopped when they saw her, wagging their tails and crowding at her, making themselves into a warm, furry barrier. She bit her lip hard. "I have to go and see Mam," she told them, but saying the words out loud made her feel as if she were too close to a high cliff edge.

She hesitated and thought about putting the locket back. Billy licked her hand and whined a little. Rage looked into his warm brown eyes and felt like crying. Worry for the dogs was mixed up with fear for Mam. If only there were someone to tell her what to do.

At that moment the goat stopped eating the fruit

tree and jumped down from the brick wall and into Mr. Johnson's backyard. Seeing the poor, bedraggled thing climb so easily over the barrier seemed like a sign to Rage. After all, she wouldn't be running away. She was just going to visit her mother in the hospital, and no one had actually forbidden it.

She pushed through the dogs to the gate, shooing them away. But when she slipped through, they surged past her as if they had been waiting for the chance to escape. Rage stared after them, horrified.

Opening her mouth to cry out, she realized that she couldn't, because then Mr. Johnson would come out and the moment for going would be lost. She closed her mouth and the gate, heart beating fast. The dogs would have to come with her. She did not know what she would do with them once they reached Hopeton, but the fact that she would not be making the journey alone lightened her heart.

They cut across the property alongside Winnoway Farm and kept away from the roads, because that was where the police would go when Mr. Johnson rang them. He would not call the police until he was certain she was gone, and it would take time for him to be certain. Maybe he would even wait until morning.

"We have to get as far as we can before that," Rage told the dogs.

She could see the water glimmering ahead and wondered if the reservoir behind the dam really was bottomless, the way some of the boys at school said. It was important to keep in sight of the shoreline, because it would bring her to the little gorge leading into the next valley. It would save hours of climbing, and it led to a track that cross-country skiers used in winter. That would take her all the way to the outskirts of Hopeton, and there were huts along the way where she could sleep.

The dead trees looked more and more like claws sticking up out of the flat water as the sun fell toward the horizon, and Rage walked faster, spurred by the thought of what the dam would look like at night, under the moon.

Rage had a sudden vivid memory of Grandfather Adam standing at the fence bordering Winnoway Farm and staring over at the dam with a blank expression that had frightened her with its emptiness. She knew the whole valley had once been Winnoway land. It had been divided between Grandfather Adam and Great-Uncle Peter when their father died.

"What happened to Great-Uncle Peter?" Rage had asked Mam once, imagining another cold, hard man like Grandfather. Mam had shrugged, saying he had left after the government forced him to sell his land for the dam project. Grandfather Adam had pleaded with his brother to use the government money to buy land in the next valley, but he had refused.

"Did Grandfather want him to stay?" Rage asked, surprised.

"I think he wanted him to stay very much," Mam had answered.

"Why did Great-Uncle Peter go, then?" Rage was old enough now to know that had been a bad question, because it reminded Mam of her brother running away.

"He had to do what was right for him," Mam had answered in a low, sad voice.

Remembering this, Rage decided that she did not

believe people should do what was right for themselves without thinking about what was right for other people as well. No doubt Uncle Samuel had left Winnoway because that was right for him, but his going had not been right for Mam.

Rage realized she must have missed the opening to the gorge because she was still climbing and she had long passed the end of the reservoir. Now she would have to go to the top of the ridge to get her bearings. It would be a hard climb, but she knew she would be able to see the bleary arc of light given off by Hopeton.

It was slow going over the uneven, brambly ground. Every time they came to a rusted barbed-wire fence left from the days when this was farmers' land, she propped open the strands with the stick she had picked up to smack at the grass and frighten snakes away. The darker it got, the harder it was to walk, and she kept tripping over blackberry runners.

She began to worry about what she was going to do with the dogs when she got to Hopeton. They would stay if she told them to wait just outside the town, but after a while they would come looking for her. It wasn't disobedience. It was just that their minds weren't made to hold orders for very long.

She felt like crying again. It was too much, having to worry about the dogs as well as about how she was going to find the hospital and convince the nurses to let her visit Mam. She knew from listening to Mr. and Mrs. Johnson talk that the nurses were very strict about visiting times and about how many people could visit. They were sure to make a fuss about Rage being there without an adult.

You must get in, Rage told herself fiercely. She found herself remembering the awful night when no one had come to pick her up from school. She had sat in the headmaster's office and listened to him phoning the police. From the way his shoulders hunched she knew that it was bad news.

She made herself concentrate on watching the dogs. No matter how bad she felt, that always made her feel better. Elle was rushing ahead and coming back every once in a while to walk a few steps beside her. Mr. Walker ran round and round her in circles, covering double the distance of the others. Billy Thunder trotted at her side, behind his mother. Mrs. Johnson was right about him being the sweetest dog that ever lived. Billy was pure honey and sunlight, which was a wonder when you thought how near he'd come to dying almost as soon as he was born.

He was the only one of the dogs born on Winnoway Farm. Mam had been amazed to discover that Bear was pregnant because Bear was so old. When her puppies were born too soon, Grandfather said they were too small to feed and ought to be drowned. He might even have done it if he hadn't been so ill by then. Mam called the vet, who said he could not come until the following evening and that they must milk Bear and feed the puppies all through the night. Mam only managed to get a small cup of milk from Bear.

"It is not enough for all of them," she said. "We have to choose one."

She stood looking at the five puppies for the longest time, until Rage knew that she could not bring herself to choose. But if a choice was not made, then all of the puppies would die. Sometimes Rage thought that was the worst moment in her life: looking at those puppies and knowing that she must choose, and that whichever puppy she chose meant choosing that the others would die. Billy had begun to wriggle then, and she had picked him up because she had thought he might be stronger than the others and have a better chance to survive.

They had carried him inside, leaving Bear nuzzling and worrying at the other puppies. Mam heated Bear's milk and watered it down, then she told Rage to put her finger into the mouth of the puppy so it would suck, and she would dribble the milk into its mouth with an eyedropper. Rage obeyed and was horrified to feel that the inside of its mouth was cold. She had not wanted to touch him after that because she thought death had already got into him, but Mam said death did not always win.

Billy had lasted the night, but the other puppies died. Bear had moved them out of the garage and under the house, and that was where they found her with the poor things in the morning. Mr. Johnson came and took the bodies away, but Bear kept scratching under the house as if she thought the ground had swallowed her puppies up. Then quite suddenly she seemed to realize that Billy was inside. She howled and sniffed at the door, but they couldn't give him to her because he was too small and sickly.

It took them a long time to make him well, and when they did let him outside as a gangling, floppy boy dog, Bear had sniffed at him with disinterest.

"Perhaps she doesn't know Billy is her son," Rage said.

But Grandfather had said Bear knew all right but that she didn't care. "Love can end," he had added malevolently.

Rage tripped over a furrow. Picking herself up, she was startled to notice how dark it had become while she was daydreaming.

Now that she and the dogs were all still, she could hear something rustling through the grass behind them. Fear poured through her veins, but Elle seemed not to scent whatever was making those soft noises. Rage told herself she must be imagining things. But still she could hear twigs snapping, the sound of creeping movements through the grass. A rabbit, then, or birds?

What sort of animal would creep after a human and four dogs? she wondered with a shiver. *Wouldn't a wild creature run away as fast as it could from such a strange procession?*

She remembered the dazzling flash of orange in the orchard and wondered if a cat or another dog was following them. But if so, why wasn't Elle barking?

A branch cracked as loudly as a gunshot, and she whirled, catching Elle by the collar.

It must be a person, Rage thought. Someone following and hoping she had money or something valuable to steal.

There was another rustle, and this time something big and white emerged from the dark tangle of foliage. Rage gave a little sobbing laugh of relief when she found herself looking into the strange, square-pupiled eyes of Mrs. Johnson's goat. It shook its curls and gave a loud, plaintive bleat. Of course none of the dogs had barked. They had recognized the strong smell of the goat's wool. Elle, who liked the goat especially, trotted over to it and snuffled at its long white ringlets.

It occurred to Rage that the goat could only have

followed them if the Johnsons' gate was open. Except she distinctly remembered closing it. Shutting gates was one of the important rules on Winnoway Farm. That meant someone else had opened it.

"Don't be silly," she told herself, fighting panic. "Why would anyone deliberately let the goat out?"

There was a snicker of sound somewhere behind her, and Elle leaped up, barking frantically.

"Elle!" Rage cried, but it was too late. The bull terrier had plunged away with Mr. Walker at her heels. Bear stayed by Rage, growling softly, while Billy sniffed the air in a puzzled sort of way.

Rage stood there stupidly, indecisive, until Billy gave an urgent bark.

Spurred by the thought that Elle and Mr. Walker would head back to the farm, Rage began to run and stumble after them, pushing brambles aside and ignoring the jagged thorns scratching and tearing at her bare skin.

It was full dark now, and Mrs. Johnson would have begun to worry. Bear and Billy trotted at her heels, the goat skittering along behind them, but the others were too far away to see. "Elle," Rage yelled. "Mr. Walker!"

Rage completely lost her sense of direction as the ground began to slope suddenly down into a fold where the undergrowth was even thicker and more tangled. She could hear Elle and Mr. Walker barking ahead, but it sounded as if they had stopped running. Maybe they had treed a cat or bailed up a fox in its hole. She was scratched to pieces, even through her jeans, when at last she broke through a wall of blackberry bushes and into a small clearing.

Right then the bright crescent moon that had risen

behind a cloud bank slid out into the open, bathing the world in a silvery light.

Rage stopped dead in astonishment. Right in front of her, looming far above her head, was a high, wild wall of brambles, and in the midst of the tangled branches was a perfect archway, like the gate in the hedge at home. Spiders had spun their webs, tying all of the leaves together with a silvery lace that glimmered in the moonlight, but not a single cobweb stretched across the opening.

2

Elle and Mr. Walker growled at the strange gate. The goat trotted up to stand behind them. Beside Rage, Billy Thunder whined. When she dropped a hand to his head, she found that he was trembling all over.

"What is it, Billy? What do you smell?" Rage asked, trying to understand who had created such a thing in the middle of the wilderness, and why. It was far too perfect to be an accident of nature.

Then came another of the snickering chitters. Elle began to bark again, inching closer to the bramble gate.

"Elle!" Rage said sharply. To her relief the bull terrier came to heel, Mr. Walker following. She ran her hand along Elle's back and found all the hair standing up on her spine, stiff as bristles on a toothbrush. What was it about the strange gate that had got the animals so upset?

Studying it, Rage saw that it offered a clear path out of the brambles. But why would someone make a gateway here? Nothing could be kept in or out by it.

"Who made you? I wonder," Rage murmured aloud.

"Wizard making bramble gate," answered a purring

voice out of nowhere. "Is enchanted gateway."

Rage froze in shock. "Who said that?" she whispered.

"Am being firecat, Ragewinnoway," the voice responded, soft and rough as a cat's tongue licking the evening air.

Rage's heart gave a nervous jump as she looked around, but she could see no one. "Wh . . . who is that?"

"Am firecat," the voice repeated.

Rage licked her lips. "How do you know my name?"

"Am knowing many things," the firecat responded, its voice beguiling, but with a hint of teeth in it. "Am knowing Ragewinnoway is thinking about sleeping mother."

Rage gasped in fright.

"Not hurting Ragewinnoway," the voice said hastily.

"What do you want?" Rage wondered if someone was using ventriloquism to play a nasty trick on her. Except who could know so much about her?

"Firecat helping Ragewinnoway wake mother," the voice said.

"I . . . I don't need any help," Rage quavered.

There was a hissing laugh. "Mother of Rage being far away . . . and even if finding her, daughter-calling not powerful enough for waking mother from such deep and dangerous sleeping. Ragewinnoway needs waking magic."

Even through her fear, the sneering words cut Rage. She had been a fool to think she could wake Mam when the doctors had failed.

"Come through bramble gate, Ragewinnoway," the voice invited. "Wizard will conjure waking magic."

"How do you know about Mam?" she asked, blinking hard to stop herself from crying.

The firecat ignored her question. "Ragewinnoway must forget being careful if wanting to save mother.

Must become Ragewinnoway whose name is Courage and enter bramble gate. All questions being answered on other side."

"I don't understand what you mean," Rage stammered. "My name isn't Courage. It's Rebecca Jane Winnoway. Rage for short."

"Naming something hidden can bringing it out of its hiding place. Firecat can smell boldness hidden in Rage Winnoway. Firecat smells that Rage Winnoway can become Courage Winnoway," the firecat said slyly. "If wanting to helping mother."

"Of course I want to help her," Rage said.

"Then coming through bramble gate," the firecat said eagerly. "Wizard helping."

Rage shivered and wondered if she could be dreaming. But when she pinched the inside of her wrist, she did not wake. "How do you know the wizard will help Mam?" she called out.

"Waking magic being payment for service to wizard," the voice said briskly.

"What service?"

"Wizard needing something delivered to him. Something small. Very, very small."

"Why don't you take it to him?" Rage called. There must be a microphone somewhere because she was sure no one was concealed in the brambles. The voice appeared to be coming from the bramble gate itself.

Again the speaker ignored her question. It said, "Come through, Ragewinnoway, before too late for sleeping mother."

"Who are you?" Rage called again. "What has this to do with you?"

There was no answer.

Rage stared through the bramble gate. Who would play such a trick on her, and why? And most of all, how?

She thought of Mam lying in the hospital bed, and a tear trickled down her cheek. She had left Winnoway Farm to help Mam. The slinky voice had made her see that she had behaved as if she were in a fairy story about a girl going to save her mother, with happily ever after waiting around the corner.

But what if it really was an enchanted gateway? "Oh, don't be such an idiot," Rage cried, dashing away the tear. Of course there were no such things as magic gates and powerful wizards. Any more than daughters who could save their mothers.

Rage drew closer to the gate, and the air fizzed against her skin. Startled, she looked down at her arms. All of the hair was sticking up. Rage told herself it was only static electricity. They had done experiments with torn-up bits of paper and combs in science class at school. She was determined to expose the trick. Entering the gateway, she found herself wishing that the animals were human so that she didn't have to face this alone.

But as she passed through the gateway, the air began to glow. A slit of darkness opened under her feet like a greedy mouth, and she screamed as she fell into it.

She fell and fell.

She was in the living room, a fire burning in the small, deep hearth. Mam was on the couch with her feet curled under her, reading a thick book. Rage was on the floor, making some plasticine dinner for her plasticine fairies. Grandfather Adam was in his chair, staring into the flames just as he always did. Outside, the wind whined and rattled the glass in its frame.

"Mam, could I have a sandwich?" Rage asked.

"The girl did not eat dinner when it was offered," Grandfather said, never taking his eyes from the flames. His words were like stones set in the center of the room. A fierce coldness came off them.

"We ate early tonight," Mam said.

"The girl is not to run wild under my roof," Grandfather answered. Then he began to cough. His whole body shook with the force of those coughs. Rage waited for them to shake him to pieces, but he closed his mouth and forced them back down his throat.

Then there was nothing but the sound of a heavy, raspy breathing full of sharp points and edges.

Rage woke to find herself lying on her back and staring up into the night sky. Only a few stars and a misty sliver of moon were visible. She sat up. There was no fire, no Grandfather (because, of course, he had died), no Mam (because she was in the hospital, lost in her dreams).

Rage's head hurt, and she guessed she had hit it. The last thing she remembered was running after the dogs in the darkness. Then there had been a dream about going through a magical gate. Fingering her head for the bump, she looked around. She was on a grassy slope hemmed on all sides by a dense forest. The faint moonlight made long shadows that striped a dark patch of brambles to one side of the clearing. There was no sign of a gateway, enchanted or otherwise.

"It was a dream after all," Rage said aloud. The animals were nowhere to be seen. Had she also dreamed of taking them away from Winnoway Farm? She heard something making its way through the trees toward her, and opened her mouth to call out. Then she closed it, because whatever was pushing its way through the trees was a whole lot bigger than any dog.

A huge, shaggy black bear pushed its way out into the open.

Rage froze. She had read that bears have weak eyesight, and she prayed it was true.

The trees rustled again, and a barefoot teenager with straight, toffee-colored hair stepped into the clearing. One lock of hair flopped untidily over his left eye. He brushed it aside with a dirty hand. His other hand rested on the bear's flank.

Rage almost laughed out loud. Seeing the bear, she had thought for one second that she really had gone through a magical gateway. But the bear must belong to a circus and the boy was its keeper. Before she could call out, the bushes rustled again and out stepped a man the height of a large cat. He looked quite human but for his size and two soft, furled elf ears sticking up out of his pale golden-colored hair, which perfectly matched a silky-looking tail.

"I can't find her," the little man told the boy.

Rage couldn't believe her eyes. "I must still be dreaming," she whispered.

"I suppose she'll smell her way to us." The boy sighed.

The bear creature gave a deep groan and sat back on its haunches in a weary way. Rage saw that it was not a bear after all. Or not exactly. It was the right size but the wrong shape. It was like a bearish dog, or a doggish bear. "I hurt!" it said huskily.

Rage gaped to hear it speak.

"I don't see what you have to complain about," the little man told it querulously. "You've hardly changed at all. Look at me! I'm completely misshapen. All my lovely fur is gone, my bones hurt, and my nose has shrunk."

"You don't *look* horrible," the boy said kindly.

"I think a person ought to be asked before they are changed," the little man said, casting an accusing sideways look at Rage.

She took a deep breath and made an effort to stop her mind from reeling. Dream or not, she had to say something. "Hello. I . . . I'm Rage Winnoway of Winnoway Farm."

The trio stared at her.

"Did you hear that?" the little man demanded of the other two in his sharp little voice. His ears twitched in agitation.

"She must have hit her head," the boy said. "A hit on the head can make you very confused. I remember once when a man threw a stone at me and I forgot my name for ages."

"Amnesia!" the little man said triumphantly, then he gave Rage a severe look. "Have you lost your memory?" he asked loudly, as if he thought loss of memory also caused deafness.

"I've not lost anything. I told you, I'm Rage Winnoway of Winnoway Farm," Rage said, thinking she might as well behave as if the dream were real until she managed to wake up. "What *is* this place?"

"You must know where we are. You brought us here!" the little creature said indignantly. "You even wished for us to be human."

"I . . . I what?" Rage asked faintly.

"She's not really to blame," the boy protested. "Not completely. After all, haven't we all wanted to be human from time to time? Haven't we secretly wished it? To be free? To be able to decide? To be masters of ourselves?"

"I never wished to be human," the bear creature said heavily. "I fought the gate magic and it hurt me."

A young woman with very short, sleek blond hair leaped into the clearing. She was dressed in a tan bodysuit belted at the waist and looked like one of the warrior women in Rage's book of legends. She stretched and then stared alertly about out of deep-set, almond-shaped brown eyes.

"We were looking for you," the boy said.

"I was trying out this shape," she answered, turning her beautiful eyes on him. "It's fast, and it's strong, and it's not stiff like my old shape was. Is there anything to eat?"

Rage shook her head, for this last question appeared to be aimed at her.

The young woman appeared momentarily downcast. "That won't do at all." She brightened. "Shall I go and look for some food?"

Rage nodded in bemusement at being asked such a question by an adult. The Amazon immediately sprinted away into the trees, and Rage wondered if the denizens of this place were as mad as the White Rabbit in *Alice in Wonderland*.

"You should not have let her go," the bear creature told Rage.

"It's only right she should have to find us something to eat," the little man declared. "She started all of this by running off without thinking, as usual."

"She couldn't help it," the boy protested. "It was the smell. It caught hold of her. You ran after it, too," he added. "It was so interesting! Sly and slinky. Almost a cat smell, I thought. But not quite."

"It smelled hot," the little man said, ears twitching back and forward. "But I could have resisted if Elle hadn't run off like that."

Rage's mouth fell open. *Elle?*

25

She looked incredulously at the odd collection of beings. Was it possible that they were the dogs—her dogs—transformed into these *creatures*? The big bear-dog could be Bear, and Billy Thunder might be the barefoot boy in jeans and a bomber jacket; Mr. Walker was the little man in hooded pajamas, and Elle was the Amazon. But how could they have been so changed?

The little man had accused her of wishing for them to be human, and it was true she had wished that just as she stepped through the gate, but she hadn't really meant it. Besides, they hadn't become humans. Bear actually looked more wild than she had on the other side of the bramble gate, though she claimed to have resisted the transformation. What if each of the animals had reacted to the magic according to their nature? Mr. Walker might have resisted out of characteristic stubbornness, whereas Billy had admitted wanting to be human sometimes, and maybe Elle felt that way also.

"Bear?" Rage called softly.

The huge animal turned sad, dark eyes on her, and Billy Thunder beamed. "There now. You've remembered Mama's name. Maybe you didn't hit your head very hard after all."

"Oh dear," Rage said faintly, and sat down. Surely everything must be a dream—running away from Winnoway Farm to help Mam, the firecat and the bramble gate and the transformation of the animals. It was a dream. It must be, except that she had never had a dream that felt so true.

"It's a shock," Billy said kindly. "But at least you are yourself. I kept falling until I learned how to balance on two legs. It's easy once you get the trick of it, though. You've been asleep for *hours*."

"Look who I've found," said Elle, coming out from the trees and leading a skinny, depressed-looking young man by the hand. Only he wasn't a man because he had goat legs. He was, Rage marveled, a faun, like Mr. Tumnus out of *The Lion, the Witch and the Wardrobe.* He even had two elegant horns.

Goaty, Rage thought, feeling dazed. He would have followed the dogs through the gate. He must have resisted the gate magic, too, just as he always resisted everything.

"Look what has happened to me," he bleated. "I have become a terrible monster." He shivered violently.

Billy took off his jacket. "You're not a monster," he said gently, helping Goaty into the coat. "You've just changed a bit. Now you're partly human."

"What on earth are you doing here, anyway?" the little man demanded. "No one invited you."

Mr. Walker, Rage reminded herself. *Mr. Walker, as always scolding and worrying at Goaty.*

The faun plaited his bony fingers. "I'm sure I don't know. It's a wonder I know anything at all. Sleep in a puddle and your brains leak out. Everyone knows that. I'm dreadfully wet!"

"You shouldn't have followed," Mr. Walker said. "She never intended for you to come. She shut you in."

"She did," Goaty agreed, giving Rage a reproachful look. "She left me behind, the way everyone always leaves me." His pale eyes widened, and he shuddered. "On this occasion I might not have minded. But then that thing came and undid the gate, and I couldn't help following. It's in my nature," he added apologetically.

"What thing?" Rage asked.

"The hot thing," he answered, glancing over his

shoulder nervously. "I couldn't see what it looked like exactly. It was very bright and shifty. In the end it flew spitting at me, and I ran from it in terror."

The Amazon grabbed his arm and began sniffing his sleeve vigorously. She snuffled right along his arm and up to his shoulder. Then she stuck her nose into his armpit, sniffed intently, and gasped. "That's it! That's the smell that made me run out the farm gate." She held Goaty's arm out to Rage, inviting her to smell it.

Rage shook her head, but Mr. Walker and Billy sniffed.

"The same smell," Billy Thunder confirmed solemnly.

"Exactly," Mr. Walker said. "But what does it mean?"

"It's obvious," Bear said heavily. "Whatever let Goaty out, whatever lured Elle after it, it wants us here for a reason."

"No doubt it means to eat us," Goaty said gloomily, chewing absentmindedly at the end of his pale ringlets. "It had very sharp-looking teeth."

Rage licked her lips. "I think it was the firecat," she said.

"The *what* cat?" Mr. Walker asked.

"A . . . a voice spoke to me before we came through the bramble gate," Rage explained. "It said it was the firecat, and it told me that the gateway was magical, and on the other side of it was a wizard who could give me magic to wake Mam, if only I did an errand for him."

"Why would a wizard need your help?" Mr. Walker asked.

It was a good question and one that Rage now wished she had asked the firecat. But she had thought that the voice belonged to someone playing a trick on her.

"What errand?" Billy asked.

"I have to deliver some small thing to the wizard," Rage answered. But she was remembering how quickly and lightly this had been said, as though the firecat had been pretending that something important was unimportant. She thought of the ring in *Lord of the Rings*. That could be called a small thing, but Frodo had almost died in delivering it to Mount Doom.

"What small thing?" Mr. Walker demanded.

"I . . . I didn't ask," Rage admitted.

Billy and Mr. Walker exchanged a look. Then Billy shrugged. "She had to come if there was a way to help her mother."

Mr. Walker scowled. "Who says that the firecat was telling the truth about the wizard being able to help her mother? I've heard of magic to make people sleep, but not to wake them up."

"It all happened so fast," Rage cried. "I was running after you, and then I saw the gateway, and the next minute there was this voice telling me that the only way to save Mam was to go through to the other side! I was upset about Mam, and I thought it was some kind of mean trick. I only went through to prove it wasn't a magical gateway."

"Except it was," Mr. Walker said severely. "You ought to have thought it through more carefully, just in case."

Rage had the urge to shout that she was too young to think properly about things, but that was stupid. The dogs seemed a lot more judgmental now that they could talk, especially Mr. Walker.

"Where is this wizard, then?" Billy asked gently, sensing she was upset, just as he had done when he was a dog.

"I . . . I don't know. But the firecat said it would answer all my questions if I came to this side of the gate," Rage said, though that wasn't exactly what the voice had said. "Probably it will come in the morning," she added quickly, to forestall another pointed question from Mr. Walker.

Billy said they might as well try to sleep while they waited.

"Nice sort of creature this firecat must be, luring us here and then forcing us to sleep in the middle of a forest like this," Mr. Walker grumbled as they sat under a big tree and settled themselves for sleep.

Rage sat stiffly with her back against a tree, and the others took up sleeping positions similar to their usual animal ones, only instead of Billy trying to lie across her legs, he lay down beside her. Mr. Walker curled into Rage's lap, and Elle flung herself on the ground beside them. Goaty sat beside Elle and shyly invited her to rest her head on his fleecy lap. Only Bear moved apart, preferring to sleep under another tree.

In a remarkably short time the animals were all asleep, snuffling and snorting. Rage tried to stay awake to think, but before long she drifted off as well.

She was traveling on a train, and suddenly Mam said they must go back to Winnoway.

"Your grandfather is sick and he needs us," Mam said, but it was she who looked sick.

"What is the matter with him?" Rage asked.

"He is sad," Mam answered. "That is a sickness, too."

He is sad and sad and sad, *the train wheels whispered.*

3

The next day Rage woke to Goaty's volcanic sneezes and to the realization that what had happened was real!

It was raining, though the drops were so fine as to be more of a thick mist. Rage's coat was clammy with it. Goaty sneezed again and declared that he had a cold, only he said "code" because of his blocked nose.

Shaking and squeezing the ends of her coat, Rage tried to remember everything the firecat had said to her, but a picture of Mam lying still and silent in a hospital bed kept getting in the way.

Elle did not trouble herself with thinking. She sprang out into the rain and vigorously rubbed the tan bodysuit, which Rage could now see was part of her, like hair or fur. She was less human than she had appeared last night, which meant that she *had* resisted the gate magic. Only Billy seemed to be completely human.

Bear came out from under her tree and looked up into the drab sky. She sighed heavily and dropped her head to lick at her paw. Rage felt guilty, as if somehow the rain were her fault on top of everything else. In the cold light of day, going through the enchanted gate seemed madder than ever. Mr. Walker was right. She ought to have known no one could play such a terrible and complicated joke. She should have thrown a stick through the gateway instead of going herself.

Then a happier thought occurred to her. If the gateway was enchanted, maybe there really was a wizard with waking magic. Rage made up her mind. If the firecat was right and the wizard wanted something brought to him, she would do it, no matter what it was, just so long as he agreed to help Mam. The trouble was, like Dorothy in *The Wizard of Oz*, she had to find the wizard before she could learn what he wanted her to bring him.

In the misty daylight, she could see a sort of path through the trees on the slope above them. "I think we should go up there and have a proper look around," she said, pointing.

"What about the firecat?" Mr. Walker muttered, but Rage pretended not to hear him.

"We'll ged wed and all die of code," Goaty said. It took a minute for Rage to figure out what he had said.

"It's not really cold," Billy told him cheerfully. "And walking will keep us warmer than sitting still."

"Exercise will do us good," Elle said heartily.

Mr. Walker gave Rage his soulful look, and she automatically picked him up, just as she had when he was a little butterfly-eared Chihuahua, tucking his tail under her arm.

"No one ever carried be," Goaty sniffed sadly.

"No one ever stepped on you, either!" Mr. Walker said snappishly.

The break in the trees was not a path after all, only a natural thinning along a rocky seam, but it made walking easier. Although the rain was fine, Rage soon found she was very wet. Fortunately, Billy had been right in saying it was not cold. The rain began to ease as they reached the top of the hill, which was a cap of hard stone where nothing green could grow. They climbed down into a valley and began another hard climb, up the next hill.

Rage stopped to catch her breath and looked back. A dense, trackless forest spread away beneath them until it became a greenish haze that merged with the sky. There was not a single sign of life, just forest blanketing the hills and valleys. It was the way Rage imagined Winnoway might have looked before people arrived. It was beautiful to see a forest so untouched, but she hoped there would be something more than wilderness on the other side of the hill.

"Up," Goaty urged. He trotted ahead, and at first Rage was puzzled by his sudden enthusiasm. Then she remembered that it was the nature of a goat to climb, and for all his transformation, Goaty was still more goat than anything else. He had never climbed a hill in his life, let alone a mountain, but his wild ancestors had lived on steep-sided mountains, so perhaps this was buried in the deepest part of his mind.

Bear was making heavy work of the hill, and Billy hovered, looking worried. She stumbled slightly. When he caught at her she snarled and slashed the air in his direction with her claws extended. Rage heard the wheezing sound her breath made and felt anxious. It was how Grandfather Adam had sounded before he died.

"I'm sorry I got you into this," she told Bear, who gave her a weary look before going on climbing.

"She doesn't blame you," Billy said quietly, coming up beside Rage.

"She seems so unhappy," Rage murmured, slowing so that they could talk.

Billy sighed. "Life has been hard for her. Your grandfather was not a kind master. Mama never had a pat or soft word until you came. And then there were all of my brothers and sisters dying, and you keeping me from her. I remember hearing her calling to me when I was sick, like a voice in a dream. Calling and calling."

"But you would have died if we hadn't taken you. . . ."

"She knows. I know. But it doesn't make any difference to the hurting of it."

"She hates me, then," Rage said, devastated.

"Oh no," Billy said. "Hating's a human thing. She's just all filled with grieving, and sometimes when it gets too much, she lashes out. But she cares very much for you and your mam."

"And you? Doesn't she care for you?" Rage asked.

Billy Thunder looked up the hill after his mother. "I think it hurts her to look at me," he said, very softly.

Toiling up the last bit of the hill, Rage was weighed down with a sadness as heavy as her sodden coat. It seemed so unfair that Bear could care for her and Mam but not for her own son.

"Hey!" Elle yelled. Rage looked up to see that she and Goaty had reached the top of the hill. "I see a road and there's a river alongside it, and over there, in the forest, is a big house with pointy bits."

The top of the hill was a perfect vantage point. Before them an enormous valley opened like a seam between parallel ranges of towering, white-streaked mountains. Thick masses of clouds rested on their peaks, concealing what lay beyond. A river emerged from the farthest mountains and wound its silvery way the length of the valley. To the east of the river, the valley was densely forested but for a castle on a hill—Elle's big house with pointy bits. A faint track ran from the castle, through the forest, and around the foot of the hill they were standing on, before joining a road that ran beside the river.

Rage noticed a small settlement not far along the river road. "What do you see there?" she asked, pointing it out.

"Houses and gardens," Mr. Walker answered, wriggling to be put down.

"A stone well in the middle of a little square in the middle of houses and streets," Billy said.

"People," Elle said.

"*People* people?" Rage asked.

Elle squinted. "People of some sort," she said at last. "What difference does it make?"

"Oh, it makes a great deal of difference," Bear said thickly. "People only care about people who are exactly like them."

Rage was hurt by the scorn in Bear's voice, but she only said, "I was thinking we could go there and ask about the wizard."

"If there are people, they will want to send me to the abattoir," Goaty said. He sneezed, very wetly.

Mr. Walker looked at him in disgust. "Do you mind! You spat on me just now."

"No one will dare to send us anywhere!" Elle declared. She bounded into the trees and emerged with a dead branch. "I'll make a spear!" She waved the stick around so wildly that it poked Goaty in the eye.

He rubbed it and said mournfully that it didn't matter. "I have another eye, and I doubt three eyes would be enough to see all the trouble that we're bound to find if we go down into that valley. Going down is a bad thing."

"Why don't we go there instead?" Mr. Walker said, pointing to the castle on the hill.

"It's a castle," Billy said.

"Of course it is," Mr. Walker snapped. "And in it there will be a king or queen or a wise advisor who will be able to help us find the wizard. Perhaps even the wizard himself lives there."

Rage was startled to find that Mr. Walker and Billy knew what a castle was. Then she remembered that Billy and Mr. Walker had always sat with Rage when Mam read her stories.

"That track leading to the castle doesn't look very clear," Rage said.

She did not want to admit that she was afraid to go to the castle. In fairy tales there was always something dramatic and violent happening in a castle—somebody being stolen away or put to sleep for a hundred years, somebody getting his head chopped off or being usurped. She wasn't actually sure what being usurped was, but it sounded at least as bad as having her head chopped off.

"The village is closer," she argued. "They can tell us who the castle belongs to, and if the wizard owns it, we can still go there."

Mr. Walker looked mutinous.

"What if we vote?" Rage suggested, thinking it had been easier when they were dogs.

"I vote for the village," Billy said promptly.

"I vote for the castle," Mr. Walker said.

"I vote for the castle, too," Elle said enthusiastically.

"Oh dear, oh dear." Goaty sighed and wrung his hands. "I suppose each way will be as bad as the other. In fact, surely the most sensible thing is to stay right where we are. That's what I vote for."

"We can't just stay here forever," Rage protested. "We ought to try to find the wizard."

"I expect he will just want to eat us when we find him," Goaty said in a depressed voice.

"I think a wizard would have better ways of getting food than cooking his visitors," Mr. Walker said coldly.

"I would like to see what a castle smells like. Let's go there at once," Elle said impatiently.

"No use in going to castle," said a familiar slinky voice. "Nothing there but spiders scuttling. No food. No treasure. No sleeping princess."

"Who said that?" Mr. Walker demanded, his high-pitched voice barely audible over the ferocious rumbling growl of Bear. She looked much more like a bear than a dog now that she was curling back her lip and showing her teeth.

"It's the firecat," Rage whispered.

"It's the thing that unlocked the gate for me," Goaty observed gloomily.

"I don't like this one bit," Mr. Walker whispered loudly.

"Not liking hairy little man-dog, either," the firecat said.

"Where have you been?" Rage asked. "You said all of my questions would be answered when I came through the bramble gate!"

"Firecat is having many things to do. Many important things," the voice said sulkily.

Rage bit her lip to stop herself from saying that since it had convinced her to come through the bramble gate, it ought to regard *her* as important. Instead she said, "Where is the wizard and what does he want us to bring to him?"

In answer there was a lurid flash of purple smoke. A tiny hourglass full of pale, glittering sand appeared on a stone knoll. Rage bent down and gingerly pinched its waist between her finger and thumb. It was surprisingly heavy for such a small object because the bottom and top were capped in densely patterned silver. The glass felt thick and was faintly discolored. A few glimmering grains of sand fell through the neck of the hourglass as she watched.

She turned it upside down, but instead of the grains running in the other direction, a few more gleaming fragments floated up from the bottom chamber and into the top.

"A magic hourglass," she murmured, glad it was not a golden ring.

"Hourglass telling how to find wizard," the firecat said.

Rage examined the hourglass and found there were two lines of ornate lettering engraved into the silver:

BRING ME TO THE SHORE OF THE ENDLESS SEA
STEP THROUGH THE DOOR THAT WILL OPEN FOR THEE

"These are not proper directions!" she protested.

"Ragewinnoway clever. Figuring out riddle," the firecat said.

"No!" Rage said. "You send us back home at once."

"Home?" the firecat echoed with a tinge of mockery. "Home-going needing powerful enchantment. Only wizard having such magic."

Rage's anger turned inward once more. Why had she

chosen to go through the bramble gate? The worst thing was knowing that she had gone through it solely because she hadn't believed it was magic. Now they would not be able to get back home unless she could figure out the wizard's whereabouts from the riddle on the bottom of the hourglass.

If only she had not gone through the magic gate . . .

If only she had not run away from the Johnsons' . . .

If only her mother had not been in an accident . . .

"I wouldn't trust that cat thing one bit," Mr. Walker said.

Bear said shortly, "Any fool could tell it was a liar. It smelled like a liar, and it sounded like one."

Rage hung her head and said nothing.

Billy put his arm around her shoulders and said stoutly, "We should go into the village to see if anyone knows anything about the wizard. Maybe it won't be as hard to find the Endless Sea as it sounds."

Rage feared it would be every bit as difficult as it sounded, but before she could say so, Bear growled impatiently and began to descend the hill.

"We'll all be killed," Goaty sighed glumly as they set off after Bear.

It was midday before they reached the road. Going down had turned out to be a lot more difficult than going up, especially where the steep rock face was slippery from rain. At least the weather had warmed up, but Rage was beginning to feel dreadfully empty. The animals must be as hungry as she was, and she feared they would expect her to feed them, just as she always had. Maybe they would be able to get something in the village. In books, people always begged, or chopped wood for their supper. Sometimes they stole it. Rage had never stolen anything, but in stories it never seemed as awful to steal as it did in real life.

"We must be careful, though," she muttered to herself when they were in sight of the road. She had got them into enough trouble by failing to think things through. She could not make the same mistake again.

"I'll protect us!" Elle declared, brandishing her stick.

"Put that down before you do poke someone's eye out," Mr. Walker said crossly.

Rage peered along the road in both directions. It seemed to be deserted, but she looked to Elle, whose superb bull terrier eyesight seemed to have been carried over into her new form. "Do you see anyone coming?"

Elle looked along the road in the direction of the castle and shook her head, but when she looked toward the river, she frowned. "Something is coming. . . ."

"Some*one*, you mean," Mr. Walker corrected.

"It's not a people," Elle said slowly. "It's . . . something biggish and brownish and it has . . . a lot of legs."

"Probably a giant poisonous jumping spider," Goaty said.

Rage resisted the urge to smack him. She was not afraid of spiders exactly, but she preferred them to stay on the ceiling or on the other side of the room. It occurred to Rage, rather horribly, that whatever was coming might be something worse than a spider—some sort of monster. Unlike Goaty, she kept this terrifying possibility to herself. They agreed to stay hidden until whatever it was came nearer and they could judge if it was dangerous.

"Probably it will sniff us out," Goaty said.

"At least if it eats us, *someone* will have a full stomach," Mr. Walker said, giving Rage a sideways look.

She bit back a retort and shifted to a spot that

allowed her a clear view of the road. As she waited, Rage was surprised to find her eyes growing heavy despite her apprehension. Mr. Walker climbed into her lap and fell immediately asleep. Beside her, Billy was silent, lost in his thoughts. Only Elle seemed wide awake, standing and rubbing a stone along her stick to smooth it. Goaty, who was as fond of her in this shape as in the other, held the stick steady for her, from time to time looking back up the hill with dreamy longing.

Rage's eyelids grew leaden, and finally she could not resist letting them close. She drifted into a dream of her mother crying, only Mam was a little girl, younger than Rage.

"Sammy! Sam! Don't go!" Mary wept.

"Let him," her grandfather said coldly, his hair black instead of silver. "He does not care that he is leaving you. People who go never care what they leave behind them."

Rage woke with the queer, unhappy thought that by falling into a coma, Mam had gone away and left *her*.

Mr. Walker growled.

"It's nearly here," Billy whispered to Rage, and a thrill of terror ran through her veins.

She listened hard, but what she could hear did not sound the least bit spiderish. It sounded more like a horse clip-clopping lazily along. She pushed Mr. Walker off her lap and got up just as a woman on a horse came riding into view. It took a second more for Rage to realize that the woman and the horse were a single creature. The bottom half of her was a horse, but from the waist up she was human.

"It's sort of a horse," Goaty whispered.

"It's a centaur!" Rage breathed, enchanted.

"Is it really? I can't see," Mr. Walker complained, and Billy picked him up. "It *is* a centaur," he said, sounding delighted. "I wonder if they really do have a human stomach and a horse stomach."

"Stay here. I'm going down to talk to it," Rage said, determined to be Rage-Winnoway-whose-name-was-Courage, as the Firecat had advised. After all, if anyone would know about magic, it must surely be this legendary beast. In the stories she had read, centaurs were always noble and honorable creatures. She slithered down the last bit of the hill overlooking the road, meaning to stop herself at the edge and climb down with dignity, but it was steeper than she thought, and she flew out and landed hard on her bottom.

"What in the wild!" exclaimed the centaur, coming to an abrupt halt.

Rage could feel her face growing very hot. She got up with as much dignity as she could muster and brushed her clothes off. "Good afternoon, centaur," she said, noting that the fur from the creature's horse half grew up into a sort of shirt for her human half.

The centaur lifted beautifully arched brows. "Good afternoon to you, too, girl. What are you doing here without any sort of keeper?"

Rage felt this rather a rude thing to say. Somehow she would have imagined a centaur to have a high and poetic way of talking, with lots of *thee*-ing and *thou*-ing. "I am looking for the shore of the Endless Sea. Do you know the way?"

The centaur snorted in a very loud and horsy way. "I have never heard of it."

"What is this place called?"

"We are on the road that runs between Wildwood

and Deepwood and leads to the River of No Return."
She tilted her head. "How is it that you know so little
about where you are?"

"Because I don't belong here!" Rage burst out. "It's all
a mistake. I came through an enchanted gateway that
disappeared, so I couldn't get back."

"Ah yes, well, they do that. Many gates in but only
one out," the centaur said absently. "Enchanted gate, you
say? That means you used magic?"

"You said there is a gate out?" Rage asked eagerly.

"I was just repeating an old song my dam used to sing
to me. But tell me, you used magic to come here?"

"I said the gate was magic," Rage said.

"But there is magic where you come from?"

"There are lots of *stories* about magic, but I didn't
know it really existed." Rage hesitated. "I . . . I heard
there was a great wizard this side of the gateway who
could work powerful magic."

"Once, long before my creation, a wizard lived in the
castle on the hill in the middle of Deepwood," the
centaur answered. "He made Valley, they say, so he must
have been very powerful."

So Valley was the name of the world they had come
to, Rage thought. "Where does the wizard live now?"

The centaur shrugged. "No one knows. The witch
women say he got sick of the keepers coming to the
castle for advice all the time when he was trying to do
his spells, so he magicked Deepwood into a thick tangle,
to make it hard to get to the castle. Then one day he just
wasn't there anymore."

Rage's heart sank. Witches! And who or what were
keepers? And how on earth was she to find a wizard who
had disappeared ages ago? More importantly, why had

the firecat told her the wizard wanted something brought to him? She remembered uneasily that Bear had said it smelled like a liar.

She thought over all that the centaur had said. "If the witch women are magical . . . ," she began.

"They *work* magic," the centaur corrected her. "Only a wizard can make magic. Terrible curious the witch folk are about him. But the wizard became a recluse before they moved to Wildwood, so they never really had much to do with him. You would need to ask the keepers in Fork about him. Time was, there used to be a lot of coming and going between the castle and Fork."

"Fork?" Rage echoed in bewilderment.

"Fork City. Other side of the River of No Return. Just follow the road to the crossing place."

"Who lives in Fork?"

"Humans, of course. It and all of the villages along the road are keeper territory. It is the road that marks the land ruled by the keepers, not the river." She stopped and suddenly glowered at Rage. "You're not a keeper spy, are you?"

"Don't touch her!" Elle cried, and bounded onto the road between Rage and the centaur. Billy jumped down, too, and stood boldly beside Elle, who was brandishing her spear.

The centaur stared at them both, then all at once the stiffness went out of her bunched muscles and she chuckled. "You are clearly not from Valley, for here no one would be foolish enough to provoke a centaur." Without warning she reared up and drove lightning-fast hoofs into the earth between Elle and Billy.

Rage screamed in fright.

"Fear not, girl," the centaur told her. "You are lucky

that I am not one of my brothers, for they are far more warlike." She turned to Elle. "Put aside your weapon, little warrior, for I mean no harm to your friend. What sort of things are you?"

"I'm a dog." Elle was staring up at the centaur in admiration.

"Me too," Billy said.

The centaur frowned. "There are dogs in some of the villages, but they do not look like you."

"We were dogs before we came through the enchanted gateway that brought us here," Billy explained. "It changed us."

"There must have been a mighty magic in that gate," the centaur said.

"I was told that the wizard made it," Rage said.

The centaur shrugged her massive shoulders again. "Maybe he did. I don't suppose gate making can be much harder than the making of Valley." She gave a shiver, as if her skin were impatient to get moving. "Well, I must go. The witch women have summoned all wild things to a grand council at the heart lake in Wildwood. Would you like to come with me? I'm sure they'd be interested to hear about your world."

Rage shook her head firmly. "We will go to Fork."

"Be careful, then. Keepers rule their territories with hard hands and cold eyes. They don't like anything out of the ordinary," the centaur added, seeming to forget that it had been her idea to seek out the keepers. "Best not to call any attention to yourself. And obey all their rules." Her skin twitched again. "Now I will say goodbye, for I doubt we will meet again."

Rage watched the centaur vanish into the trees beside the road. A moment later she wished she had thought to ask about the firecat. She had no doubt now that it had deliberately lured them through the bramble gate with its promise of magical help from the wizard. The question was, *why?* It hadn't told them about the wizard disappearing, but it had given them the magical hourglass with its riddled directions, so maybe the wizard was hiding somewhere, waiting for someone to unravel the riddle. Rage saw that they had no choice but to look for the wizard since he was their only way home.

"What a lot of words saying nothing," Bear growled, lumbering out of the trees.

"I'm hungry," Mr. Walker said, jumping down.

"Me too," Goaty sighed, following him.

"Shall I go and look for food?" Elle volunteered.

"No!" Rage almost shouted. "I just need to think for a minute before we do anything."

"Thinking is very useful," Elle said doubtfully.

"I don't like the idea of witches," Billy said.

"Me neither," Mr. Walker agreed. "Witches fatten you and eat you, or poison you with apples."

"I don't think we'd better rely too much on what fairy tales say about them," Rage said, thinking that the centaur had not been much like centaurs in stories.

"There's no need for us to go near the witch women," Billy said. "After all, the centaur said that they didn't have much to do with the wizard. We need to talk to the keepers."

"What is a keeper?" Goaty asked.

Rage frowned. "I don't know. A human adult, I suppose, since the centaur asked why I was without one."

"They live in Fork, and the centaur said humans live in Fork, so they must be human," Billy pointed out.

"They *rule* Fork," Mr. Walker said. "Maybe the witch

women rule the wild parts of Valley."

Goaty looked around as if he expected a witch to leap out of a bush.

"She asked if we were keeper spies," Billy murmured. "The keepers wouldn't spy on the witch women unless they didn't like them. Maybe they're at war."

Rage sighed impatiently. "It doesn't matter whether keepers and witch women are at war! We're not on either side. We're only going to Fork to find out about the wizard."

"I still think we should go to the village first. We have to get some food, and we can ask about the keepers and the wizard at the same time," Billy said.

"I vote for food," Mr. Walker agreed promptly.

4

The village they had seen from the top of the hill was less than an hour's journey away. It lay in a place where the road curved inland from the bank of the river. As they approached, Rage could see that it consisted of about twenty houses and smaller outbuildings arranged into four twisty streets that radiated from a central square. A couple of men sat on a step smoking pipes, and another man was chopping wood. A group of old women went down a street carrying baskets and chattering. There were a lot more houses than people. Rage guessed that most of the villagers were inside or had gone off to work somewhere else.

"I'll go in. The rest of you wait here for me," she said.

"Not alone," Billy yelped.

"Mr. Walker can come with me, in my coat pocket. If anything goes wrong, I'll send him for help."

"No," Billy said. "I will come, too."

"Let him go," Bear growled before Rage could argue. "I don't want to hear his whining."

Rage and Billy entered the village, leaving the others

hidden in bushes behind them. "Why does Bear talk to you like that?" Rage asked.

"I don't mind," Billy said.

Rage bit her tongue to keep from saying *she* minded, because how could she when Billy didn't? She would have minded very much if Mam had been as cold and sharp with her. But Billy seemed to accept his mother's treatment and to love her anyway. Was that because he was a dog or because he was sweet-hearted?

Bear as a bear was both a lot angrier and sadder than she had been as a dog. Rage tried to imagine living her whole life with Grandfather Adam's stone eyes on her. She decided she would have run away like Uncle Samuel. Of course, being a dog, Bear couldn't run away. Animals didn't have the same freedom as humans. Then again, maybe humans didn't have much freedom, either, because if she had left, she would have had to leave Mam. She could never do that.

I would have taken Mam with me, Rage thought.

An approaching red setter regarded them expectantly. "Good day," it said cheerfully.

Both Billy and Rage stopped and stared.

"You can talk," Billy said.

"So can you. What of it?" the setter said, then it sniffed and tilted its head. "You look human but you smell like dog."

"I am—" Billy began, but Rage elbowed him in the stomach to remind him that they had agreed not to tell anyone else that they were strangers. "I mean, I—I have a dog as a friend," he stammered at last. "That's probably what you can smell."

The dog tilted its head at Rage.

"We're travelers," Rage said quickly. "We came to see

the wizard who lived in Deepwood, but we have learned that he has moved away."

"I wouldn't know anything about wizards," the dog said.

"We heard that he used to visit the keepers in Fork," Billy said.

"I wouldn't know about that," the setter repeated. It studied Rage for a time. "You smell like a human she-pup."

Rage gave up trying to get information about the wizard. "We were hoping we might be able to work for some food here." The dog flapped its long ear to dislodge a fly. "Do you . . . I mean, whom should we speak to about getting work?"

"I play with the baker when he smells in need of a bit of frisking," the setter said easily. "He feeds me for that. Maybe you could play with him and he'll feed you as well."

Rage blinked at the thought of getting fed for romping with a grown man. "Maybe he'll have something else for us to do. Where is he?"

"I'll show you." The dog rose and stretched enormously, then clawed violently at a spot behind an ear. Billy scratched the spot obligingly, whispering to Rage that he knew just how that felt. The dog gave Billy a lick on the feet, and Rage noticed that there were toffee-colored tufts of hair on Billy's bare toes. These seemed to be the only reminder that he really was a dog.

The setter led them down one of the streets to a small round dumpling of a cottage on the bank of a stream. A wooden waterwheel was turning slowly beside it. The dog bid them farewell and trotted lazily away.

"He had a nice smell," Billy said, looking after him wistfully. Rage couldn't help but smile. Sometimes Billy was so doggish.

They found the baker inside the round building. He turned out to be a thin man wrapped in a huge white apron, kneading bread on a marble counter.

"Excuse me, sir," Rage said hesitantly. "We are in need of food, and a dog told us you might have some work for us."

The baker stopped his kneading and stared at her. "Well, well. I suppose you have come a long way."

It sounded more like a statement than a question, and though it didn't seem to make much sense, Rage nodded politely. Then she said, "The dog . . ."

"Ah, that dog is a fine, playful beast," the baker said, returning to his kneading. He shot her a speculative look. "I've heard them as lives in the outer villages hold loose to keeper ways."

Rage smiled and shrugged, sensing danger. Given the centaur's question about her being without a keeper, she wondered if there was a rule in Valley about children traveling alone. It struck her that she had not seen a single child or young person in the village.

"You say you're prepared to work for food?" the baker asked, and Rage nodded. "Happen I do have something needing doing, but it's hard, dirty work." He gave her and Billy a searching look. "I need someone to clean out my ovens. It'll take a bit of muscle."

"I can work hard," Billy said eagerly.

The baker beamed. "I like to see a lad prepared to put his back into a job. Just let me finish this and I'll show you where the ovens are. They're all cool now because I don't bake until night. Too hot in this weather."

They watched him shape the dough into loaf tins. "They'll need a good few hours of rising now." He laid a damp cloth over them, then wiped his hands on his apron and looked at Rage. "You're too small to do this

51

work, but you can pick your pay while the lad labors. There are berries all along the back of the hedgerow, and I've also got tomatoes and potatoes growing out back. And there are pots of jam and relish and some cheese and butter in the cellar store. And some bread, of course. As much food as the two of you can carry for the job."

Soon Billy was up to his waist in the enormous ovens, and black with soot from head to furry toes.

Rage went to a hedge on the pretext of picking berries and let Mr. Walker out so that he could tell the others what was happening. She began collecting berries, pleased to find they were firm as plums. It would have been impossible to carry real berries without squashing them. The berries tasted rather like vanilla custard, and Rage ate as many as she picked for her bucket. She had just finished digging up a small pile of potatoes and was wondering how they would manage to cook them when the baker called her to the porch. He had assembled several jars of jams and relish, a stone dish of butter, some small crusty loaves of bread, and two fat wheels of cheese wrapped in cloth. Beside them were two cloth bags to pack everything in.

Rage thanked him profusely for his generosity.

"You're a pair of workers, I'll say that," he said, showing Rage a pump where she could wash her hands. "My sister will bring a bite of supper before I start the evening's baking. You're welcome to share that if you like, and stay the night in our barn. It's nice to see a couple of young faces around the village."

Rage thanked him, but hearing him refer to the lack of children made her nervous. "We ought to get on," she said, trying to sound diffident.

The baker nodded. "I suppose it's best not to dawdle on the road. It's not often you see girls traveling without keeper guardians these days." He grinned. "To tell you the truth, I thought you were wild things when I first set eyes on you. Sprites do wander over the road from time to time, poor things. I'd feed them if I could, but as you know, they can't eat ordinary food."

Rage was thrilled at the idea of sprites. She would have liked to ask what they ate, but feared this might be something that was commonly known. "We saw a centaur," she said, thinking it safe to contribute.

The baker sighed. "Used to be a great herd of them hereabouts, but not anymore. What I say is, it's a shame."

"You'd best hold your tongue, brother," a sharp voice said.

Rage turned to see a thin, dark-eyed woman carrying a basket over one arm. Her clothing was gray and plain, her hair pulled into an enormous severe bun. She wore a pair of heavy silver bracelets, one on each wrist. They looked very strange with her workaday attire.

"It's not treason to have an opinion, Rue," the baker said mildly, rising to take the basket from her.

Rage felt the woman's eyes bore into her. She resisted the urge to fidget, since that always made adults think you were guilty of something.

"How do you know this girl will not report to the keepers on which villagers secretly support the witch women and their activities?" Rue asked.

"Activities? It's not like there can be more than a skerrick of magic left for them to work with. I daresay they think more of their dying pets than of intrigue."

Rage was startled. What did the baker mean by saying there was little magic left? Surely magic was not something that could be used up, but was a force to be summoned by spells and incantations.

The baker's sister spoke again. "The witch women

would do anything to feed those unnatural creatures they created."

The baker laughed at his sister. "Ah, Rue, the city has made you cold and hard. Have some compassion for the poor wild things. Is it their fault the witch women created them?"

"You are a fool," the woman said to her brother. "Your careless talk will see us both dragged up before the High Keeper and cast into the River of No Return when this girl tells what she has heard."

"The girl is not banded yet, so how could she be a keeper spy?"

Rage wished Billy would hurry up. She didn't like the talk of spies and being thrown into rivers. And what was banding?

"Who said anything of spies? She's bound for Fork, isn't she?" the woman snapped. "The keepers will question her. They always interrogate new girls to find out if the witch women have tried to recruit them."

There was a charged silence.

"Have you been to the city?" Rage asked the baker lamely, trying to change the subject.

"Never been, never wanted to." He gave his sister a pointed look. "I was born right here in this village, back when it was still common for children to be raised this side of the river. If you want to know about Fork, it's Rue you should ask."

"I do not take kindly to being discussed as if I were not here," the thin woman said. She turned one of the metal bracelets on her wrist and rubbed at the delicate patterning with her thumb. "Where do you come from?" she demanded of Rage.

The baker laughed and flapped a floury hand in his

sister's face. "Now, Rue. You're starting to sound like the keepers, worrying about everything being in its place."

"There is much to worry about," his sister said icily. "As you would see if you ever looked past the dust on the end of your nose, you bumpkin!" She flounced back into the cottage and slammed the door behind her.

The baker sighed. "Don't mind her," he advised. "'Tis her time in the city made her all sharp and nervy-like. She fought being taken to Fork, but she was a girl who might become a witch, so she had no choice. Rue talks proud of the city now, but all that stone and cold water in Fork left its mark on her."

Rage pretended to rearrange the food in the bags, but her mind churned with the knowledge that girls were forced to live in the city of Fork by the keepers, to stop them becoming witches. That must mean the witch women were humans who had learned to work magic. Rage willed Billy to hurry, and this time, to her relief, he appeared. When the baker went to check his ovens, she whispered that they must leave as soon as ever they could. The baker came back beaming and renewed his offer of supper and a bed. But they thanked him and took their leave. Only when they were out of earshot of the village did Rage tell Billy what the baker and his sister had said.

"So there are hardly any children this side of the river because keepers take all girls to Fork," Billy mused. "But I wonder how being in the city stops a girl becoming a witch. It must be because there are no witches there to teach them how." Seeing Rage's look of admiration, he flushed. "It's easier to think in this shape."

"You don't mind being turned into a human?"

"Sometimes it feels very strange," he admitted. "I

can't do some of the things I used to do as a dog. I can't run as fast, and my nose seems to be almost useless. That's the worst thing. But I can remember things better now. There is more space for keeping things inside my head. I'm not completely human, though. Humans can do more things with their minds than I can. But the longer I am this shape, the more my mind grows."

Rage tried to imagine what it would be like if she were transformed into a dog. She realized with shame that much as she loved the dogs, she wouldn't want to be one. Mostly because it meant she would belong to a human, who might be like Grandfather Adam or Mr. Johnson. And because dogs weren't allowed to decide things.

"I don't think I'd like to be completely human," Billy went on apologetically. "I thought I would, but now I can see that human minds are growing all the time, until they are like enormous houses with thousands of rooms and twisty passages and dark hallways all full of cobwebs and shadows and forgotten things. No wonder there is so much confusion in humans. Dog minds are like standing outside. There are no walls, the wind blows freshly, and light falls everywhere. The best thing about being human is that I can talk with you."

Rage wondered if her mind was full of twisty passages and dark shadows. She didn't feel like it was true, but maybe that was only because she was not grown up. Certainly she could imagine Grandfather Adam being full of dank, secret niches, and even Mam's mind must be full of hidden corners.

"How do the others feel about being changed?" she asked curiously.

"They don't talk about it much. Mama doesn't know

how to be happy, so being changed doesn't seem to have made much difference to her. Mr. Walker complains, but he likes complaining, and Goaty is just as scared as he was before. Elle likes being human-shaped because it's something new."

They lapsed into silence. It was hard work carrying the heavy bags. When they arrived, the others greeted them with hungry delight. Soon they were enjoying a hearty sunset picnic on the bank of the river. Rage told them what had happened, then she took out the hourglass and they all studied it.

"It's strange that the wizard would want such an old-fashioned way of telling time," Rage said, noting that the grains continued to float from one side of the hourglass to the other. But most of the grains had yet to fall.

"I suppose he needs it because it's magic, rather than because it tells the time," Billy mused.

"I wonder why the firecat wants to help the wizard, anyway," Rage murmured.

"Why *us*, is what I'd like to know," Goaty muttered.

"Maybe it wanted strangers," Billy said. "If it had tried to get someone from Valley to look for the wizard, they would just refuse or give up when it became too difficult, but we can't."

Rage couldn't help but be impressed by Billy's perception. He must be right, too. No one in Valley could possibly want to find the wizard as much as she did.

"Maybe the hourglass measures something other than time," Mr. Walker suggested.

"Whatever it measures is running out," Goaty murmured.

That made Rage think of Mam in her dangerous sleep, which might last forever. Whatever the risk, she must decipher the wizard's riddle and find him. She put the hourglass back in her pocket and looked around at the others.

"I think we must still go to Fork," she said. "One of the keepers must know where the wizard is. We should be safe enough as long as we obey the rules." She was confident she could do this. She was good at being obedient.

"But we don't know what those rules are. And they won't let you leave again, because you're a girl," Billy objected.

"I don't see how anyone can guard a whole city properly," Elle said. "I'm sure we could escape if we had to."

"Cities are no place for animals or even for half-animals," Bear pronounced grimly.

"That's true," Goaty said. "I vote for what Bear votes for."

"She didn't vote for anything, you nitwit," snapped Mr. Walker. His tail twitched in irritation.

"I don't see what else we can do but go there," Rage said, feeling more troubled than ever. "We have to find out where the wizard is if we ever want to get home. And I'm sure Elle is right and we can slip out of Fork again when we want to leave."

"Even if these keepers know all about the wizard and where he went, they might refuse to tell us," Mr. Walker said.

"What do you think we should do, then?" Rage asked.

The little man opened his mouth, then closed it, looking slightly self-conscious. "I suppose we have to go to Fork," he said at last.

"So let's go!" Elle said impatiently. When no one argued, she packed up the remaining food into two bundles, neatly tying this to that until she and Billy could sling them over their shoulders. Rage said she was amazed that Elle was so *hand*-y, given she had spent most of her life with paws. This seemed to her a very funny joke, though the animals stared at her in puzzlement when she laughed.

"I guess you have to be human," she muttered as they set off again. Even Billy looked bemused, and she supposed that his mind hadn't grown enough to make space for jokes. She had a painful longing for Mam, who had always laughed at her jokes, even when Rage messed them up and said the funny bit in the wrong place.

By the time they left the village behind, dusk was deepening into night. When Rage looked back at the village, she could make out lights in a few of the cottage windows, and little dribbles of smoke coming from the chimney stacks. They heard the setter barking—not in anger, but in a casual way. The barking faded as they went on. The road drew nearer the river until Rage could smell its dank odor and hear it slap and gurgle against the bank.

"I hope we don't walk off the edge into the river," Goaty fretted.

"Stay close to me," Elle said heartily. "If you fall in, I'll save you."

"Once upon a time there were rivers where one sip of the water was poison, or where falling in meant forgetting everything you ever knew," Mr. Walker said dreamily.

"That wasn't this river," Billy said.

"You never know with rivers," Mr. Walker said.

Rage was surprised once more at how much Mr. Walker's thoughts revolved around the stories and myths her mother had read to them.

The narrow moon was setting when they stopped for

the night, having decided it was too dangerous to go on in the darkness. Rage studied the moon curiously, wondering if it was a different moon from the one that shone over Winnoway Farm. It looked exactly the same, but how could that be?

Rage was very glad when Elle found a huge, hollow tree trunk with a dry, woody floor that was big enough for them all to take shelter in. Even Bear could fit in, and though it was a tight squeeze, they were glad to cuddle together. A chilly mist had risen off the river and drifted just above the ground, luminous in the darkness.

Sleep came almost at once. Rage dreamed that she was walking through a jungle looking for Uncle Samuel. Though he must be a grown man now and she had no idea what he looked like, it didn't seem to matter in the dream. After a bit she thought she could hear a man's voice in the distance, calling her name, but no matter how long she walked, she never seemed to get any closer.

Sunlight woke her, slanting through the leaves and into the hollow, insistently poking at her eyelids. Rage found herself cuddled warmly between Billy and Bear. It felt so safe and nice that she wished she could stay like that forever. Mr. Walker was asleep in Billy's lap, snoring.

None of them woke as she eased her way out from between them to go to the toilet. She found a place a short distance from the others and dug herself a shallow hole. It was a nasty, messy business. Covering it over, she thought it was much better in stories, where no one ever had to go to the toilet or eat or bathe. The need to wash her hands drew her to the river, and she was startled at how close it was to where they had slept. The bank was steep, but she found a flat stretch where the river had slopped over the bank to form a quiet lagoon. The river was wide and the current looked strong and swift, but the lagoon was calm and inviting.

She stood gazing at it for a time, remembering Mr. Walker's words about the dangers of unknown rivers. A poisonous river seemed unlikely, but where there was magic, anything might be possible, even if the magic was dying out. It would be truly awful if she found the wizard only to discover he had no magic to send them home or save Mam.

Sitting on the bank, Rage took out the hourglass again. As before, the grains floated from one end to the other without interruption, no matter which way she held the hourglass. Even when she shook it gently— thinking about Mr. Walker saying that the fall of sand might measure something other than time—it did not seem to affect the inner motion of the sand at all. If it was sand. She held the device close and peered into it, wondering if the grains of sand were magic and what would happen if the glass broke.

"Has Ragewinnoway guessed riddling of wizard yet?" a familiar smoky voice asked.

Rage started violently. "I wish you wouldn't creep up on me!" she snapped. "I'm not talking to you anymore unless you show yourself."

There was a faint sizzling noise, and the water in the lagoon began to boil. Rage stared warily into it as the bubbling subsided, but instead of seeing her own face peering back up at her, the water was stained red and orange and flecked with slivers of light that might have been eyes or sharp teeth.

"What does seeing say to Ragewinnoway?" the firecat asked, and the water seemed to shimmer mockingly.

"I can't see you properly," Rage complained.

"Ragewinnoway seeing only what is to be seen."

There was the suggestion of a shrug in the voice. "But does she see what wizard is telling in tricky words?"

"I haven't figured his riddle out yet. But there are some things I want to ask." Rage was determined to get some clear answers from the elusive creature.

"Maybe answering and maybe not answering," the firecat said contrarily.

Rage counted to ten. "Where is the Endless Sea? Is it beyond the mountains?"

"If firecat knows where is Endless Sea, firecat can bring hourglass to master," it sneered.

Rage blinked. The firecat had called the wizard its master! "How long has the wizard been missing?" she asked.

"Long time," the firecat said vaguely.

Rage guessed from this that it didn't understand how to count time. "They say here that he disappeared from his castle. Is that true?"

The firecat made no response.

"Did he ask you to bring the hourglass to him before he went, or did he send a message to you?"

"Hourglass belonging to wizard. But is dangerous. Be careful. Not breaking," the firecat warned, and for the first time there was nothing but seriousness in its tone. Perhaps it was even telling most of the truth for once.

"What does the hourglass do?"

There was a hesitation. "All wizard knows is in hourglass," it answered finally in a purring voice.

"Why didn't the wizard take it with him?"

"Firecat not knowing. Wizard saying obey words on hourglass and be rewarded with what you deserve."

Rage didn't like the sound of that at all. It almost sounded like a threat. She had intended to ask if the wizard was good or bad, but now that she knew he was the firecat's master, she doubted that it would answer truthfully—especially since it wanted them to deliver the hourglass. It was clear, though, that the wizard had instructed the firecat *before* disappearing, which meant he really must want the hourglass. But why hadn't he simply taken it with him, or given simple instructions, instead of creating a difficult and mysterious riddle?

"The wizard told *you* to bring the hourglass to him, didn't he?" Rage guessed. "He promised to give *you* a reward if you would bring it to him. So why do you need me?"

"Hurrying," the firecat hissed, then the water began to bubble and spit, and gradually the colors faded.

"I should have asked it if magic is really running out in Valley," Rage muttered aloud, although the firecat seemed to have no shortage of the magic necessary for appearing and disappearing. She thought over its answers and decided it really did not know where its master was or how to find him.

The urgency of its final, hissed word made her think of the sand in the hourglass. What did it measure? The firecat had warned her not to break it, saying it was dangerous. No doubt it had only said this to make her careful. The wizard would probably be furious at it if the hourglass was damaged. The biggest puzzle was why the wizard had asked the firecat to bring the hourglass to him at all.

Unless the riddle was a test for the firecat itself!

Rage bit her lip in excitement, certain she was right. It was the only explanation that made sense. It even explained the firecat's evasive manner—by getting Rage to try to figure out the riddle, it was obviously cheating.

Another thought occurred to her. If she was right about the quest for the hourglass being a test, maybe the sand in the hourglass represented the amount of time the firecat had been given to solve its master's riddle.

Rage wondered how the wizard would feel about *their* solving the riddle, if they managed it. Maybe he would be angry. He might turn them all into frogs or river slime. The firecat had said they would be rewarded, but it was clear the creature would say anything to get them to do what it wanted.

A drab little bird fluttered to the ground and tilted its head to drink from the tea-colored water. Flinging off her clothes, boots, and all thoughts of the firecat and the hourglass, Rage climbed gladly into the lagoon. The water was warm from the sun or maybe from the firecat, and she was still paddling in her underclothes when Billy appeared. He ran at the lagoon with a whoop of delight and plunged in with a great splash.

"You ought to have taken your clothes off," Rage spluttered, laughing.

He looked embarrassed. "I forgot." He climbed out and peeled off his T-shirt, jeans, and jacket and jumped in again in cotton shorts. Rage studied him curiously for signs that he was really a dog, but there were none, other than his hairy toes. His skin was creamy pale, and his shoulders were broad and muscular. There were little patches of toffee hair under his arms and a fuzz of hair down his legs, but grown men had those. In human years, Billy appeared to be about sixteen, but as he looked over the small sandbar that separated the lagoon from the river, his expression of longing seemed very young to Rage.

"It's dangerous," she said firmly, remembering how he had always been attracted to water as a dog. He sighed and came away from the edge. As they paddled, she told him about the firecat's appearance. He agreed that it was very likely that the riddle on the base of the hourglass was a test that had been set for it.

"But it doesn't make any difference to us if it is," Billy said. "We still have to solve it if we are to find the wizard, get home, and help your mam."

"The wizard might be mad that *we* solved the riddle," Rage pointed out.

Billy frowned. "I'm more worried about the keepers than the wizard, to tell you the truth. That centaur said we ought not to draw any attention to ourselves in Fork, but if we tell them how we came to be in Valley, it's sure to cause a fuss."

"I know," Rage agreed.

"I wonder if the wizard setting a test for the firecat could have anything to do with his disappearance," Billy murmured, now floating and staring at his hairy toes. "Maybe he made the riddle and went to the shore of the Endless Sea to wait for the firecat to solve it, and he's still there waiting because the firecat can't figure it out."

"Why would he wait so long? He'd use his magic to come back and see what had gone wrong," Rage said.

"What if he couldn't?" Billy countered, turning onto his stomach. "What if, instead of the hourglass containing a record of all he knew, it actually held all of his power!" His brown eyes glimmered with excitement.

"It doesn't make sense," Rage objected. "Why would the wizard risk his power to set a test for the firecat? Besides, like you said, maybe the firecat was lying about the hourglass. That riddle on it doesn't say anything about the wizard, after all."

"Then what on earth does the firecat want of us?" Billy dog-paddled neatly around the lagoon, looking glum. Coming back to Rage, he said, "That centaur said the keepers kept annoying the wizard for advice—advice about what?"

"Maybe about everything. I suppose it was because of him making Valley. He must have been like the king here," Rage said.

"Only he didn't like being the king, so he became a hermit and then he vanished."

"I wonder why he made Valley in the first place if he didn't want to live here," Rage pondered.

"I've just thought of something!" Billy pushed his hair out of his eyes. "What if he put the magic in Valley when he created it, and it's dying out because he has disappeared?"

They were distracted from this interesting idea by the arrival of Elle and Mr. Walker. Rage climbed out of the water because her underclothes needed time to dry out. Fortunately, the sun was shining brightly and the air was pleasantly warm.

Elle and Billy romped and splashed in the pool. Mr. Walker drank daintily and washed his hands and face but otherwise avoided the water with a shudder. Rage spread out her coat and laid out a breakfast of slightly squashed berries, bread, and cheese. Bear was nowhere to be seen, but Mr. Walker said he could smell her nearby.

After they ate, Rage dressed, checking to be sure the hourglass and Mam's locket were still safe. She went through the ideas that she and Billy had discussed, but there was no way of knowing which were right. Talking had got them no closer to unraveling the riddle of the wizard's whereabouts, and in the end that was really all that mattered.

The others were having a last romp on the bank

when Bear came out of the bushes. Rage offered her food, but the old dog shook her head and sat down to lick at her paw.

"Why do you keep doing that?" Rage asked.

Bear regarded her through tiny black eyes. "A thorn from the bramble gate got into me."

"Why didn't you say so?" Rage asked, undoing a pin she kept in the hem of her coat and taking the huge paw firmly in her hand.

"A dog's pain is a dog's pain. Dogs don't complain," Bear said with melancholic poetry as Rage probed the swollen flesh.

When she found the shiny black top of a thorn driven deep into the pad, she looked at Bear with concern. "I am afraid I will have to hurt you to get it out."

"It is in the nature of humans to hurt," Bear said, staring bleakly into her eyes.

Rage swallowed and stuck the pin into the paw, forcing it under the thorn and levering it out. The breath hissed through Bear's lips, but she did not growl or groan.

Rage drew out the long, sharp thorn with dismay.

5

The road wound along companionably with the river, sometimes going right along the edge of the bank, other times turning away to avoid a thick clump of trees. Late in the morning, they came upon a group of little stone houses between the road and the water, but they had clearly been abandoned long ago.

"We could stay a night here," Mr. Walker said. Rage could see he was attracted to the smallness of the houses.

"We don't want to stop again so soon," Elle said firmly, striding ahead.

"Probably those little houses are so old they would fall on our heads and squash us flat," Goaty said.

Rage glared at him, wondering if this was what came of being around Mr. Johnson, who always saw the worst side of things first. Mam used to say that you could show Mr. Johnson a pretty wisp of cloud and he would see the end of the world.

"Like Grandfather?" Rage had asked.

"Like Grandfather." Mam's eyes had grown sad.

Rage remembered that this conversation had happened on a train. Mam loved trains. "They're so much gentler than cars. They don't roar through cities; they wind politely around them. They stop to let people in and out. People exchange newspapers or talk or just sit together. People sleep in trains and walk in them. They drink cups of tea and eat scones in them. Trains are for sharing."

"I like trains," Rage had said earnestly.

Mam laughed. "Imagine a city where all of those roads were turned into green paths. People could stroll and eat their lunches. Imagine looking out of a high building and seeing paths with big trees growing along them, fruit trees with masses of blossoms and huge cedars. There'd be no car noise, no pollution from the engines. People could lie under trees or watch buskers or just read. You wouldn't feel like you were in the city at all."

Mam had been like that. She would have an idea about something, and suddenly it would turn into a much bigger idea. Everything would be sucked into her idea and turned into something better. After they came to Winnoway, they had taken few train trips. There were no more talks or sing-alongs, no more stories or laughing tumbles together. Mam had become silent and distracted. She went on long walks alone, or she sat for hours gazing out the window. Sometimes she had smiled at Rage without really seeming to see her.

Rage shivered, remembering what Mrs. Johnson had said about Grandmother Reny growing more and more silent until she had just faded away, and the cold seemed to go inside her bones.

She tried to think about something she and Mam had done together after they shifted to Winnoway, something that they had really enjoyed, but she could think of nothing except those wonderful train journeys before they had come to Winnoway. Rage was startled to discover that Winnoway Farm, and even her own bedroom with its lilac wallpaper, was hard to picture. The farm seemed as if it belonged in someone else's world, in a story.

Did people in stories feel themselves to be real? How would she know if somebody had made her up? Then she wondered if maybe all that had happened was a story she was telling herself.

Thinking like this made her feel dizzy, as if she were turning round and round on the spot. She grinned, remembering how she had done that while holding Billy when he was a puppy. He had sprawled and lurched and sat down hard when she put him on the ground.

She looked at Billy and found him watching her.

"You were smiling," he said.

"I was remembering how dizzy you were after I swung you round and round when you were a puppy."

He threw his head back and laughed. "I thought the ground was jumping under me. I felt so sick in the stomach."

It occurred to Rage that what she had done was cruel.

Seeing the look on her face, Billy said, "It was no worse than when a puppy bites his brother or sister too hard on the ear."

"You weren't angry at me?"

"I love you," Billy said simply.

Rage opened her mouth to tell him that she loved him, too, but Elle interrupted to warn them that she could smell someone coming along the road behind them. They hurriedly decided that Billy would stay on the road with Rage while the rest of them got out of sight behind some bushes a little back from the road.

Before long, a gray donkey appeared. It was harnessed to a small open carriage bearing several very little girls in spotless white tunics and stockings and three women in long, colorful tubelike dresses. The women carried elaborately painted parasols to shade them from the sun. At first Rage thought the women were all deathly pale, but when they came closer, she could see that their faces were painted white, like those of Japanese ceremonial dancers. Their dresses even looked a bit like kimonos. The children had been laughing and chattering gaily, but they fell silent when they noticed Rage and Billy.

"Wild things!" piped one.

"Stop," shouted another, and the donkey obeyed. "Ahoy there. Are you wild things?"

"I'm just a girl like you," Rage said.

"You are almost a woman, yet you *are* like us, for you wear no bands," the girl chirped, lifting both of her bare arms up for Rage's inspection.

"Why don't you come in the cart with us?" one of the other girls invited.

"Impossible!" the eldest of the women said sternly. She waved an arm in an imperious gesture, and Rage noticed that she was wearing heavy metal bracelets like the ones worn by the baker's sister, Rue. Being banded must mean having to wear such bracelets, which seemed to mark the wearers as loyal keeper subjects.

"Why shouldn't she come with us?" another of the children asked defiantly.

"Perhaps she does not go to be banded," hissed the plumpest of the women. "Perhaps she is a witch woman."

The children stared at Rage solemnly.

"Don't frighten them with foolish talk, Ramis," the older woman said in a no-nonsense voice. "Witch women do not venture from Wildwood. This girl is clearly from one of the outer villages and is traveling with her escort to Fork to be banded. They often come in somewhat older. It was so with you, was it not, Ania?" she asked the youngest of the women.

Ania nodded meekly, but when she spoke, it was to the children. "Even if the girl is a wild thing, you have nothing to fear. You will see many wild things in the city."

Rage heard this with puzzlement. Hadn't the baker said that wild things were not supposed to enter keeper territory? To her delight, one of the children voiced this very question.

"The High Keeper has given wild things leave to enter Fork," the plump woman said piously.

"But why? They're so strange," the girl complained.

"I do not know why, but they do no harm with their strangeness," Ania said. The other two women stared at her askance. She shrugged. "Well, it is not as if they can draw magic from the earth without a witch woman's help, and witch women are forbidden to cross the river."

"They cannot be permitted to drain the other side of the river of magic as well," said the older woman icily.

Rage blinked, wondering if she had heard correctly. The woman seemed to be saying that there was still magic on the other side of the river, although it had almost died on this side. Was it possible that magic could be in one part of a land and not another? Did it form in the ground like gold or silver? And how could the witch women have used it all up?

"I think wild things should be stopped from coming

over the river," said the plump woman. "It is so depressing to see them drifting about looking sick and starved."

"More depressing for them to be starving, don't you
think?" Ania asked.

"The wild things are only dreams the witch folk
brought into being. We should rather pity them than fear
them," said the little girl who had invited Rage to ride in
the cart.

"I should not voice such opinions when you are in
Fork," advised the severe woman dryly. "Now, let us
continue. I'm sorry we cannot take you and your friend,"
she added to Rage. "But you ought to go along as quickly
as possible."

"There really isn't room," Rage pointed out when the
little girl looked as if she might argue. Belatedly, it
occurred to her that she was wasting a perfectly good
chance to get more information. "Uh, before you go, we
met another traveler who spoke of the Endless Sea. Do
you know where that is?"

The plump woman snickered rather meanly. "She is
from the outermost village in Valley, surely, to ask about
a child's myth as if it were a real place."

"I heard that the wizard who made Valley had gone
to the shore of the Endless Sea," Rage persisted.

Ania opened her mouth as if to speak, then seemed
to think better of it.

"I do not know where the wizard has gone, but it is
said he will return when things are properly in Order
again." The severe woman spoke these words as a chant,
then bid the donkey continue.

"The wild things must eat magic," Billy said when the
cart had drawn out of sight. "They're starving because it
has run out on this side of the river."

"It's horrible being hungry," Elle said. "Why don't the keepers let the witch women give them some magic from the other side of the river?"

"They're probably afraid it will all be used up," Billy said.

"How do you eat magic?" Goaty asked.

"How do you get it out of the ground?" Mr. Walker muttered.

Billy's mind had been going along a different line. "I wonder what that woman meant by saying the wizard will come back when there is Order here. What is Order?"

Rage could see Billy was enjoying his new ability to think complex thoughts, but she was sick of questions with no answers. The women in the cart had laughed at her for asking about the Endless Sea, calling it a child's myth. Rage wondered if they were going to find the answers they needed, even in Fork. She was beginning to be afraid they would never get back home and that she would never see Mam again, asleep or awake. That thought made her throat ache.

"I wonder what is over the river besides the city of Fork," Mr. Walker said.

"A dangerous, wet land, probably," Goaty said.

Rage lost her temper and rounded on him. "Why do you always have to imagine the worst?"

Goaty hung his head and looked so pathetic that her anger drained away. After all, she was really angry at herself for getting them into such a mess. "I'm sorry I shouted at you, but all those bad things you keep saying are like stones we have to carry. They just make everything harder."

"I know," Goaty mumbled. "That's why no one wants me around. I make everyone feel bad and sad. It is because of the hole in me that comes from never having a name."

"But you have a name."

He looked up at her. "Would it be a name if you were called 'girly,' or Elle were called 'doggy'? Goaty is not a name. It is the name given to a thing no one cares about enough to name."

Rage swallowed hard, remembering that her grandfather had always called her "the girl."

"We will give you a name," Elle said enthusiastically. "What shall it be?" She looked at the rest of them.

"A name can't be decided just like that," Billy said admonishingly. "Naming is a serious business." He sounded so like Mam that Rage felt perilously near to tears again.

"We will think of the right name for you," she told Goaty thickly.

"What I want to know is how we are supposed to cross the river," Mr. Walker muttered, for they had reached a part of the road that ran right along the very edge of the swift-flowing water.

Rage was carrying him because his little legs could no longer keep up.

"I'm sure there will be a bridge," she said, and she was sure, for how else would the women and children in the cart get to the other side?

"There will be guards on it," Mr. Walker said. "Rulers always have soldiers to make people obey them. The more rules, the more soldiers are needed to keep them."

"Maybe the keepers keep their own rules," Rage said.

But Mr. Walker shook his head authoritatively. "In stories, the makers of rules are never the ones to force people to obey them."

"No one said anything about soldiers," Rage said.

"Where there are rules, there are soldiers," Mr. Walker insisted.

"I'm afraid Mr. Walker is probably right," Billy said. "Humans are fond of rules and even fonder of giving people the power to make sure they are obeyed. Besides, there are bound to be guards at the bridge, if only to stop witch women from going over."

Rage thought of something that one of the white-faced women had said. "How will they know *I'm* not a witch woman?"

Billy shrugged. "When we reach Fork, you must say you have come from one of the outer villages to be banded. I just wish we knew exactly what banding meant."

"It's getting metal things on your arms, like the bracelets those women in the cart wore," Mr. Walker said. "Like getting a dog collar."

"If that were all, what would stop witch women putting on the same sort of bands and coming to steal magic from Fork for the wild things?" Billy asked. "I think the keepers have some way of making sure magic can't be taken from the ground, and I think the bands are part of it."

A chill crept up Rage's spine as she understood what Billy was trying to say. "You think being banded is more than just getting those bracelets?"

"I don't know," he admitted.

"If banding stopped women from working magic, why would they be kept in Fork for so long?" Mr. Walker asked.

"So they can't have daughters who might be recruited by the witches?" Rage suggested.

"Maybe," Billy said. "Anyway, if we see anyone else on

the road, we must be sure to ask about banding. When we get to Fork, they will want to band you, and we need to understand what that means."

They did not meet anyone else until it was almost dusk, and by then Mr. Walker was asleep in Rage's oversized coat pocket and Bear had disappeared into the trees alongside the road.

A wild-looking girl came round a bend in the road in front of them. She was flanked on either side by two coppery red winged lions, only slightly bigger than Bear in her dog form. The lions could only be wild things. Rage's heart beat fast at the sheer wonder of them.

Goaty moaned in fright and stopped, trembling from head to cloven hoofs.

"Good dusk," the girl greeted them in a thin, high voice. Up close it was clear that she was a wild thing, too. Her eyes were an impossible hue of violet, and her great tangle of black hair rippled as if breezes blew through it. She wore a ragged bit of a shift that showed a lot of her skinny greenish limbs, and her wrists were unadorned.

The winged lions began sniffing Billy, who laughed. "It tickles," he said apologetically.

The sprite cocked her head at the lions. "They ask why you do not answer their greeting. And they ask what manner of thing you are."

"I'm a dog," Billy said.

One of the lions licked his toes, then looked at the sprite. "He says you smell like and not like a dog, as does your friend." She pointed to Elle, who was now being examined by the lions. Fearless as ever, Elle ran her hands through their manes. The sprite laughed and danced across to caress her golden hair. "Pretty. Strong. And what are you?" she asked, coming to Goaty and tugging at his ringlets. "Soft. Pale. Half human, half beast. Are you not a wild thing?"

Goaty tried to speak, but the winged lions converged on him, and he fell into a quaking silence.

"They say you stink of fear," the sprite said, tilting her head curiously. "You do not need to be afraid. We will not hurt you. Why don't you come with us to Wild-wood? I will make a crown of living ivy for your hair, and you shall learn to dance and ride on my friends as I do, and you will forget fear." She threw her arms around his neck and kissed Goaty passionately on the cheek.

"Oh, please don't eat me!" he shrieked.

"Don't be a fool! She's trying to kiss you, not eat you," Mr. Walker said crossly, poking his head out of Rage's pocket.

The sprite stared at him in delight. Sighing, Rage let him out onto the ground. The lions sniffed at him, and the sprite knelt to look at him. "I thought you one of the little people, but my friends say you are like that one and that one." She pointed to Billy and Elle. "A not-dog." Her face grew puzzled. "The witch women ask us to tell them of things that smell of magic but are not wild things."

Rage felt even more wary of the witch women now that she knew they were responsible for draining magic from the land. "We are not magic, but magic has been worked against us," she said carefully, knowing the cen-taur would tell the same story if the witch women asked. Better not to speak of the firecat and the hourglass. "We are looking for the wizard, to see if he can undo what has been done to us," she added.

"The witch women also seek the wizard, for they say

only he can restore magic to Valley," the sprite said. She bent to pet Mr. Walker. "You are a pretty thing, with your soft ears and big eyes. Magic has made you into this shape, and whence comes the magic?"

"An enchanted gateway brought us here and changed us," Mr. Walker said, twitching his ears.

"Where is this gateway?" the sprite asked. Mr. Walker started back in alarm from the sudden hunger in her eyes. The sprite looked abashed. "I did not mean to frighten you. It is just that magic is so scarce here now, and we are hungry."

"You haven't come from Fork?" Billy asked.

The sprite nodded. "Wild things cannot eat unless food is magicked for us, and there are no witches there. My friends and I went to the High Keeper to ask if they would not allow the witch women to come to Fork and create food for us. We had to wait a long, hungry time. Then he looked down from his seat of dead willow and said it was best that we fade, since we were never natural things and upset the Order of the land."

"I'm sorry," Rage said. "I wish we could help, but we really don't have any magic."

The sprite nodded sadly. "My friends say your words smell of the truth." Then she stopped and listened to the lions again. "My friends say there is another. . . ."

Bear came lumbering out of the trees lining the road, and the lions turned as one to regard her with their flaring golden eyes. Rage suddenly felt frightened that they might hurt her. But before she could say anything, she saw that the lions were merely sniffing Bear, who strangely allowed it. They then withdrew and sank on their bellies before her, purring loudly and spreading their glowing scarlet wings.

"They humble themselves before your companion," the sprite told Rage. "They say your companion is . . . I do not know a word for it. Greater magic? My friends can see a little into the future, and what they see makes them honor this great dark beast. Can you not hear them?"

"I can," Mr. Walker said with uncustomary shyness.

The sprite touched his face, then drew a deep breath. "Well, we must go back to Wildwood." She turned to Bear and made a low, graceful curtsy. "Farewell, Great One. If I have done naught in my life but look on you, it is enough."

The lions rose, and all three of them went on down the road.

"Well!" Elle said, staring after them. "What was all that about?" But no one answered, for they were staring at Bear.

She growled at them to leave her be. "I don't know why those creatures acted like that. There's nothing special about me. Nothing at all." She turned away and went back into the trees. She disliked being in the open now, even more than when she had been a dog.

"Could you really hear those lion things talking?" Elle asked Mr. Walker, as they set off again.

"I said so, didn't I? But it wasn't exactly talking. It was sort of a deep, purring music. A bit like the firecat's voice, but not so sneering and sly."

"We should have asked that sprite about the firecat, and we forgot to ask about banding, too," Billy said, but his eyes were on the bushes where his mother had gone.

"I don't suppose she would have known much about banding," Rage said. "And I don't think we should tell anyone anything about our business anymore."

"Maybe the firecat is a wild thing," Elle said.

"It couldn't be," Billy said. "Wild things can't work magic to feed themselves, and the firecat uses magic every time it appears."

"Maybe it can work magic because the wizard made it, and he is more powerful than the witch women," Mr. Walker said.

Rage said nothing. The encounter only seemed to have produced more questions. The sole interesting thing they had learned was that the witch women believed the wizard could restore the lost magic to Valley and were searching for him.

"Dangerous wild beasts," Goaty said, looking down the road after the sprite and the winged lions.

"She was very small," Mr. Walker said, and he sighed.

Not long after, the sun sank. They were beginning to think about finding a place to sleep when Billy pointed out an arc of light on the horizon.

"I bet the bridge to Fork is just over this rise," Rage said, excited.

But she was wrong.

6

It wasn't a bridge but a river port. Rage and her companions looked down on it from a low mound beside the road. The gray donkey and cart were tethered to a wooden pier with a hut built at the end of it. Obviously the little girls and the women in kimono dresses had already gone across the river. Rage noticed a big metal winch with thick, twisted iron cables stretching out across the water, which pulled the ferry across the currents to the opposite bank.

The darkness and width of the river meant that she could not see the other side. "Elle?"

"I see nothing, but I smell water and stone on the other side," Elle reported.

"I have been thinking," Billy said when they had been standing there staring down silently for some minutes. "The High Keeper told the sprite that wild things ought to be allowed to die because they upset Order here, and the woman in the cart said the wizard would not return until Order had been restored. What if the keepers are letting the wild things die because they think that will bring the wizard back?"

Rage stared, beginning to feel just a little bit awed by the way Billy was able to figure things out. She did not know what to say to his grim idea, but it struck her that a lot of people in Valley were looking for the missing wizard.

"Let's go down," Elle said impatiently. "We have done enough thinking, and talking about thinking."

"Going down is always a bad idea," Goaty murmured.

"I don't think we should go down just yet," Rage said. "Let's wait until a boat comes."

The others agreed. Billy suggested they travel in two groups when the time came to cross the river. "Rage will go as a human girl I am escorting to Fork to be banded, and the rest of you can pretend to be wild things," he explained. "You can be going to plead your cause to the High Keeper, like the sprite and the winged lions."

"I don't want to see the High Keeper," Goaty protested. "He sounds horrible."

"He does," Billy admitted. "But remember how the sprite said they were made to wait a long time to see him? He won't see you at once, and that woman in the cart said there were lots of wild things in Fork, so they must be able to move around the town."

"What about the other wild things?" Mr. Walker protested. "They will smell that we are not wild things."

"You'll just have to avoid them," Billy said, sounding exasperated. "You have to go as wild things, otherwise we will have to explain about the bramble gate and admit to coming from another world."

"I don't understand," Elle said. "I thought we were going to see the keepers about the wizard. Surely we'll have to tell them everything."

Billy glanced at Rage, and she saw that, like her, he had come to the conclusion that they had better avoid the keepers. "I think we should learn a bit more about the keepers before we reveal ourselves to them," he said.

Elle cast herself down on the grass with an expression of utter boredom and said she might as well sleep if they were not going anywhere. Goaty lay neatly beside her, and Bear and Mr. Walker curled up to sleep, too. Billy stayed beside Rage, gazing down at the pier. Several people were moving around the hut and the winch. They looked like workers, not passengers.

"What do you suppose the lions smelled on Bear?" Rage asked Billy.

"I don't know," he said. "It was very strange. That sprite said they saw something in her future." He shivered. "I could not bear it if something bad happened to her, Rage. Her life has been so hard already."

Rage understood. She felt the same about Mam. But she was beginning to see that something had been wrong with Mam even before the accident. That was why they had moved so often, and why Mam never made any friends. Rage had thought they went back to Winnoway for Grandfather Adam's sake. Now she wondered if they had come back because Mam hoped to heal whatever had been hurt inside her.

But Grandfather Adam had been just as cold and hard as ever.

Strangely, instead of hating her grandfather for the way he had been, she found herself trying to imagine what had happened to make him so blind to joy and laughter, so stony to Rage and her mother. It couldn't be because of Mam and her brother running away, as she had always thought—Mrs. Johnson had said Grandfather Adam was like that even before he married Grandmother Reny. That meant something must have happened to him even before Mam was born.

Later, as Rage laid out a supper of what remained from the baker's supplies, Elle vanished for a time. Returning, she shook herself mischievously, showering Rage and Billy with water. She had been for a moonlight swim. Goaty woke from his nap with a shudder as Elle and Billy fell into a wild romp. They were scolded happily by Mr. Walker, whom they almost squashed. Remembering what Billy had said about the difference between being a dog and being human, Rage wished she had their ability to put aside cares and live in the moment. But she was too human. Billy had once said that to be human was to be free to make choices, but really, being free only meant you had to worry about everything your choosing might cause.

She leaned back against a tree and closed her eyes. Listening to their puffing and panting, she could almost pretend she was home with Mam.

She wondered what the kids at school had thought when she didn't come to classes. They knew her mother had been in an accident and had been awkwardly kind when Rage returned to school, but she hadn't wanted anything from anyone except to be left alone. One of the boys had asked why her father didn't come, and the teacher had shushed him, but Rage wasn't offended. There were lots of kids in the school who did not live with their fathers, and at least one other boy who didn't know his father. Unlike him, Rage never thought about who her father might be. She didn't know why, but his absence hadn't hurt her at all. She had Mam, and that was enough for her.

After they had eaten their fill, Rage suggested they all sleep. It was unlikely another boat would arrive before morning. There were some bushes on the side of the mound farthest from the road, where they would not be seen. The animals curled up readily enough, even Billy, but Rage found she could not sleep, despite being tired. She wrapped her coat around her shoulders and thought about Mam, wondering how she was.

She could hear Mrs. Somersby: *Mary Winnoway will die if she doesn't wake and exert some will to heal. . . .*

Rage found she was crying, but it didn't much matter because it was dark and all of the animals were asleep. Then she noticed Bear watching her with dark eyes that caught the light of the moon in twin points.

"You are thinking of your mother," Bear said in her soft, gruff voice. "I smell your remembering. Long ago, I cried for my son. It is hard when you call and no one comes."

Bear's words made Rage feel guilty, but they also reminded her of a time when she had wakened to a cry in the night and had gone into her mother's room to find her asleep and dreaming. "Sammy!" Mary had cried, turning to the window. Moonlight poured onto her wet cheeks. "Don't leave me. . . ."

"Life is full of calls that are not answered and people who go away and do not return," Bear went on.

Rage nodded, her thoughts jumping to Grandfather Adam and his brother, Great-Uncle Peter. Mam told her that Great-Uncle Peter had fought against the creation of the dam in their valley. He and a lot of other people had marched and chained themselves to bulldozers and written letters to politicians, but it had been useless. The day the river was dammed, the water flooding what had once been his property, he left Winnoway forever. Could Great-Uncle Peter's departure have hurt Grandfather, just as Mam's brother's leaving had hurt her?

Rage looked at Bear, blinking back tears. "I'm sorry we took Billy away from you, but at least he lives and he is with you now."

"Sometimes it is too late," Bear said, so softly that Rage thought she might have imagined it.

Rage shivered and thought with longing of Mam, and of the times she had crawled into bed beside her on cold nights and had been kissed and cuddled close to her. More than anything in the world, she wished that she were home and that Mam were sleeping an ordinary sleep, safe in her own bed.

"I have to find the wizard and get home," Rage whispered to herself. The whisper fled before her into a dream of boots crunching along the river road.

She heard a voice calling her name and thought it was Mam's voice, faint because it had to travel from one dream to another in all the confusions of sleep.

"Help me. . . ."

"I'm coming, Mam," Rage muttered.

"Beware . . . dangerous . . . magic . . ."

Rage frowned and came closer to waking. The voice was not her mother's after all, but that of a man.

She opened her eyes to find Billy kneeling in front of her. Behind him the sky was still pitch-black.

"You were calling out," he said softly.

"I was dreaming." Rage rubbed her eyes and looked around to see Elle, Mr. Walker, and Goaty all cuddled up together, still asleep.

Billy helped her up. "Sometimes I used to dream I was chasing a ball. I would wake and find myself biting my own tail."

"Do you miss being a dog at all?" Rage asked, putting

her coat on properly.

He sighed. "Life was very vivid and simple. I didn't think so much. Once you start thinking, it is hard to stop." He shook his head as if that was not quite what he had meant. "The world you make in your thoughts is brighter than the real world." Again he shook his head.

Rage stuck her hands in her coat pockets to keep them warm and turned to look down at the pier. She was surprised to find a square, flat-topped boat tethered there. A cabin in the middle of its deck had an enormous wheel on each side, where the iron cables that stretched across the river were attached. The water was barely visible, for a thick, impenetrable mist lay over it like a ghostly eiderdown. There were torches lit around the pier and on the ferry, the mist smearing their brightness.

From the activities of the crew on deck, it looked as if departure was imminent, though there did not seem to be any passengers.

"We ought to go," Billy prompted her gently.

Rage hesitated. The centaur had called the water the River of No Return. Now that the moment of crossing was upon them, she hoped that the name would not prove to be an ill omen. *Maybe I should go over alone*, she thought.

"We must stay together."

She turned to find that Bear had spoken, and wondered if it was possible that the old dog could read her mind. She knew better than to ask. Since they had come to Valley, Bear had communicated almost as little as when she was a dog, though she had given up bossing the other dogs.

Rage drew a deep breath. "Billy and I will go first. Remember, you three must convince them that you are wild things wanting an audience with the High Keeper."

"What about me?" Mr. Walker asked sleepily.

"You can go in my pocket."

"What I want to know is, how are we going to find out about the wizard if we don't ask the keepers?" Elle demanded.

"We have to go to an inn, of course," Mr. Walker said. "Then we'll find a keeper who doesn't like the other keepers, or one of their servants, and they'll tell us what we need to know."

Rage looked at Mr. Walker and wondered if he was ever going to realize that life was never as easy as stories made it out to be. She did not voice her fears about the nature of banding or of keepers. She glanced over Billy's shoulder and saw that there was an increase in activity around the winch. She wondered if they ought to wait and catch a later boat. But if there were more passengers, it would be more dangerous. Better to use the cover of darkness while they could.

"We'd better go before we miss the boat," she said.

Mr. Walker climbed into Rage's pocket. Then she and Billy set off, having instructed the others to wait a little before following.

A big-bellied man, wearing a white cap and a thick black jumper that matched his wooly beard, watched them come down the hill.

"We would like to cross," Billy announced.

The man jerked his head at a small ramp running from the shore to the deck of the ferry. "Get aboard, then. Ferry casts off in ten minutes."

The ferryman's eyes slid down to Rage's wrists, but she had deliberately let her coat sleeves fall down over her hands. Then he looked up and past her, his eyes narrowing a fraction, and she knew the others must have arrived already.

"You together?" he asked Rage.

She turned and made a play of looking behind her vaguely, then shook her head. "Of course not," she said, and went aboard, followed by Billy.

"We three wild things wish to see the High Keeper," Elle announced to the ferryman, exactly as Rage had bidden her.

"Three, you say?" Rage turned in time to see the ferryman's eyes harden as they settled on Bear. "What is a true animal doing this side of the river?"

"What is the matter?" Rage asked, trying to sound like a curious bystander.

He slanted her a look. "Surely even folk from the outer villages know that keeper laws allow only cats and dogs and domestic true beasts this side of the river. A bear belongs in the provinces. The stone mountains, maybe, or the greenland. The keepers are bound to want to know how it got out of Order and into the hands of the wild things."

Rage swallowed. "I heard its friend say it was a wild thing."

"It's a bear, or my life on it."

Bear lumbered forward and gave a rumbling gurgle that was almost a growl. The man paled and held up his hands. "Take no offense, bear! It's keeper business, keeping Order. I'm a riverman, and river folk go with the flow. I'll take you, for there's no law against natural creatures crossing from the wild side, but you won't be allowed back."

Bear came aboard, followed by Elle and Goaty. The man kept a wary eye on them all as he untied the ropes that held the boat stable against the pier.

Once they got into the middle of the river they lost sight of both banks. They could hear the creak of the winch pulling them along the cable, the slap of water on the hull, and the occasional sneeze from Goaty. Even Elle's eyes could not penetrate the mist. It was eerie and clammily cold. Rage had the feeling that they were not moving at all.

They drifted separately along the deck to meet behind a pile of crates, out of sight of the ferryman and his crew.

"I am afraid there might be trouble on the other side," Rage said in a low voice.

Bear grunted. "There is always trouble when humans are involved."

"Mama, you must convince them that you are a wild thing," Billy said urgently, stroking her arm. "There's no use just growling at them."

"I will do what needs doing," Bear said, shrugging away his hand. She moved to the edge of the ferry, sat down, and stared across the swirling water. She looked very bearish in the dull light.

"That man said Mama is out of Order," Billy murmured. "Seems like Order covers a lot of things."

"I think in this case it means Bear is not in the place the keepers want her to be," Rage whispered. "Let's talk to that ferryman and see if we can find out anything that will help us."

After making a few meaningless, casual comments about the river and the mist, Rage asked the ferryman, "What will happen to the bear on the other bank?"

He shrugged. "If it is a true beast, it will be sent to the provinces."

Rage said lightly, "What if it turns out to be a wild thing?"

"It will be set free." He gave her a speculative look. "What's it to you what happens to the beast?"

"Nothing, except I thought it was a wild thing and pitied it," Rage answered. "But if it is a natural animal, I guess it will be well looked after in the provinces."

To her surprise, the man's face darkened and he opened his mouth. Then he seemed to think better of what he had intended to say. He finally said mildly, "Some say there is sickness in the provinces."

Rage did not know what to say to this, but the ferryman returned to the previous subject awkwardly. "Time was, everyone petted and marveled at the wild things. Keepers didn't much like the magicking of them. Felt it showed disrespect to the true animals the wizard had put here. Maybe people did think the true beasts dull in comparison to wild things, but that was just the novelty of them, see? There were no rules or laws about who could go where and do what. No objections if a girl wanted to study magicking, and no provinces, either. Humans, natural animals, and wild things went where they liked it best. Live and let live."

"Why did things change if everyone got along so well?" Rage asked, curiosity making her forget caution.

The ferryman frowned at her. "Don't the folk in your village teach history to their children? The keepers never liked the making of wild things, like I said. Rumbled and complained enough that the women who did the magicking left Fork and set up their own settlement in Wildwood. Keepers didn't like that, either. Eventually they set up the provinces on the other side of the river and moved all the natural animals there. The witch women, as they came to name themselves, paid no heed to the keepers. Claimed the wizard would have let them know by now if he objected to their doings. By then the wizard had got reclusive and difficult anyway. Matters stayed that way until magic started to dry up on the wild side of the river. The witch women went to see the wizard about it. A hard, strange journey it must have been, through that Deepwood the wizard magicked around his castle, but when they got there, there was no one home. He had gone."

"So the keepers accused the witch women of driving him away with their magicking," Billy guessed.

The ferryman gave him a strange look. "Stands to reason, eh?"

"Do *you* think the wizard left because of the witch women?" Rage asked.

"Why else would he go?" the ferryman asked, but Rage had the impression he was being careful rather than truthful. She wondered suddenly if, like the baker's sister and the centaur, he suspected them of being keeper spies.

"Then what happened?" Billy asked. "Girls started being forced to come to Fork?"

The ferryman looked at him. "Are you not bringing this young lady to the city for banding of her own free will?"

Billy looked taken aback, and Rage could tell that he had become so interested, he had forgotten their ruse. "Of course I am," he said boldly. "But in the outer villages we never hear much of how things come about. We were told girls had to come to the city and stay until they were too old to have babies. That it was now keeper law."

"Well, it is," the ferryman said, apparently mollified.

Maybe he had decided they were not spies, for now he said, "The keepers had cause to clamp down hard on the witch women, what with them draining the wild side of the river of magic. Folk supported the laws, which said they must come to the city and give up magic, but the witch women refused to leave Wildwood. So the keepers formed the blackshirt brigade and set them to hunt down the witch women and bring them in to be banded. But of course they still had woodcraft enough to evade their followers. All but a few escaped, but they have a price on their heads."

"How exactly does banding stop the witch women doing magic?" Billy asked lightly. "I've always wondered."

The ferryman shrugged. "Don't rightly know myself. It's something about iron. Once a girl's hands are banded, she can't draw the magic up into her mind for the working of it. Welded on, they are, and there's no way of removing them, save with the same heat that sealed them. The first couple of bands are only lightly welded because they have to be replaced as the wrists grow. But once girls become women, the weldings are made to last."

Rage felt sickened at the thought of the heavy bands she had seen on the arms of the baker's sister being welded onto the arms of the little girls in the cart. "If all the magic is gone from the wild side of Valley, I don't suppose the witches will bother the keepers for much longer."

The ferryman shrugged. "There are still a few pockets of magic left, but the fact that the witch women have begun sending the wild things to beg for keeper mercy tells how desperate they have become. Mercy is as scarce in Fork as magic is on the wild side of the river. The keepers won't stop until all wild things have faded and all witch women are dead or in chains. That female wild thing and her faunish friend we've got aboard don't look too bad, but most of the creatures that come over the river to plead are pale and hunched in their bits of rag, and near faded away."

Despite her own worries, Rage's heart went out to the wild creatures she had met—the centaur, the laughing sprite, and the winged lions. All her life she had loved to read of such fabulous things, and here she was in a world where they existed, only to discover they were dying. Not that they had looked sick to her, but perhaps she had been too dazzled by their beauty to notice. She felt a surge of anger. Her desire to find the wizard had been for her own reasons, but now she thought that she would ask him why he did not help the wild things, since it was his magic that had made Valley and everything that lived in it.

"You can't help but pity the poor things," the ferryman said. "But cold as the keepers are, I don't see they have any choice. If the witch women were allowed to use up the magic on the tame side of the river to feed their pets, they'd die soon enough anyway, along with the rest of us."

"Die?" Billy echoed, sounding as confounded by this as Rage felt.

The ferryman gave a great snort. "That village leader of yours ought to be whipped for your ignorance, lad. Of course all of us. What do you think holds Valley together but magic? What is left is barely enough to keep Valley intact. The River of No Return is nibbling at the edges of Fork even now. I don't wish harm on the wild things, but like I said, if they don't die now, they'll die later when the magic runs out. But we have a choice. We don't need to use the magic up."

"What has the river to do with anything?" Rage stammered.

The man gave her a look of disgust. "Valley was taken from the bottom of a great and terrible river. The River of No Return is a small part of that river, bound to flow through Valley by magic. If the magic is used up, Valley will return to the bottom of the river. Everything here will be engulfed by the waters from which the wizard took it."

"The wizard could stop it, couldn't he?" Billy asked.

When the ferryman spoke, he was blunt, as if they were too stupid to be spies. "The witch women claim he could restore magic to Valley, but the keepers say he won't return until the wild things are all gone and there are no more witch women. My own opinion is that the wizard left for his own reasons. Who knows what moves a wizard to do anything? It is said that he loved Valley above all things, yet he abandoned it. Why should we imagine he means to return?"

His words gave Rage a peculiar feeling. Here was another man who had gone away, leaving those behind to suffer.

"Why would the witch women use up the magic if they will die when it is gone?" Billy murmured. "It doesn't make sense."

The ferryman glared at them and said loudly enough to make Rage jump, "Do you accuse me of consorting with the witch women? I did not say I spoke to them. Nor do I know their business. I have heard rumors, is all." He turned away, muttering about work to be done. Several crewmen cast furtive looks at Rage and Billy.

"Look!" Elle cried, distracting them. Rage turned to see the other bank materializing out of the mist. It was immediately clear that this side of the river was vastly different from the wild side. A stern promenade of black cobblestones ran in a wide path alongside the water. Beyond this lay an enormous, dark city. In the distance, stone skyscrapers were swathed in mist. Between the skyscrapers and the river were a higgledy-piggledy mass of small black-roofed houses and twisting streets. There was not a spot of green anywhere—no trees, no flowers, no grass. The air smelled of wet stone and rust.

Rage went to the edge of the ferry and stared out in disbelief. She had known Fork was a city, yet this was so huge and uniformly dark that it seemed less a collection of streets and buildings than some vast, slow, cold creature. Unlike Leary City or even Hopeton, there were no lights in windows, no flashing neon signs, no helicopters, and no traffic noise. No ambulance or police sirens. No music. No sign of life despite the fact that most of the population of Valley lived here.

Rage shivered, thinking how hard it must have been for children to come from their pretty, sunny villages to this gloomy metropolis. She did not wonder that Fork left its mark on those who dwelled there. She wondered if the wizard had created the city, and she shuddered at the thought of a mind that could spawn such a place. Not for the first time, she tried to guess what they would do if the wizard turned out to be evil or indifferent. But he was their sole hope, and so she must go on searching for him. She didn't believe the ferryman's suggestion that the wizard had left Valley altogether, and wished that they had asked him about the Endless Sea. Too late now.

Just then it came to Rage with a little shock that the

lines of verse on the hourglass might actually refer to something other than the real shore of a real sea. After all, the verse spoke of a door. How could there be a door on a beach? It was far more likely that there was a tavern or a shop called the Endless Sea, maybe even named for the children's myth the woman in the cart had mentioned. The wizard might be living there under another name. Though why he would stay hidden when Valley was in danger, she could not imagine.

Unless he planned to appear at the last minute to save his creation.

Goaty and Elle had shifted closer. Rage didn't have the heart to tell them they ought to keep their distance. The city, looming ever nearer, drew her eyes again. It was like Mam's imaginary city without cars and roads, but it was also without light and brightness and greenness.

"Where are the people?" Elle asked in a surprisingly timid voice.

"It's too early for humans to be up from their beds," Billy said.

All too soon they were approaching a wall of blackened boards that formed a solid barrier between the bank and the ferry. There was a metal gate in the barrier, and through it Rage saw a group of men in black trousers, boots, and shirts. Her skin rose into goose bumps at the sight of them. Blackshirts! Mr. Walker had been right about people who made rules needing soldiers.

The men she glimpsed had a grim resemblance to the visitors from the child-welfare department who had come to talk to Mrs. Johnson after the accident. One was a man and the other a woman, but they had been alike, even down to the dark suits they wore. When Rage said she could look after herself and had often done so before, it was as if she had not spoken. If Mrs. Johnson had not insisted on having her, she would have been taken away and put who knew where.

The iron cables drew the ferry with a thud against fat rubber bolsters alongside the barrier. An authoritative voice called through the iron gate, "Any passengers, riverman?"

"Aye. Humans and wild things," the ferryman answered.

Rage leaned forward in time to see surprise register on the flat features of a blackshirt. Perhaps it was unusual to have passengers so early in the day. The surprised man's shirt had a thin red line down the front, and she guessed he was the leader of the group.

The ferryman told Goaty and Elle that wild things had to disembark first. Then he asked, "Where is the bear?"

Only then did Rage realize that Bear was nowhere to be seen.

7

There was no place that a creature of Bear's size could be hiding aboard the ferry. Even as Rage saw how Bear had solved their dilemma, Billy gave a howl of anguish and rushed to the edge.

Rage ran at him and caught his arm, afraid he might hurl himself over. "You have to stay calm," she told him fiercely. "We still have to get off this ferry."

"But Mama—"

"Can swim," Rage said, squeezing his arm desperately. Fortunately, the gate was narrow enough that they were hidden from the blackshirts. Billy was pale as milk, and she could feel him trembling. She turned to find the ferryman watching them.

"The bear went overboard," he said in a queer, emotionless voice. "Keepers won't like that. I'll be blamed for it."

"You needn't tell them," Rage said, abandoning any attempt to pretend they were not traveling with Bear.

"Maybe not, but the crew won't keep quiet without reason for it."

Seeing he wanted some sort of payment, Rage's heart

sank. There was only one valuable thing she possessed apart from the hourglass, and that was Mam's locket. One day it was to be Rage's to give to her own daughter, just as it had been given to Mam by her mother. It was precious because it was a link between all of those mothers and daughters. But if the ferryman told the blackshirts about Bear, they might never get home. Mam would have given the locket up in a second for Bear.

In the end, things are just things. They don't care about you. They don't love back, Mam's voice whispered to Rage.

Rage dug the locket out, took the photographs from it, and slipped them into her pocket. Then she held the empty locket so it dangled on its golden chain and glimmered in the light of the ferry lanterns.

"A pretty trinket," the ferryman said, making no move to take it.

Rage saw that he was trying to make her offer something more. "I have nothing else," she said desperately. She could hear Billy's teeth beginning to chatter with the strain of controlling himself.

"That bear is old," the ferryman said. "Why take her to Fork? You could have let her live out her life on the wild side of Valley."

"We had to come," Rage said desperately.

The blackshirts shouted to the ferryman to lower the ramp so that the passengers could disembark. Rage took a deep breath and did something she never would have dared do before. She reached across and dropped the locket into the ferryman's pocket.

"Say nothing of the bear," she said.

She feared he might fling it back at her or shout out to the blackshirts, but he only gave the whey-faced Billy a final, penetrating look before turning to instruct his crew to let the ramp down. Elle and Goaty went down it and through the gate in the barrier. Rage moved so that she could see what happened. Her heart was in her mouth as the blackshirts inspected them, but the men made no attempt to touch or even speak to either of them. It was as if they were afraid of being contaminated. One of the blackshirts was pointing away from the river, and Rage guessed the animals were being directed to the High Keeper.

She breathed a sigh of relief. She had been afraid that wild things might be escorted directly to the High Keeper. "Three to go," she muttered, praying no one would search her. It had seemed simpler to hide Mr. Walker. But if he had pretended to be a wild thing, he would be safe now. Beside her, Billy was rigid with tension.

"You'd best make haste," the ferryman advised, coming to stand beside her. "The bank is steep this side of the river." He said all of this without looking at her, without expression.

Thinking that she had taken such risks that another scarcely made any difference, she said, "I am not banded. Will they take me away immediately?"

There was a short silence. The ferryman asked in the same quiet voice, "Are you from the witch women?"

"No," Rage said, startled. "The bear is my friend."

"Then it must be great need that brings you all here. You might not be taken to a banding house if you can convince the blackshirts you have family or relatives to stay with. Go ashore now, lest they grow suspicious." The ferryman turned away.

Rage gathered her wits and whispered to Mr. Walker, who had begun to wriggle, that he must be still now or see them all thrown into the River of No Return.

Steeling themselves, Billy and Rage made their way across the ramp, through the metal gate in the barrier, and onto the bank. The blackshirt with the red stripe stepped smartly forward and asked Rage's name. He had thick, powerful arms and small, cold green eyes.

"My name is Rage Winnoway," she said meekly. She had rolled up her sleeves so that it was immediately apparent she had no bands.

"You are almost a woman," he observed.

"I am from an outer village," Rage answered, hoping he wouldn't ask which one.

"Who are you?" the leader of the blackshirts demanded of Billy. Rage crossed her fingers, but he answered well.

"I am Billy Thunder, protector of Rage Winnoway until she is banded. The leader of our village sent me with her to make sure no witch women tried to recruit her."

The blackshirt nodded approvingly and turned to Rage again. "I will assign two men to escort you to the banding house. The next banding is tomorrow evening at the Willow Seat Tower. You will not need this fellow any longer."

The obedient part of Rage almost wanted to do what the blackshirt ordered, but the new, stubborn part of her silently asked what right he had to tell her to do anything. Aloud she said calmly, "We are to stay with my uncle." Behind the blackshirts, she could see the ferryman ordering his crew to make ready to depart. There were no return passengers.

The guard frowned. "Your uncle should be here to collect you, then. Where is he?"

Her heart felt as if it were thudding in her throat. She thought fast, fingering the tiny photographs in her pocket. "I could not tell him exactly when I would come because I did not know how long the journey would take. His name is . . . Samuel Winnoway. He will be expecting us." She was afraid that the guard would ask where her uncle lived. She must not be separated from the others, especially with Bear lost.

Pleasepleaseplease. She willed the blackshirt to let them go on their way. Perhaps if there really was magic in the land, she could draw it up with her longing. *Please let us go.* She grew hot, and a bead of sweat trickled down her spine.

To her stunned delight the blackshirt suddenly shrugged, seeming all at once bored. "Very well. Be with your uncle by nightfall and make sure you register at the nearest banding house early tomorrow."

Rage felt physically weak with relief as she and Billy walked away from the pier and down the nearest street. The minute they were out of sight of the blackshirts, Billy stopped and said in a hoarse voice, "I must find Mama."

Rage bade him go ahead and let Mr. Walker out of her pocket. He shook himself, then trotted alongside her as she hurried after Billy, who had vanished around the nearest corner. Despite her concern for Bear, Rage could not help but stare at the houses. They looked like buildings out of an old storybook, except that they were all black. The uneven cobbled road—empty of cars, buses, or even horse-drawn carts—was black as well, and it twisted here and there like an eel. It struck her that there were no lights nor any other signs of life from the houses: no sound, no smoke from a fire, no door closing. The silence of the city was as palpable as the mist coiling along the cobbles.

They made their way back to the riverbank. It was very dark away from the ferry lanterns. Would morning light never come? The bank turned out to be every bit as steep as the ferryman had warned. It was set with big, smooth green-black stones to stop it from eroding. Rage knew there was no way Bear could climb it without help. Yet there was no sign of her in either direction.

Billy sniffed frantically, then said in an anguished voice, "I can't get her scent!"

They made their way downstream, peering anxiously out into the river, but after some time Billy stopped and turned to look back upriver. Rage guessed he was wondering if Bear had managed to reach the bank closer to the pier. She did not like to say that such a swift river could have carried Bear some considerable distance if she had not got to the shore quickly.

"Maybe she swam to the other bank," Mr. Walker said, but without great conviction.

"No," Billy said. "It is too far. We must go back and search nearer the pier."

There was no point in arguing that they might be seen. As they retraced their footsteps Rage noticed that the houses facing the water had dark windows that showed nothing behind them. She shuddered at the thought of unseen eyes watching them, though she had the queer sense that the houses were empty.

Once the pier and the departing ferry were in sight again, Rage caught hold of Billy. "We must not let the blackshirts see us!"

"I have to find Mama," Billy cried.

"You know she can swim," Rage insisted. "It is just a matter of—"

"Look!" Mr. Walker hissed, and they both turned to

ISOBELLE CARMODY

see a dark bulk move within a mass of shadowy reeds at the waterline, not far from where they stood.

Billy gave a groan of relief. "Mama!"

Bear emerged from the reeds and used her claws to drag her sodden mass onto the flat lip of the bank. It took all of their combined strength to push and drag her the rest of the way up onto the cobbled promenade. By the time they had managed it, their breathing was nearly as labored as hers.

"We have to find somewhere she can rest and get warm," Rage said, alarmed by Bear's utter exhaustion.

"I'll see what I can find," Billy said determinedly.

He ran off, and Rage reflected on how independent the animals had become. Was that because they had been transformed, or had they always been that way, without her knowing?

Trying to squeeze some of the water from Bear's thick fur, Rage felt her begin to tremble in shock. How much punishment could the old dog endure without being permanently injured? The journey was clearly taking a harsh toll on her, yet there was nothing Rage could do but push her to continue.

Elle and Goaty arrived, the latter looking deeply relieved.

"It is hard to smell far here," Elle said. She looked at Bear and sniffed. "She smells bad."

For once Goaty had nothing awful to add, which made Rage feel even more worried. What did *bad* mean? Sick? Tired? Dying?

"It took us a while to find her," Rage managed to say calmly. "She was in the water too long."

There was the sound of running feet and they all froze, but it was only Billy. He had found a small park farther along the riverbank. "It's not much better than this, but at least there is shelter," he panted.

Bear was in no state to be moved, but they dared not delay. They roused her enough to get her on her feet and led her to the park. This was filled not with real green trees but with black stone carvings of trees. Of all the things she had so far seen in the city, this horrified Rage the most. Why would anyone prefer black stone trees to living trees? On all sides of the park more of the small houses clustered together like black, crooked teeth. Again, it seemed to her that they were not separate houses but part of the same entity: this black city that seemed to have some sort of malevolent life of its own.

"I don't smell any people," Elle whispered uneasily.

Bear cast herself down under a stone tree with an overhang of drooping branches and lay as one dead. She had not said a single word since coming out of the water. Billy lay his jacket over her and lifted her head onto his knee. He stroked her fur, his face haggard with fear.

Rage knelt down beside them. "Billy, stay here with Bear and the others. I'll go and see if I can find out anything about the wizard."

Billy looked up at her, eyes brimming with unshed tears. "I'm afraid for Mama," he whispered.

Rage saw that all of his new power to think, and his delight in it, had been consumed by fear for Bear. She thought of her own mother but dared not dwell on her. She was responsible for herself and the animals being in Valley. It was time for her to think and act instead of letting everyone else do it for her.

"Bear's old and the water wasn't good for her, but she'll be all right if she rests," Rage told Billy with a mixture of Mrs. Johnson's kindness and Mr. Johnson's gruff certainty. She had to be firm because she knew the voice of fear must even now be whispering to Billy. "You must keep her warm. I will be as quick as I can."

She motioned to the others to withdraw and talk.

"The river did it," Elle said, looking more troubled than Rage had ever seen her before.

"It got inside her," Mr. Walker added.

Drawing a deep breath, Rage told them her plan. "I'm going into the city to see if I can find out where the wizard has gone."

"But we know that already. He has gone to the shore of the Endless Sea," Mr. Walker argued.

"Yes, but maybe the Endless Sea in the riddle isn't the real Endless Sea, if there is such a thing. Maybe it's the name of a place right here in Fork."

"Wouldn't those women in the cart have told us if it was?" Elle objected.

Rage shrugged. "It's a big city. And I asked about the Endless Sea, not about a place called the Endless Sea. Anyway, we have to do something." She directed a pointed look at Bear.

"All right," Elle said. "But you'd better not go alone. It might be dangerous."

"I'll take Mr. Walker in my pocket," Rage offered.

"He can't fight for you! He can't protect you!" Elle cried, but Rage was firm.

"Mr. Walker can hide in my pocket and come back for help if I get into trouble. Billy will need you here."

Rage felt a lot less sure than she sounded. But there was no point in burdening the others with her uncertainties. And maybe luck was on her side. She still found it hard to believe that the blackshirts had simply let her find her own way to her uncle's house.

Once she was out of sight of the park, her steps slowed and she tried to decide which direction to take. All of the houses looked exactly the same, and there was no sign of any people, nor of the circular, black Willow Seat Tower, to which the animals had been directed by the blackshirts.

Rage made up her mind to keep the river at her back and the skyscrapers in front. Surely such imposing buildings would be at the heart of the city, and among them she would be bound to find groups of people in which she could mingle and eavesdrop. She had no fear that she would not be able to find her way back to the others because the river would be her guide.

She had been walking for perhaps an hour when she entered a street that ran up a steep incline. At its apex, a perfectly round black tower stood in the center of a flat, open area paved in blocks of gleaming black marble that glittered as if studded with pieces of mirror: the Willow Seat Tower.

There were no signs of shops or stalls or anyplace where one might buy food or clothes. But here, for the first time, were people. Most of them were clad in long white gowns. Rage guessed these were keepers.

The thought of the High Keeper rejecting the pleas of the sprite and the winged lions made a cold, cruel picture in her head, even if it was true that Valley would be doomed if the wild things were fed any more magic. Still, something drew her toward the tower. Obeying the compulsion, she was careful to stay in the shadows and move as slowly as everyone else.

Rage was close enough now to see that all the people in the white gowns were men. But there were also men, women, and groups of boys and girls in plain gray tunics and trousers. Not a single spot of color was worn by anyone. No one spoke loudly or moved quickly. This crowd of harmoniously dressed people moving slowly and silently ought to have been beautiful, but the scene was strangely stiff and unreal. Everyone moved as if they were part of an old and complicated dance with many rules and tiny, intricate steps. No one looked happy.

This was a dance of obedience, Rage thought, each person doing only and exactly as he or she was bidden. This was Order, and clearly there was no joy in it.

"Have you noticed there have been no streetlights these past few nights?" Rage overheard a man observe to his neighbor in a low voice.

His companion nodded. "I heard there were orders that they should not be switched on, to conserve magic."

"Powering the lights doesn't consume magic any more than the enchantments that keep the provinces in Order. Besides, we don't need to conserve magic. It's those witches who need to do that."

There were indeed unlit streetlights—balls of glass on iron stalks attached to the walls lining the streets. Rage was intrigued by the news that there was more than one way to use magic. Apparently the keepers had some way of working it to organize the provinces where natural animals were kept. If what these men said was true, the keepers' working of magic did not deplete it. Rage wondered if the creation of the wild things was what had used magic up on the other side of the river. It must take more complex enchantments to create a living, thinking being than to organize animal habitats. If she was right, it would explain the keepers' dislike of wild things. But unless the witches were mad, there had to be more to it than that.

An ornately carved litter, borne on thick poles by eight muscular men, drew up beside the entrance to the tower. Rage watched closely as it was set down carefully by its bearers. Two men emerged from it, both elderly and clad in white. One, bent almost double with the weight of the years he carried, wore a tunic edged in gold trim. A troop of blackshirts marched toward the tower and saluted the two men. Rage scuttled hurriedly into a lane. It was too dangerous to stay here. She turned her back on the circular tower and began to walk in the direction of the black skyscrapers again.

"Where are we going now?" Mr. Walker asked, poking his head out to look around. He was a bit pale, but she supposed it was none too comfortable riding in her pocket.

"I am looking for a place where there are people. A market or a square," she told him.

"We must find an inn," Mr. Walker insisted. "You can buy some ale for someone, and they will tell you about the wizard."

Rage felt exasperated. "I haven't seen anything that looks like an inn, I don't know if they have ale here, and I have no money to buy it, even if they would serve someone as young as me!"

Mr. Walker looked disgruntled. "Those sorts of things never matter in stories."

"Well, this is not a story," Rage snapped. She had gone only a few more steps when Mr. Walker spoke again.

"You could knock at one of these houses and say you are trying to find your uncle Samuel, who lives near the big market. Then you could get directions."

It was a good idea, but before she could say so, the

little narrow street ended at a broad avenue, and as if at some hidden signal, dozens of front doors opened simultaneously, and dozens of gray-clad men and women emerged. The doors closed behind them soundlessly and almost in unison, and Rage had a dazed vision of all the doors in Fork opening up at the exact same moment and hundreds and hundreds of gray-clad people pouring into the streets in a silent flood.

Glancing around, she was shocked to see the black Willow Seat Tower in front of her again. How could that be possible when she had been walking away from it? Yet there was no mistaking the tower. The streets must twist about very strangely for her to have come back so close to it.

Not daring to walk boldly along the avenue, she peeped out and sought another lane. When there was a gap in the flow of people, she darted across the avenue and ran down the lane, until once more it ended at a broad avenue. This happened three more times before she recognized a pattern. The avenues all radiated out from the tower, while the lanes ran around it like the concentric rings in a tree trunk. But no matter how far she ran along an avenue before entering another lane, there was the Willow Seat Tower again, the exact same distance away!

Finally she gave up trying to make sense of the city. It had been built in an enchanted valley, so perhaps ordinary rules didn't apply. Taking any turn not filled with people, she walked and walked, always turning her face away from the Willow Seat Tower. But the black tower proved as hard to leave behind as the skyscrapers were to approach.

Then, all at once, she turned a corner, and there they

were, the skyscrapers, right in front of her. They were not modern skyscrapers after all, but ancient-looking towers made from huge blocks of rough-dressed, greenish black stone, with only a few unglassed windows set high up. Each tower had a tall iron door at street level, with a long lever worked by a complicated mechanism of cogs and meshed teeth instead of a doorknob. Over the doorways were spidery markings that reminded her of a picture she had seen in a history book of the writing on the walls of Egyptian tombs.

As Rage stood dumbfounded, a woman in gray came rushing around the corner and cannoned into her.

"What on earth are you doing here?" the woman demanded crossly. Her eyes fell to Rage's wrists, and in a flash she pounced. Rage found herself being marched briskly back the way she had come. In minutes they were approaching the black tower.

Rage began to struggle, though she could not bring herself to scream and draw the attention of all the silent walkers.

"Be still, child," the woman snapped, tightening her already viselike grip. "You are out of Order. By the look of your barbaric attire, you come from one of the outer villages. I suppose, being a bit older, you just thought you'd slip away from the banding house and do a bit of exploring."

Rage opened her mouth to tell the woman about the uncle she was supposed to stay with, but then she found herself being marched smartly *past* the door to the Willow Seat Tower!

Her relief that she was not going to be made to face the High Keeper was so great that she felt dizzy. She decided that she would not try to get away from the woman after all. She had no idea how to negotiate the strange, magical city, nor how to find information about the wizard. The banding house might be the very place to learn what she needed, especially if it was as easy to slip away as the woman's words implied. Far better to go there than wander stupidly in circles looking for some sort of public place. Anyway, if she did wrench her hand free and manage to get away, the woman would just summon the blackshirts and they would begin to comb the city for her, perhaps finding Bear and the others as a result.

They had walked no more than fifteen minutes when the woman stopped at a wooden door in a high stone wall and rapped at it imperiously. A young woman wearing a white apron over her gray clothes appeared.

"This girl is unbanded!" Rage's captor announced accusingly.

The young woman's eyes fell to Rage's wrists and widened. "I see, but what do you wish me to do? She was not registered here by the blackshirts. We are not expecting any new children before the next ceremony."

"She ought not to be wandering the streets! Look how close she is to womanhood."

"Her placement is the responsibility of the black-shirts," the younger woman said stubbornly.

"I will tell the brigade captain that you said as much. No doubt he will investigate the lapse in Order," the older woman snapped. "Meanwhile, the girl will remain here." She gave Rage a push that sent her stumbling into the arms of the younger woman, and departed triumphantly.

Inside the dimly lit hallway, the woman took a small notepad and pencil from her apron pocket. "What is your name?" Rage told her, and she wrote it down. "You may have to sleep top-and-tail tonight. The banding house is growing smaller, and there is less space than usual."

Rage was hardly listening. Instead, she contrived to drop a little behind as they walked so that she could ask Mr. Walker if he could stand to remain hidden a while longer.

"Not for too much longer," he whispered in martyred tones.

"In here," the woman said, and they entered a large, bare room with high, slotted windows that let in daylight, though Rage could not look out of them. Like everything else in the city, all of the surfaces were black and unpatterned.

The woman turned to Rage again. She was beautiful, with dark, lustrous hair smoothed into a bun and big, long-lashed eyes.

"My name is Niadne," she said. "I am one of the banding-house attendants. Are you hungry, child Rage?"

"A little," Rage admitted, puzzled that the woman did not ask how she had come to be wandering the streets.

"Nearly everyone is hungry when they arrive in Fork. And you have come very far. I don't suppose you were properly provisioned for the trip?"

"Not really," Rage said. "I didn't know how far I was to come when I set out."

"That is often the way of journeys," Niadne said serenely. "Especially journeys that lead to Fork. But come. You must wash your face and hands before you eat, and perhaps I can find you a gray tunic. You will have a proper gray gown for the banding. You will need to be fitted for it today, since the ceremony is tomorrow night. We must also find time to cut your hair. The High Keeper does not like hair to be so wild and curly. Too witchy."

Rage said nothing. She had no intention of being in the banding house long enough to have her hair cut.

8

Splashing her face and arms with warm, scented water, Rage was delighted to hear Niadne ask if there was anything she wanted to know. "I am aware that little is known of Fork in the outer villages," her companion added.

Rage's mind swarmed with questions, but she decided to begin simply, and asked if Niadne had been born in the city.

"I came from one of the villages on the other side of the river. Not an outer village like yours. But that is so long ago, it seems a dream."

"I suppose you love Fork now?"

There was a silence. "No. I could not say I love it, but I have grown used to it here." A hovering attendant handed Rage a simple gray shift and a pair of sandals, and watched as she stripped off her clothes to don them.

"These are queer garments," Niadne said, examining one of the ripple-soled hiking boots curiously.

"Can I keep my old things?" Rage asked.

"Of course you may," Niadne said kindly, which saved Rage having to try to think of what to do about

Mr. Walker, who was still in her coat pocket. Niadne watched her bundle the clothes up very gently before saying, "You probably won't ever wear them again, but there is no reason you should not keep them as mementos."

"Why does everyone in Fork wear gray or white or black?"

"The High Keeper wishes us to live in harmony with one another. To do so, we must give up selfishly asserting our individuality, even in our attire."

"What will happen after I am banded?"

"You will live in one of the childhouses, or if you have family here who claim you, you will be assigned to live with them. You will be given work to do and classes to attend each day, for idle hands make much mischief. But because you are older, and indeed almost a woman, an offer may be made for you. If that happens, you will go to live in the house of your future husband."

Rage's feelings must have shown clearly on her face. First they kept saying she was on the verge of womanhood, and now they were talking about marriage. She had barely begun secondary school! Niadne gave her a look of mild pity. "I suppose in your village girls and boys still choose their own partners, but here we are more efficient. The keepers will listen to proposals from boys or their fathers and then choose the most appropriate match for you."

"I'm too young to get married," Rage protested.

"You will not be wed immediately, but it is the High Keeper's belief that women are better growing in the will of their husbands from an early age."

All the better to stop them leaving Fork, Rage thought, wondering if Niadne had any thoughts or opinions that

were not given to her by the High Keeper. But she reminded herself that she was supposed to be finding out
about the wizard, not making judgments.

"Where is the Endless Sea?" she asked baldly, sick of
trying to find clever ways to avoid asking outright for the
information she needed.

Niadne smiled indulgently. "There is no such thing. It
is part of a myth about the River of No Return. The story
claims that once the river leaves Valley, it pours into a
vast sea that laps between all worlds."

Rage's mouth fell slack. The ferryman had claimed
that the River of No Return was connected by magic to
the very river from which the wizard had drawn Valley.
But what if it did flow to the Endless Sea? Common
sense told her it was more likely that the Endless Sea was
an inn, but this was a world held in place by magic! Why
shouldn't it contain a river that flowed to a magical sea?
In fact, where else would a river that flowed endlessly
from a magical land go but into an enchanted sea?

"What is the matter?" Niadne asked.

Rage discovered that she had stopped halfway
through putting on a sandal. "Nothing. I was just
wondering about boats."

Niadne's eyes widened in outrage. "Who would
speak to an innocent, unbanded girl about such dreadful
things?"

Rage blinked, confused. "A boy on the road said I
could see them here," she said quickly. In her experience,
boys said all sorts of outrageous things, only some of
which were true.

"Oh, a *boy*," Niadne said, looking both relieved and
exasperated. "Well, it would be best if you forget what
he said. Other than the river ferry, boats are only used by

the blackshirts. I will not speak of the purposes to which they are put."

"I just wanted to see them," Rage said, twisting her face childishly in the hope that this would cause Niadne to elaborate.

Niadne just pressed her lips together in disapproval. "Your mother will have told you something of her own banding, but you should know that this High Keeper is very strict. He will not look tolerantly on mistakes. You must be very careful to move slowly and keep in Order with the other girls as you walk up to the Willow Seat, and do not speak to any of the other supplicants during the banding. The High Keeper does not like women to talk. He believes it is a flaw in womankind that we chatter rather than think deep thoughts. Do not speak to the High Keeper at all. And do not look into his eyes."

Rage was surprised at how much she resented all of the rules made by the High Keeper. Back home, rules had always made her feel safe. It had not occurred to her that there might be bad rules as well as good ones, and she had obeyed them without question. The High Keeper sounded as harsh and mean-minded as the rules he made. *What would he do if I refused to obey them?* Rage wondered hotly, then realized she had spoken aloud.

Niadne regarded her gravely. "This is not a game, child Rage. The High Keeper might see your boldness as an omen. The best thing is not to be noticed. Make yourself utterly inconspicuous."

Or what? Rage wanted to ask, but she only said, "You can be sure I won't speak to the High Keeper." She had no intention of even seeing him. The more she thought about it, the more certain she felt that the River of No Return flowed into the Endless Sea. It made strange but compelling sense. She couldn't wait to hear what Billy thought.

Niadne was still regarding her anxiously. "Can I have something to eat now?" Rage asked.

Her question wiped the lines of worry from the woman's lovely face. "Children are always hungry," she said happily. "Come."

A little later, eating horribly sweet porridge out of a thick earthenware bowl, Rage studied the girls seated at her table. Most were a lot younger than her. Other than being slightly subdued, they appeared content to be in Fork. Maybe they took comfort from the company of their friends. From what she could gather, they had all come from their villages in twos or in groups, having been collected by the white-faced guardians.

The little girls Rage had seen on the road recognized her at once, and the one who had invited her to ride with them insisted she join them. Her name was Ninaka, she said, and her two friends were Sarry and Bylan.

"Where is *your* friend?" Bylan had asked pertly after Rage introduced herself.

"Friend?" Niadne asked. "There was another?"

"A boy," Rage said quickly. "He came to escort me, but now he has gone back."

Niadne seemed mollified and told Ninaka that boys did not come to this childhouse, which was a temporary refuge for those to be banded.

"My brother is coming to Fork soon, but he will not stay in a childhouse," another girl said. "He will go to the keeper academy. He says the villages are dead and one day Wildwood will just be another province ruled by the keepers."

"My brother wants to be a blackshirt," another said.

"My brother *is* a blackshirt!" yet another offered.

"Hush," Niadne said. "Good girls do not boast or speak loudly, even of their brothers."

The little girls exchanged abashed looks.

"What *do* girls do?" Ninaka asked. "Can we be keepers and blackshirts, too?"

Niadne shook her head. "Keepers and blackshirts must be strong and give orders and make rules. Girls are not good at such things."

Rage gritted her teeth and vowed that she would never obey another rule or voice without first deciding that it was wise.

"Why is everything so black and dark in Fork?" Sarry asked in a mournful voice.

All of the little girls sat cross-legged in a circle around Niadne, who folded her hands neatly in her lap. "In the beginning," she said primly, "the wizard used his great magical power to draw Valley from time. He made it to be fruitful. He filled it with natural beasts, and he made the river to flow through it and the moon and the sun to shine on it. He brought high-minded men to keep Order, and women to be their obedient helpmates. He made the great city of Fork for them to live in. At that time, Fork was shining and filled with music and color, and there were bridges of glass and sculptures of silver and gold."

"Why did it become black?" Sarry asked, sounding sadder than ever.

Niadne gave her a reproachful look. "You must not interrupt in such a rude and aggressive way, child Sarry. You must wait until I have finished speaking, and then, if no one else is speaking, you may speak."

"Why *did* it become black?" Rage repeated in the silence that followed this soft scolding.

Niadne looked at her in disapproval, but this time she answered. "The city blackened to reflect the disappointment the wizard feels at what became of Valley."

"You mean, because of the magic being used up?"

Niadne pressed her lips together for a moment, then nodded stiffly.

"But how could Fork reflect what the wizard feels when he left Valley so long ago?" Rage asked.

"Valley is held in place by the wizard's magic. He knows what is happening here. That is why we must strive so hard for Order. Perhaps, in time, he will forgive us and return," Niadne said piously. "Only then will the city grow light again."

She rose and directed them to rinse their plates and spoons and dry them. Another attendant summoned them to practice the banding ceremony. Rage began to follow the other girls, but Niadne asked her to remain behind.

"The ceremony is not so very complex that you need worry about lacking practice," she said. She led the way through a door and down a passage that brought them to a long room where women sat sewing and ironing. "Practice is needed for the little ones, since they forget things easily. But you are old enough that you need only be shown once or twice. Tonight and tomorrow morning there will be practices, and those will be sufficient. Now you must be fitted for your banding dress."

"Why do the little ones have to be banded so young?" Rage ventured.

Niadne gave her a quick look. "Well, it was not

always so, of course. In your mother's time and mine, as I am sure she told you, only women who came to Fork were banded. The keepers would not have magic worked this side of the river. But when magic began to die on the other side of the river, the High Keeper announced that all girls must be banded, so that there was never any possibility of their drawing magic from the land and harming Valley."

"The keepers use magic in the provinces, don't they?"

Niadne shook her head. "They do not work magic. They channel it."

Rage was confused. Maybe channeling was like making a river flow to a different place, while the making of wild things and magical food was like taking the water away in buckets and drinking it or letting it evaporate. But even then water was never really used up. It was transformed into mist or moisture and eventually would return as rain.

"I don't understand why the witch women keep on wanting to work magic if it is destroying Valley."

Niadne looked aghast. "Child Rage, you must not speak of . . . of those women here. The High Keeper has decreed that they are not to be mentioned. You must learn to curb your tongue. There are many unpleasant punishments for women, and even children, who speak or behave in forbidden ways."

Rage was puzzled that mention of the witch women seemed to occasion more alarm than the possibility that Valley would be destroyed. "If the wizard comes—"

"He will not come until Order is restored in Valley."

Rage was suddenly sick of hearing about Order. "It seems to me that Order is whatever the High Keeper decides it is. I can't believe a wizard who made all of

Valley and Fork would want all curly hair to be cut and everyone to wear gray."

Niadne paled. "You must not speak so, child Rage. The wizard is not here, and so the High One keeps Order in his absence. It is not for us to question the rules he imposes."

Not even if they are stupid, mean rules? Rage thought, but she held her tongue and kept her face meek as she was measured by two slender young women with downcast eyes. She thought darkly of how, in stories, people left in charge often ended up wanting to go on being in charge. Sometimes they even plotted to murder or imprison the true ruler, to make sure they would not return to claim their place. What if the keepers, who seemed so fond of making rules, had done something to the wizard? But the keepers would be no competition for a powerful wizard. Yet it did seem possible to her that the keepers might be glad that the wizard had gone, despite what they said.

Rage remembered the two men she had overheard talking about the loss of magically produced power in Fork and the rumor of sickness in the provinces. A queer thought occurred to her: what if the magic on *this* side of the river was fading as well?

"How does anyone know there is magic on *this* side of the river?" she asked without thinking.

Niadne's lovely face grew stern. "You will suffer the discipline of silence if you go on speaking so thoughtlessly, child Rage," she said.

Rage decided she had better not provoke the woman and tried to look penitent. Besides, if the magic *had* died on this side of the river, Valley would have gone back under its river and they would all be dead. If it had begun to fade, the keepers who looked after the provinces would have noticed.

The two women who had measured her knelt and unrolled a bolt of gray silk. Their scissors flashed through the lengths, then they pinned the pieces together around her, their hands darting like quicksilver, their touches as light as a butterfly landing. At last they stood back and surveyed their handiwork with tilted heads. Turning her to face a mirror, they began to unbind her matted plait and comb out the snarls with fine combs and slim, gentle fingers.

Rage stared into her own face and realized she had not seen herself since leaving her own world. Was it her imagination, or did she look different? Certainly her face was less round and her chin more pointed. Her eyes were more watchful, too. But she knew she had changed inside much more than outside. She was less frightened of things. She could hardly remember why she had been so nervous of leaving Winnoway, talking to the other children at school, or telling the Johnsons she wanted to visit Mam. Was it possible that the journey through the bramble gate had changed her, too, if not as obviously as the animals? Or was it just that she had come so far alone and had faced so many difficult decisions and dangers that many of the things that had once frightened her seemed silly?

Like Niadne's, the hair of the two attendants was plaited and fastened closely and sleekly about their heads so that not a single stray hair floated free. They clearly intended to do the same to Rage's hair, but before long it stood out all around her head in a wild aureole of moonbeam-colored spirals.

Finally one of the seamstresses murmured, "I do not

think this will be tamed into Order."

"It will be cut tomorrow when she is being readied for the banding," Niadne said dismissively. "It is not the sort of hair that will lie down and be still."

Nor will I, Rage thought. Her amber eyes flashed in the mirror.

"As she is older, we will embroider silver and pearl beads all over the hem and here at the neckline," one of the seamstresses told Niadne. "It will glitter and shimmer in the sun. She will be so beautiful, an offer will surely be made."

"The High Keeper will be pleased," Niadne said.

I bet he will be, Rage thought. She wanted to tear the lovely gown off and flee the cloying, perfumed air, but she made herself stand passively while they removed the dress, piece by careful piece.

Collecting her bundle of clothes, Rage felt Mr. Walker stir, and hoped he was all right. She yawned widely and asked Niadne in her meekest voice if she could sleep.

"Of course," Niadne said kindly. "You may rest until supper, and then you will be fresh for the evening practice."

She brought Rage to a tiny, cupboard-sized room containing a single pallet bed with white sheets and gray blankets, and a bucket with a lid. Rage had expected to find herself in some sort of dormitory, and her heart sank when the door was locked from the outside. It would be impossible to escape the windowless cell at night. That meant she must risk slipping away during the evening practice or at suppertime. It would not be long before her absence was discovered and an alert sent out to the blackshirts, but there was no alternative.

When Niadne's footsteps had faded, Rage shook her clothes, and Mr. Walker came out, looking cross and rather ill. "That is the last time I am going in anyone's pocket," he announced. "It is *too much*."

Rage smoothed his disheveled fur and made soothing noises until he calmed down, then she gave him a piece of bread she had hidden in her sleeve. When he had eaten, Mr. Walker sighed and said, "We must get away before they cut your hair. Once a woman cut my fur and nipped me on the ear. Having your fur cut is a very bad thing."

"Having your hair cut is not quite the same thing as having your fur trimmed, though I expect the High Keeper would make sure it was a very ugly haircut. But I don't suppose it would be the end of the world," Rage said.

"You never know when magic and hair might be mixed up together," Mr. Walker said. "Hair is very odd stuff. Look at what happened to Samson when his was cut. Then there was that princess who grew into a giant when her hair was cut."

"Ragewinnoway whose name is also Stupid!" a voice taunted.

Mr. Walker began to growl ferociously. Rage woke, wondering where she was. Memory flooded back, and she hissed at Mr. Walker to be quiet. "What do you want?" she asked the firecat softly.

There was a pause full of anger, then the wall began to glow red above the bed. Mr. Walker gave a yelp of fright and launched himself into Rage's arms.

"It's only the firecat," Rage assured him.

"Only! *Only?*" it mimicked furiously.

"Yes, only," Rage snapped, wondering why it had ever made her feel nervous. After all, other than tricking her into coming to Valley and setting them to find its master, it had done little but sneer and refuse to answer questions. Incredibly, she had hardly thought of it since coming to Fork.

"Not taking hourglass to shore of Endless Sea!" the firecat said vehemently.

"I am doing my best," Rage answered.

"Not taking. Locked in little room! Stupid, stupid Ragewinnoway!"

"I may be locked in, but at least I know how to get to the shore of the Endless Sea," Rage said sharply.

Mr. Walker looked up at her. "Do you really?"

"How getting there?" the firecat asked warily.

Rage considered refusing to answer, but after a hesitation she said, "We have to go down the River of No Return."

"Ragewinnoway will go down river?" the firecat asked in such a queer, tense voice that any doubts Rage felt about whether the river would bring them to the Endless Sea vanished. But if the firecat had known this, why hadn't it said so? She decided not to antagonize it by asking it directly.

"I'll go down the river if I can find a boat to carry us," she said. "Maybe you could help us find one."

"Clever Rage is finding out all things on ownsome," the firecat purred. "Doing what must be done. Good. Brave."

Its voice seemed to be fading, and Rage remembered she wanted to ask it about the magic in Valley. "Is magic really dying here in Valley?" she asked.

"Of course not dying. Why such stupid thinking?" It

scoffed so firmly that Rage thought it must not know about the magic fading.

"Can you get us out of this place?" she asked, but the glow on the wall winked out. "Wretched creature!" she muttered.

Suddenly the key in the lock turned. Mr. Walker barely managed to dive into her coat before the cell door swung open.

9

Instead of Niadne or one of the other attendants, a gray-eyed girl only a few years older than Rage entered.

"We meet again," she said.

Rage was startled to recognize the voice of the youngest of the three guardians who had been in the cart that brought the little girls to Fork. Last time they met she had been masked in the white paint that made her teeth look yellow, and she had seemed much older.

"You are . . . Ania?" Rage said.

"You have a good memory, Rage Winnoway. I have come to help you escape the banding house. But we must make haste, for the blackshirts will soon arrive to check the names against their list of all who dwell here."

"Niadne has written down my name already, and the blackshirts have it, too."

Ania smiled. "I can do nothing about the blackshirt list, but names in Niadne's book do not necessarily remain there. As long as we hurry, the blackshirts will never know you were here. Quickly, gather your belongings."

"You work for the keepers!" Rage accused.

"I may work here, but I assure you that I do not serve the High Keeper or his minions."

Rage hesitated. The last time she had accepted an offer of help from a stranger, she had ended up in Valley. On the other hand, she would be a fool not to jump at the chance to be free of the banding house. She dragged her coat on over the gray shift and gently bundled up the rest of her clothes. Despite her care, Mr. Walker groaned. "Where are we going?" she asked quickly, to cover the noise.

Ania was not listening. She walked over to the nearest wall and peered at the seam where it joined the floor. Glancing in both directions first, she knelt and pressed her palms flat to the floor. Rage could see no lever or button, yet there must have been one, for a section of the floor slid soundlessly aside, revealing a set of rough-hewn steps leading down into darkness.

"Where do they go?" Rage asked.

"Down," said Ania. She might have said more, but they heard footsteps coming along the corridor. "Quick!" she hissed urgently, slipping into the opening. Rage followed, and the moment she was clear, the floor above slid shut, leaving her standing in pitch blackness.

Several sets of boots sounded directly overhead, and gradually the voices of their owners became audible.

". . . latest arrivals have been fitted with their banding gowns and are now practicing their movements for the ceremony." It was Niadne. Rage tensed, but her name was not mentioned.

When the boots and voices had faded away, Ania's hand pressed at her shoulder. "Make no sound as you climb down, for this stairway runs by places where we could be heard." She sounded breathless and apprehensive, which did much to reassure Rage that she was not working for the keepers.

The steps led to a tunnel, which led to more steps and finally to some kind of cellar. Ania bade her wait. A thick, dank odor rose in her nostrils, as if Ania had opened a trap door in the very earth. Then Rage smelled something sharp and acrid that made her want to sneeze. Ania told her to kneel and pushed her toward a wall. "There is another tunnel in front of you. It is low, so you must crawl. I will follow."

Rage obeyed awkwardly, trying to be careful of Mr. Walker. Under her hands, stone became mud. Rage wished she weren't wearing a tunic, for it made crawling difficult. They crawled for miles, or so it seemed, turning now left and then left, then right, in no discernible pattern. At last she felt stone under her palms again, and Ania stood up, panting hard. Rage stood, too, her knees and palms stinging. It was still very dark, but chinks of light penetrated the small room into which they had crawled. Rage could dimly see Ania's features and dark-pupiled eyes.

"Here we can talk without fear of being overheard," Ania said, holding up her arms to bare her bands. "These are not metal. They are made by magic to seem so."

"You are a witch woman?"

"I will deserve that title when I complete my apprenticeship, but I can already draw magic from the land and work it in small ways," Ania admitted.

"You are here stealing magic for the wild things?"

"Magic cannot be stolen or used up by what I do, Rage Winnoway."

Rage did not want to go into this argument. "Why you are helping me?"

"I was bidden to do so by my mistress, the Mother of the witch folk. But tell me, where are the five that traveled with you? Are they safe?"

"They are hiding." Rage decided not to bring Mr. Walker out and complicate matters. "Why does your mistress want to help us?"

"I do not know," Ania admitted. "But I am not the only one in Fork who was bidden watch for a girl called Rage Winnoway who traveled with five nonhumans that smelled of magic."

Rage had told the centaur and the sprite that they were trying to find the wizard. She supposed they had reported it to the witch Mother.

Ania continued, "I was told only to say that what you desire, the Mother desires also: the finding of the wizard so that Valley may be saved."

"I thought Valley would be safe as long as no more magic is used up."

"Magic is not like a loaf of bread that can be used up, Rage Winnoway. It is a flow like water. Better to say that the flow of magic here is afflicted. First it was afflicted in Wildwood, and now it is the same here in Fork. Each day the River of No Return becomes more ferocious as it begins to rejoin the great water from which it was taken. When magic ceases to flow, the river will consume Valley."

"The keepers think that the witches—"

"At least some of the keepers know that the magic flow in Fork is fading," Ania interrupted sternly. "They will not tell the people, for it means admitting they were wrong about the witch folk. Or that they lied. But in time, all will know the truth. Our only hope is that the wizard will return to save Valley."

"Wait," Rage said, and she wriggled out of the sodden gray tunic and pulled on her own clothes. She turned to Ania. "Show me where the boats used by the blackshirts are kept."

Ania looked as shocked as Niadne had been at the mention of boats. She took a deep breath and seemed to brace herself. "I will take you, but it means traveling through the oldest part of Fork, to the other side of the city. Are you willing?"

"What do you mean?" Rage said suspiciously. "The river flows this side of the city."

"The river goes on both sides of the city because it splits above Fork," Ania said. "The part you crossed to come here is only a portion of the flow. Farther down, it splits into many smaller threads and feeds the wetlands. The main strength of the river passes to the other side of Fork, and soon after flows out of Valley."

"All right. Let's go," Rage said, barely able to control her excitement. With Ania's help, she might even be able to steal a boat and hide it before fetching the others.

Again Ania knelt and put her hands flat against the floor. Beside Rage a block of stone swung away, revealing a set of ascending steps. In minutes they were both standing in the open. It was twilight, and the sky was a brilliant swirl of cloud and color, the sun visible between buildings and low in the sky. Rage was horrified to think she had wasted almost the whole day in the banding house. "You know the way?" she asked as Ania set off briskly.

"It is not a matter of knowing the way," the other girl said over her shoulder. "With Fork, one must know one's destination. Then you need only walk and the city will bring you there."

Rage was fascinated. "You mean, if I thought of the boats, I would just be able to walk and end up where they are?"

Ania shuddered. "The boats are artifacts. They are not part of the city. You must know the *place* you are seeking. You see, the city understands itself. If you do not know where you want to go, the city cannot fathom your desire. If you are confused, you will find Fork confusing."

It gave Rage an odd feeling to think of the city as some sort of living, thinking entity, and yet hadn't she felt exactly that when she first saw it? She had not only thought of it as a live beast but also a sinister one. "Is the city's magic good?" she asked.

"One can no more think of magic as good or bad than one can call an ax good or bad. But the purposes to which they can be put may be good or bad. Fork's magic reflects what occurs within its walls and streets."

Niadne had said something similar about Fork being made from responsive magic, but she had claimed that the blackness reflected the wizard's disapproval at what had happened in Valley. Rage did not know which version to believe. She was more concerned with finding a boat to take them out of the city and, she hoped, out of Valley. "Why does everyone act so strangely when I ask about boats?" she asked.

"You will see soon enough." Ania refused to be drawn out further on the subject.

They were now moving along narrow, cobbled paths that ran between the somber stone towers with their queer markings and levered doors. There were no people around, and Rage asked the witch girl about the emptiness of the streets.

"There are only certain times when people are permitted to leave their homes or places of work or training," Ania explained. "Of course, that is one of the High Keeper's rules."

"Of course," Rage muttered darkly.

"A lot of the houses and towers are empty," Ania continued. "The city grows and shrinks and changes shape constantly."

Rage wondered what would happen if one was standing in a bit of the city that decided not to *be* anymore. But maybe the city always knew where people were, and left them alone. "Those tunnels and stairs we just used . . . ," she began.

"Oh, the city made them because I asked it with my own magic," Ania said casually.

"You mean, when you put your hands on the ground, you were drawing magic out of it?" Rage asked excitedly.

Ania smiled. "I know exactly what you are imagining now—all manner of wonders that magic could let you do and be and have. But magic is not so easy to hold nor to shape in your mind. It is like trying to remember a very, very difficult and tricky tune. It takes much training and discipline to learn how to perform even the smallest working. And you have to be in touch with the earth the whole time. The moment you stop, the flow ceases and so does the working."

"Is that why you made the tunnels so low back there?"

Ania nodded. "I can just manage to reach the flow through floors. It is better if I can touch dirt. Or mud." She grimaced at her filthy dress and hands.

"But what about the wild things? How do they exist if the witches who created them aren't constantly touching the ground? Why don't they vanish?"

"Their creation is the result of a different way of using magic. But what they do does not use magic up."

"Why did the witch women make the wild things in the first place?" Rage asked.

Ania shrugged. "Why does anyone create anything that is beautiful and difficult? It is the striving that counts, and the making of something wondrous and exquisite. And the witches who used this magic had to bind the spell of creation up with a little of their own souls. One cannot create life without cost. But they don't make them now."

"Because of the wild things starving?" Rage guessed.

Ania smiled slyly. "The wild things are hungrier since magic stopped flowing through Wildwood, but we do not let them starve. They are sent here by the witch Mother to petition the High Keeper for mercy, and he allows it because he is cruel and proud and it pleases him to see them fading. Once their pleas have been rejected by the High Keeper, we witch folk who dwell here in secret feed them and they return to Wildwood."

"The keepers think the wild things are dying out."

"That is what the Mother wishes them to think. When they come to Fork, the wild things carry enchantments that make them appear sickly. They also avoid humans so as to seem scarce. The real reason witch women no longer create wild things is because Valley is in danger and they do not wish to create beasts only to see them perish."

"Did the wizard really take Valley from time?"

"So they say."

"*Why* did he?"

Ania shrugged again. "Who knows why a wizard does anything? Some say he saved Valley from a terrible flood. Others say he wanted a place to use as a sanctuary for the animals he brought here. But if that was so, why bring humans?"

"To keep everything in Order?"

"So the keepers preach, but what need have wild animals of Order?" Ania stopped to survey another of the wider streets, then said as they crossed it, "I have told you I work magic, but you should not think I will be able to use it to protect us if we are caught by blackshirts. The keepers believe a girl must be full grown before she can work magic. In reality, we have the potential for magicking from the moment we can think and imagine. If the keepers understood this, they would band us from birth. If we are caught, I will admit to being a sympathizer, but no more than that. I will deny all that I have told you, no matter what they do to us."

Rage realized with a sick feeling what Ania was trying to say. "You mean they'd torture us?"

"It is better not to voice such possibilities," Ania warned. "But if we are caught, remember that you would only be punished for being a sympathizer. There is a much more terrible fate for anyone caught working magic in Fork, and it may be that the keepers would judge your use of magic to come here as a high crime."

If mere sympathizers were tortured, Rage did not dare to imagine what the punishment might be for a "high crime." It terrified her to think that someone might deliberately hurt her. She didn't know how she would have the courage to keep silent about Ania if that happened. *I'd better not get caught*, she told herself.

They walked several more blocks between the stone towers in silence. She thought about the hourglass in her pocket and considered telling Ania about it, but some part of her rejected the idea so forcefully that she felt disoriented. Maybe it was because the hourglass was her sole link to the wizard and her only means of winning his help for Mam.

Thinking of her mother made Rage feel strange. It had been so long since she had seen her. Guiltily, it came to her that she was getting used to making decisions and being on her own. Sometimes many hours went by without her even thinking of Mam. "Tell me about the provinces," she urged Ania, because if she thought any more about her mother, she would cry.

"What about them? A place for everything and everything in its place, that's what the provinces are about. The keepers say that is what Order means. They made the provinces so that each animal has its own place. Habitat magic in the land keeps any animal from hurting another or straying out of its own territory. But it is no different from cages. We witch folk think all creatures, natural and magical, should be left to run wild and free. There should be no keeping and no territories but the ones animals carve for themselves. The Mother says that is what nature and the wizard intended. The keepers ask, what are keepers for if not to keep Order?"

Poor Mr. Walker began to fidget violently in Rage's pocket, which was his way of saying he needed to get out. When they turned the next corner Rage hung back and set the little man down, whispering for him to follow but stay out of sight.

"What is the matter?" Ania called back.

"A stone in my shoe," Rage answered, and caught up with her.

A group of adolescent boys in white robes came out of a street. Several glanced at them, frowning.

"Why did they look at us like that?" Rage asked when they had gone out of sight.

"They're keeper apprentices, and they looked like that because we are girls. They've been taught that the seed of dis-Order is in all females."

This did not accord with what Niadne had said about the keepers saying girls were naturally weak and obedient. It made Rage see all over again that the High Keeper's rules were shaped to punish girls who were strong. In a way, Mam had done the same thing in telling her over and over to be quiet and good, Rage thought sadly.

She was so busy with her thoughts that she did not notice it was getting more and more damp until she slipped on the wet cobbles. Before she could ask if they were nearing the river, a man in a black robe crossed the street in front of them, leading an elephant and its baby. Rage was dumbstruck by the sight. It was only after the trio had vanished down another street that she saw the hides of both elephants were marred by livid, scabby patches.

"They were sick," she murmured, remembering what the ferryman had said about sickness in the provinces, and wondering if the fading of magic was the cause of that as well.

"Animals are brought in from the provinces to be treated at the conservatorium when they are ill so that if they are contagious, an entire species won't be wiped out," Ania murmured.

Another group of boys entered the street and marched slowly toward them. One smiled fleetingly at Ania, though the rest gave her disapproving looks.

"That was my friend," Ania said shyly when they had gone.

"A keeper's apprentice is your friend?"

"Not all of them think keeping is about controlling and Ordering. Some, like my friend, think it just means watching over and healing. He became a keeper because he believes you can't change things from the outside. Maybe he's right, but I'm afraid that by the time he's high enough in keeper ranks to make a difference, it will be too late for all of us."

Rage was very much surprised to hear that all keepers were not harsh and controlling. "Does he know that the flow of magic is dwindling here?"

Ania shook her head and looked troubled. "The Mother has forbidden us to speak of this to anyone but witch folk. I do not know why."

The street they were walking along ended suddenly at the edge of a wide canal running swiftly with water. Ania turned and followed the path running alongside the canal until they reached a small bridge that allowed them to cross to the other side. They had not gone far when they came to another canal, and then another. All of the canals were bridged and before long it seemed to Rage that there were more canals than streets.

"This part of Fork is built over the river," Ania explained.

Rage lost count of the canals and bridges they crossed after that. The air and the buildings became increasingly wet, and in some places the stone was so eroded that it had a diseased look. As they moved deeper into the canal district of Fork, there were fewer of the forbidding stone towers and more buildings with turrets, cupolas, differently shaped windows, and funny flights of stairs and balconies. The stone here seemed less black than gray, and the area was more run-down than the rest of Fork. Rage wondered why the city had not repaired itself, but perhaps it did not see the erosion as ugly. Nor was it, any more than the wrinkles of an old woman made her ugly. In truth, Rage thought the area far nicer than any other part of the city she had visited.

"This is Old Fork," Ania said. "The new part, where the Willow Seat Tower stands, is called Outer Fork or

Newfork. Then there's Lower Fork, which goes down to the wetland provinces, and a section that goes up to the desert and mountain provinces, called Upper Fork. I like this part best because even though it is so damp and crumbling, there are no people living here anymore and the city may be whatever it chooses."

"Is it true that the wizard made Fork?" Rage asked, again wondering about the mind that had created such a city. Niadne had said it was beautiful in the beginning. Did the degeneration of the city mirror that of the wizard?

"Don't judge the wizard by what Fork has become," Ania said, seeming to read her mind. "It was very different when he made it. There were gardens and trees and lawns, white cobbles rather than black ones, and all of the buildings were different. They say it was so lovely a melding of nature and city that bridges sang and natural animals lived in it as easily as in a forest."

"Niadne said Fork is like it is now because the wizard became disappointed with Valley."

The other girl shook her head. "The city reflects what exists within its boundaries. It was infused with accommodating magic, for the wizard intended it to be a city that shaped itself to people who lived in it, and their needs. He thought it would go on being lovely and light and beautiful, but he did not reckon on the keepers. Fork altered gradually to match their stony hearts. It became dark, and the black towers started appearing. The bridges fell silent and the birds vanished. Some parts of Fork are very bad," she added in a low voice. "Especially where blackshirts and keepers gather."

The pier, Rage thought, remembering the malevolent feel of the city as they had approached the bank. She glanced at a wall and wondered if the city was listening

to their words, if it was capable of resenting them or taking revenge. But even if it was, this part of the city
seemed less malicious than sorrowful.

"Why do you think the wizard brought people like
the keepers here?"

Ania shrugged. "Perhaps for companionship. They
were not like they are now, I suppose. But if company
was what he wanted, he soon enough regretted it. The
witch women say the keepers almost drove him mad,
going there and wanting him to decide this or that, or to
judge their disputes and mediate their arguments. To
keep them away he made Deepwood grow and
enchanted it so that it would be almost impossible for
anyone to reach his castle."

Glancing behind, Rage caught sight of Mr. Walker
lifting his nose and concentrating intensely. She sniffed,
too, and noticed a strong seaweed odor in the air. It must
come from the reddish lichen that grew on the walls of
the canals just above water level, for there was no other
kind of plant life. Certainly, it was not caused by the sea,
and yet the smell reminded her vividly of the windswept
seaside town where she and Mam had lived before they
went to Winnoway. Rage had been small, but she clearly
remembered the massive crash of the breaking waves,
the cries of the seagulls as they dived for leftover bits
of food.

The memory was so clear she seemed to hear the
roar of the ocean. Then she realized she *was* hearing it.
"What is it?" she asked.

Ania merely pointed ahead. They came to a corner,
and when they turned it, Rage stopped and gaped.

There was a handrail in front of her. It was all that
stood between them and a broad, savage river that

rushed to the rim of an abyss, then roared in a tumbling white broth over the edge and out of sight. There was nothing at all beyond it. It was like being at the top of the world's highest waterfall. The air shimmered with a mist that made the river look as if it were steaming, and droplets clung to Rage's skin and hair. Under her feet the ground vibrated with the sheer force of the water thundering past and under the city.

It was both thrilling and terrifying to witness the elemental force of the river and the waterfall after the quiet of the somber, black city. Rage's hair blew back from her face in the wind coming off the water. She felt breathless.

Looking back along the river's banks, she saw that the city was built on platforms that stood on immense pylons sunk into the riverbed. There must once have been many more buildings, but the platforms that supported them had been eroded by the water until they crumbled. Not far away half a building stood sagging on the edge of a platform, and even as she watched, the water tore at its jagged edges.

"Be careful." Ania pointed to the rail, and Rage saw that it was almost rusted through where she was leaning. She swayed back, the blood draining from her face.

Fear thickened into despair as she saw the end of her quest. The death of hope. No one could sail a boat down the River of No Return and live. It was not possible to reach the Endless Sea. She felt too sick with despair even to be angry at the firecat or to wonder why it had bidden her to do the impossible. Maybe it had hoped there was another solution and that she would be smart enough to find it. But if there was, Rage did not know what it could be.

Ania plucked at her arm and pointed to an un-manned raft careering wildly along the river. There were no passengers aboard, but a dark bundle was lashed to it. The raft was drawn inexorably to the outer edge of the fall, where it teetered at the very brink before being smashed to splinters on hidden rocks. The shattered remnants and the bundle were swept from view over the falls.

A second later the sun fell in orange splendor into the horizon and gray dusk fell like a cobwebbed cloak around them. Ania tugged at her arm. Numb, Rage let herself be led back down the lane and through an open doorway into the ruined shell of a building. There was nothing inside but a mess of moldering timber and wet, broken stone covered in spongy black moss, but the walls cut the din, so they did not need to shout.

"The boats are tethered upstream, near the blackshirt towers. They are used for the execution of ultimate sentences meted out by the High Keeper," Ania said.

Rage shuddered in horror, thinking of the bundle. "There . . . there was someone alive on that raft we saw?"

Ania nodded grimly. "Let us go from here. I cannot imagine why you wished to see the boats."

They abandoned the ruin and went back through the streets and over the canals and bridges to Newfork, the roar of the river slowly fading behind them. Even after they had passed out of hearing of the water, Rage's ears still hummed, and her heart beat too fast. Now what were they to do?

They came in sight of the Willow Seat Tower, gleaming darkly in the wan light of a rising moon. The city had bent to bring them here quickly. It struck Rage that the moon was exactly the same size as the night before and the one before that. Though it rose and set, it had neither waxed nor waned. What did that mean? Then she wondered what it mattered, since she would never be able to go home again. Never see Mam.

"There will be a search when you do not appear at the banding tomorrow evening," Ania said. "I removed you from Niadne's list and from her mind, but I do not know which blackshirts to deal with, and I am not sure their minds would be weak enough to mold."

Part of Rage still wanted to ask questions about Niadne and about Ania's use of magic, but the knowledge that there was no hope of returning home kept getting in the way.

Ania broke into the unhappy flow of Rage's thoughts, saying, "I must go now, but be very careful. The Mother bade me cast a spell to make you hard to see. Give me your hand. The spell will work best if you stand still when you are in danger of being seen."

Too depressed to speak, Rage offered her hand. Ania took it and dropped to her knees, pulling Rage down with her. She pushed Rage's hand flat against the earth between the cobbles and spoke a word.

In an instant, Rage was thrown across the lane and against a stone wall. Still kneeling, Ania gaped at her in horrified disbelief. "I—I don't understand," she stammered. "I felt something push against the magic. . . . That couldn't happen unless you are . . . a wizard."

Rage stood up, her head spinning. She felt sick and her whole body tingled, but she was otherwise unhurt. "I promise you, I'm no wizard," she said shakily. "It's probably because I'm a stranger to Valley. Thank you for . . . for trying to help me, but I . . . I have to go." She really felt dreadfully ill and had only walked a little distance out of Ania's sight before she vomited.

Mr. Walker came running up to her. "What did she do to you?"

"She tried only to work some magic, to make me hard to see, but somehow it backfired," Rage gasped. Then she thought of what she had seen. Mr. Walker must have seen it, too. "It's hopeless," she said bitterly. "There is no way we could survive a journey down that river."

"Let's go back to the others. Maybe Billy will know what to do," Mr. Walker said, his tail drooping.

Rage nodded and scooped him up. It took little time to return to the stone park because Rage knew where she wanted to go. But there was no sign of the others. Then Goaty emerged from the shadows and waved frantically. Rage heaved a sigh of relief. But when she was close enough to see him clearly, she saw that his long, thin face was pale and he wept.

"What's the matter?" she demanded, setting Mr. Walker down. "Is it Bear?"

"It's all of them. Bear and Elle and Billy—they have been taken away!" Goaty cried.

10

"Who took them?" Rage demanded. She ought never to have left them alone!

"Men in black clothes, like the ones that met the ferry," Goaty wept.

Blackshirts!

"Tell me exactly what happened," Rage told him. "Start from where Mr. Walker and I left."

"We were hungry and Elle wanted to go and search for food, but Billy Thunder said no one must go anywhere until you came back. Bear was awake, but she started coughing and some blood came out of her mouth. Elle said she was going to find you, but Bear said no. Elle tried to leave and Billy ran after her, and then the men in black came and saw them. Elle fought, but there were too many of them. One hit her over the head, and she fell down. Then some more of them came to the trees. I ran back to Bear. I tried to make her get up and run and hide, but she had gone to sleep again and she wouldn't wake. I was so scared. I . . . I hid, and I saw them take her, too."

"They carried her?" Rage said in disbelief.

"They fetched a board and a whole lot of them carried her on it, grunting and groaning. They took her one way, and some other blackshirts took Elle and Billy another way."

"Did they say where they were taking them?" Mr. Walker asked urgently.

"They said Bear must go to the conservatorium, but Billy and Elle were to be imprisoned. I heard one of them say that the High Keeper would have to decide what is to happen to them, since wild things are supposed to be harmless and Elle bit one of the blackshirts," Goaty said miserably.

Rage patted his arm, thinking that Bear was safe enough for the moment. Ania had said sick animals were taken to the conservatorium to be healed. "We'd better find Elle and Billy first," she announced. The blackshirt prison was sure to be close by the place where the rafts carrying condemned prisoners were launched, and she would use her memory of the river to bring them to that side of the city.

"Even if we do find them, how will we free them?" Mr. Walker asked. "There will be blackshirts guarding them, and they might even be in chains!"

"We'll figure it out once we see where they're imprisoned," Rage said. If she had to, she'd find Ania and demand the help that the witch girl had offered on behalf of her mistress.

"I'm coming with you," Mr. Walker declared.

Rage agreed, but she told Goaty to wait in the park. He hung his head in shame. "It's because I'm a coward, I know."

"It's not that at all. Someone has to be here in case Elle and Billy manage to escape on their own and come here."

Goaty only looked more depressed than ever.

Rage debated what to do. Her instinct was to rush off at once, but there would still be people awake and out in the streets. Better to wait until later, when the streets would be dark and deserted. Mr. Walker must have been exhausted, for when she told them what she had decided, he immediately curled up and fell asleep.

She heard Goaty sigh, and shifted closer to him. "I don't think you're a coward," she told him. "If you had done anything other than hide, the blackshirts would have taken you away as well. Then no one would have been here to tell Mr. Walker and me what happened. Hiding was the most sensible thing to do."

"Billy and Elle would not have hidden and let the blackshirts take me," Goaty said sadly.

Rage took Goaty's hand and they sat quietly, watching the thin moon rise higher and higher.

She was playing hide-and-seek. She charged at the dogs, and they raced away, barking wildly with excitement. Slipping into the undergrowth, she giggled to think how puzzled they would be, but instead of coming out on the other side of the shrub that ran between Winnoway and the Johnsons', she found herself caught in a mass of dark, rubbery leaves.

As she pushed deeper into them, their peppery smell grew stronger and the air became hot and damp. The barking of the dogs faded to a dim echo, and Rage saw that the forest was transforming itself around her, growing and thickening.

All at once she came to a clearing amid trees bigger than any she had ever seen. They soared up, their leaves high above linking and twining to block out all but a few stray beams of sunlight. The air was a deep greenish color, and shafts of light sliced through it like cables of radiance anchored to the ground.

Without warning a man stepped into the clearing. Very tall, he was, with dark-tanned, muscular arms. He wore faded jeans, a grubby T-shirt, and battered hiking boots. He carried a big, lumpy, beaten-up backpack with all sorts of things hanging off it. His hair grew down to his shoulders in a wild tangle of curls like Rage's, except it was black. This was not hair that would lie down and stay in Order, she thought, nor did the man look as if he would be easy to order around. His mouth had a harsh set, and the expression in his eyes was hidden by sunglasses that had been repaired with tape. A sweat-stained hat was pulled low over his forehead.

He stared at Rage in amazement. "Where the hell did you come from?"

His voice was muted, as if it came from behind a thick wall, but she heard it quite clearly. He looked exactly the sort of dangerous man that teachers warned against when they forbade talking to strangers, but Rage didn't feel afraid of him.

"I'm from Winnoway Farm," she said, and the man's mouth fell open with astonishment. "My mam was in a car accident and she can't wake up, so I'm trying to find some magic that will help her."

"What is your name?" the man asked urgently.

"I'm Rage Winnoway," Rage said. "Who are you?"

Before the man could answer he vanished. Billy emerged beside her, but he was no longer a dog.

"We couldn't find you anywhere," he said, pushing the toffee-colored lock of hair from his eyes.

Rage hissed at him to be quiet. She could hear a voice calling her name. Was it the dark-haired man?

"What was that?" Billy asked.

"Shh," Rage whispered. She listened hard. Sometimes when you heard a voice a long way off, it sounded like it was your name being called, even when it wasn't. But no, she was certain someone was calling her. Thinking about it seemed to make the voice louder. It was a man's voice.

"Who is it?" Billy whispered.

"Ra-age," the voice cried again.

"Who's there?" she shouted. "Who's calling me?"

The air shimmered, and the long, glowing lines of sunlight penetrating the green dimness wavered and became streamers, winding tighter and tighter into a greater brightness.

"Can . . . hear me?" The voice was coming out of the twisted sunbeams.

"Who . . . what are you?" Rage whispered, thinking of the firecat.

Beside her Billy began growling. Suddenly he was a dog again, and all the fur along his back had stiffened into a crest. She rested her hand on his head. He was trembling with tension.

"Don't trust . . ." The man's voice faded into a crackling sound, and there was a loud groan of pain.

"Who are you?" Rage asked again.

"Can't . . . ," the voice said haltingly, as if it were in pain. "Spell . . ."

Rage had read enough stories to know what this must mean. "Someone cast a spell of silence on you?"

"Yes," the voice said, sounding relieved. "Only . . . some things . . ."

"You can't say some things?"

No answer. She thought for a minute. "What do you want?"

"To tell . . . to warn . . ." The voice groaned very loudly.

"Break . . ." Another burst of static drowned out the next words.

"You want me to break the spell that is holding you?" Rage asked.

"Break . . . break . . ." The voice faded into a wheezy scream.

"How?" Rage cried.

There was a bright ruby flash of light and a violent hissing sound.

Rage opened her eyes to find she was staring up into Goaty's thin, worried face. "Are you sick?" he asked. "You were groaning in your sleep."

Rage sat up feeling very muddled. "I was having a dream," she said. She had been in a forest that kept changing. Then there had been a man wearing dark glasses, and a voice begging her to break a spell of silence. How peculiar it was that dreams stole bits of the day and wove them into stories that made sense while you were dreaming but none when you woke.

She shrugged, for she had far more serious things to worry about than a dream. Waking Mr. Walker, she told him they must go. Then she hugged Goaty, reminding him again to stay hidden until they returned.

"I'm afraid," he admitted, nearly weeping again. "I don't like being alone."

"Be brave," Rage said gently. "It gets easier each time you do it. Besides, maybe the others will escape and come back and then you won't be alone."

He took a deep breath and straightened his shoulders. "I'll try."

The streets were even darker than they had been in the

early hours of the morning. A river mist had risen, damp and clammy, blurring the edges of every solid thing with shifting shadows. In the distance the black towers again looked like skyscrapers.

Rage carefully pictured the outer edges of the city and began to walk. Her mind drifted to wondering where the wizard had got the men and women who peopled Valley, and why some of their descendants had ended up being like Ania and others like the ruthless High Keeper. Maybe there was no answer. Sometimes in a family one of the children was nasty and sullen or a bully, while the others were especially nice, but they all had the same parents and lived in the same house.

Rage stiffened as the Willow Seat Tower came into view. Thinking of the High Keeper must have been enough to encourage the city to bring her here. The street seemed too narrow and close around her, and Rage had the eerie sensation that she was being watched by unfriendly eyes. She noticed that the buildings around the Willow Seat Tower looked wrong. It was as if their shadowy outlines were distorted, so that one side of a wall was higher or wider than another, and windows were not properly square or round.

Unnerved, she turned her back on the tower and summoned up a mental picture of the place Ania had taken her to see the boats. Resisting the urge to run, she walked purposefully, and gradually the feeling of malevolence faded until she could smell the seaweed odor of the red lichen again.

She stopped when she came to the first canal and looked down at Mr. Walker. "The blackshirts keep prisoners in this part of the city, but almost no one else lives here. Can you smell people in any direction?"

Mr. Walker sniffed, turning his nose this way and that. "I think there are people that way." He pointed across the bridge.

Rage started walking toward it, but Mr. Walker did not move. "What is the matter?" she asked.

"Trolls," Mr. Walker said. "Everyone knows they live under bridges and that they especially love to eat goats. They will smell Goaty on us."

Rage wanted to shout that there were no such things as trolls and that they probably did not live under bridges even if they did exist, but she mastered her impatience. "I've already crossed this bridge today and there was no sign of any troll!"

Still Mr. Walker refused to budge, saying that everyone knew trolls only came out at night because they couldn't bear the sun.

"That's vampires, and anyway, when I came back across this bridge the sun had set." Rage and Mr. Walker were still arguing when she heard the sound of boots marching along the cobbles. Knowing there was no time to waste, she snatched him up, ran across the bridge, and pressed herself into a doorway on the other side, holding her hand over his mouth.

Not a moment too soon. A pair of black-clad men marched purposefully along the canal and crossed the bridge. Mr. Walker ceased his struggles and began to tremble in her arms as the men approached. Rage stroked his head and listened intently. She caught a snatch of the conversation and was elated to hear one of them speak of prisoners. It was too good an opportunity to miss. She set Mr. Walker down and hurried after them, leaving him to follow or not. The blackshirts walked so fast, she almost had to run to keep up. She prayed they would not hear her. Luckily, they were deep in conversation. Even so, Rage stayed close to the walls, darting from alcove to alcove and across bridges swiftly and lightly, prepared to freeze if either man glanced back.

Then, without warning, she lost sight of them.

The men had been striding along a broad street beside a canal. They had not passed any bridges, though there were a lot of tiny lanes running off to the left. Rage guessed the men had turned into one of them. She stopped and listened but could hear nothing other than her own wildly beating heart.

She went on cautiously, stopping to peer down every lane. They were all empty. A chilling thought struck her: what if the guards had become aware of her and were hiding somewhere, waiting to grab her?

Mr. Walker caught up, puffing hard. "I don't like the smells here," he whispered.

Rage swallowed her own rising panic. "Can you smell anyone hiding nearby?"

He sniffed in all directions, then began to sniff his way along the stones of a narrow lane. He stopped at the corner of another street.

"What is it?" Rage hissed. "Did they go this way?"

He didn't answer her at once. He began sniffing the building on their right—a tower like the others, except for the door, which looked new and very solid, its lever gleaming as if it had been polished.

"Do you smell that they went in there?" Rage prompted. The building was surely too small to be a prison.

Mr. Walker looked up at Rage in triumph. "I smell them! Billy Thunder and Elle."

Rage hugged herself in elation, but *finding* Billy and

Elle was a long way from rescuing them.

"Their smell is not very strong," Mr. Walker said. "I wouldn't have noticed it at all if you hadn't asked me to smell for someone hiding."

Rage took a few steps back and looked up, deciding that the men she had been following must have gone inside the tower. There was a single lit window, about halfway up. She tried the door but couldn't move the lever an inch. There was no way to get round the back of the building because it was built right up against the ones alongside.

"Here," Mr. Walker cried, peering into what looked like an air vent in the wall. "I can get in here," he announced.

Rage hesitated, not wanting him to go in alone. Bitterly she realized that she had no choice. "All right," she agreed. "Just see if you can find them and come straight back. Don't let anyone see you."

"No one ever sees me," Mr. Walker said.

Seeing his gallant, solitary little figure in the moonlight, Rage wondered for the hundredth time how the family who had owned him could have taken him to the dog pound.

"Be careful," she called, but he had already gone.

She knelt down and tried to see into the vent, but it was too dark. Then she searched along the street until she found a crumbling building where she could wait unseen for Mr. Walker. There was a hole in its rear wall that opened into another lane: a perfect escape route if she needed one.

With nothing to do but wait, she sat down in the doorway, keeping an eye on the tower. Something dug into her. She wriggled and reached into her coat pocket until her hand closed around the hourglass. It felt hot.

She took it out, and there was a gust of wind, then a sliver of mist shimmered and blew into a spiral that blushed red before her. A face appeared like a hologram; a shifty feline face with the suggestion of pointed ears and beautiful red eyes slitted with yellow, catlike irises.

The firecat.

"What do you want?" Rage demanded coldly.

The smoky image blinked at her. "Ragewinnoway not hurrying," it accused.

Rage wanted to shout that she was in no hurry to sail over the edge of a waterfall, but she held her tongue. The firecat was likely to vanish once it understood that she had no intention of going down the River of No Return.

"I can't go down the river until my friends are free," she said slyly. "They are imprisoned in this tower, and I must get them out."

"Ragewinnoway must take hourglass to wizard. Wizard helping friends."

"I won't leave the others, so if you want me to deliver the hourglass, you'd better do something to help them," Rage said bluntly.

"*Can't* do something," the firecat burst out.

Rage felt her anger fade because the firecat's frustration sounded genuine. Giving up all pretense, she said, "Look, no one can go down the river without being killed. You know that, don't you? You might as well tell me the truth about the hourglass and what it measures." She had no expectation that it would answer her question. But she was wrong.

"Hourglass is measuring life," the firecat spat. "Wizard's life. When sand runs out, no more wizard and no more magic for waking mother of Ragewinnoway."

It vanished.

Rage stared at the hourglass in horror. Most of the

sand had fallen to one side of the hourglass. She told herself that the firecat had lied to pay her back for refusing to go down the river. But what if it had told the truth and the wizard really would die if he did not get the hourglass before the sand ran out? Yet it made no sense that a wizard powerful enough to create a magical land would bind his life to the sand in an hourglass. And what part did the firecat play in all this? Despite its violent desire for her to obey the riddle etched on the base of the hourglass, it had never shown the slightest sign of love or fear of its master.

Of course there were no answers, only more questions. And the answers no longer mattered. Whether or not the wizard's life was at stake, Rage knew she would not survive a journey down the lethal River of No Return.

She thrust the hourglass back into her pocket, dismissing all thoughts of the wizard, the firecat, and the hourglass. Right now, the important thing was to get her friends out of the hands of the blackshirts. She left the safety of the crumbling building and paced up and down the street, wondering what was taking Mr. Walker so long.

She was in front of the doorway to the tower when it suddenly burst open and a group of blackshirts crowded out. Rage froze. But to her astonishment, they didn't seem to see her. Ania's spell must have worked after all, though she did not understand how Mr. Walker and Goaty had been able to see her—unless it was that she had not wanted to hide from them.

Rage dared not move as the blackshirts milled around her. Ania had said that the success of the spell depended on this. A trickle of perspiration ran down between her shoulder blades.

"Come on!" one of the blackshirts shouted back into the doorway.

Rage could see stone steps going up. She heard the sound of boots and four more blackshirts appeared.

"We should have relieved the others guarding the ferry pier half an hour back!" the man holding the door ajar said angrily. He had a red stripe on his shirt.

"It's not our fault that the tunnel collapsed," one of the latecomers said.

They marched away. On impulse Rage ran softly forward and grabbed the edge of the door to stop it swinging shut. In a twinkling she was inside and creeping up the stairs, hardly able to believe her luck.

She climbed and climbed, wondering what could be in the lower part of the building, since these steps were the only way in and they went straight up without a single doorway leading off them. They brought her to a long stone corridor, and she saw light flowing from a doorway ahead. This must be the room with the lit window she had seen from the street. Summoning her courage, she made her way to the door.

"I know what you are up to!"

Rage nearly jumped out of her skin as the voice and a burst of sneering laughter cut through the silence. But there were no footsteps. Whoever had spoken had to be inside the room.

"What do you suppose they were up to?" another man asked in a conversational tone.

Rage pressed herself to the wall and edged closer to the door.

"I've no idea. They both look human to me, but the female is furred, so she must be some kind of wild thing. The boy looks completely human, but what boy would associate with witches and wild things?"

"Maybe the witches made some wild things that could pass as human."

"I didn't think there was enough magic left in Wildwood for any more making."

"Unless Boone is right and they've found a way to get it from this side of the river. They do say the river is getting worse."

"Well, it's for the High Keeper to decide what they are, when he gets round to taking a look at them."

"Boone said there's no hurry."

"They'll die like the other ones if they're here too long. If they're wild folk, I mean."

The other man laughed harshly. "One less wild thing to bother about."

The two men were silent for a time, then there was a slapping sound.

"Is it true that the real animals in the provinces are getting sick?"

"Maybe, but who cares if a few animals die? Ahh! *Now I've got you!*"

There was another period of silence and some more slapping. The sound was tantalizingly familiar. Rage had a vision of herself playing Snap with Mam. The men were playing a card game! Figuring this out made her feel bold, and she went right up to the door and peeked into the room.

The men were seated at a table. There was nothing in the room but the table and two chairs. Rage withdrew. The conversation of the blackshirts suggested they were guarding Billy and Elle. But where were they? And where was Mr. Walker?

Rage took a deep breath, then ghosted past the door and down the shadowy hallway. It turned sharply to the left, and she peeped around the corner. There was a window in the outer wall, and in the blue-tinged moonlight she could see metal bars set in the wall opposite.

Creeping up to the bars, Rage saw a small stone cell. A man in it was sleeping soundly, his back turned to the bars. She craned her neck and saw another two cells, empty, but the third had three fairies in it, all with delicate dragonfly wings. Only one of them was facing the bars, its tiny mouth opened in a perfect O of amazement at the sight of her.

Rage put her finger to her mouth, wondering what crime the little creatures could possibly have committed. The fairy nodded and poked at her two companions. All three crept to the bars, close enough for Rage to see that they were pale and notice that they smelled bad. Her heart twisted in pity. The poor fragile things were clearly sick, despite what Ania had said about none of the wild things dying of hunger.

"Are you from the secret coven?" one of the fairies whispered through cracked lips.

"No, but I'm going to try to get you out," Rage said softly. She examined the bars. There was no lock. In fact, there didn't even seem to be a door.

"When they put us in here, the bars slid aside," the fairy said.

This reminded Rage of a movie she had seen about men in a prison. When it was breakfast time, all of the cell doors had opened simultaneously at the flick of a single switch in the office of the prison warden.

"I have an idea, but first I must see if my friends are all right," she whispered.

"The not-dogs?" another fairy asked, coming up to the bars. Then she flinched and drew back as if the metal had burned her.

"They are down at the end," the other said, pointing carefully through the bars.

Rage hurried along the corridor to the last cell,

where Billy and Elle stared out at her happily, their fingers curled around the bars. "We could smell you," Elle said joyfully.

Rage put her hands on theirs and squeezed hard. "I am so glad to see you both," she said fervently, blinking to stop herself from crying out of sheer relief.

"How did you find us?" Billy asked, bringing her down to earth.

"Mr. Walker sniffed you out," Rage answered. "Have you seen him?"

Billy shook his head. "I thought I could smell him ages ago, but not now."

Elle nodded confirmation. "He was near and then he had a going-away smell."

Rage decided that the vent Mr. Walker had used to enter the building must have led to the lower level of the tower. He'd probably gone outside by now and was heading back to Goaty. At least she hoped so.

"Have you found Mama?" Billy asked eagerly.

"She's been taken to a place where they look after sick animals. We'll search for her when I've got you two out of here."

"What are you going to do?" Billy asked.

"Just be ready to run," Rage said. She went back to the fairies. "Are there any more wild things in here?"

The fairies shook their heads. One said sadly, "There were others, but they faded. It was the iron bars."

"What about the man in the other cell?" It would be a problem if all of the cells opened and he attacked them or started shouting.

"The blackshirts brought him in last night," a fairy said. "He was groaning, but he hasn't made any noise today."

The smallest of the fairies held out a tiny bag to Rage. "It is witch's dust," she whispered. "It's for making us look sick when we come to Fork, but you can use it to wish the guards asleep. You have to throw it over them, and you mustn't breathe any in yourself."

"It doesn't last very long," another warned.

Rage pocketed the tiny bag and crept back to the room where the blackshirts were playing cards. This time she noticed another open door behind the one to the guards' room, and stairs going down. She wondered if this led to the tunnel the departing blackshirts had talked about.

". . . don't see why we can't just go in and clean Wildwood out once and for all," one of the men said. "It would be more merciful than letting the creatures die slowly, and it would teach the witches a lesson. That's what Boone thinks we ought to do."

There was the sound of cards being shuffled.

"Keepers would never abide it. They don't want their hands dirtied with violence."

"Their hands wouldn't have to be dirtied, would they? Besides, wasn't it the High Keeper himself who wanted to see what would happen if wild things were kept behind iron bars?"

Another slapping sound.

Rage peeped around the corner again. The men hadn't moved from their seats. She poked her head right into the room and saw that there was a big wheel set into the same wall as the door. It might be a central control for the cell gates, but even from that distance she could see that there was no way to turn such a wheel quietly. She thought of the little bag of witch's dust.

"I heard the witch folk claim it's not them using up

magic from the land," said the guard with his back to the wheel.

Rage took a deep breath and stepped into the room. The lanterns hung on the wall gave off a bright but flickering light, but if she could move quietly enough, perhaps Ania's spell would stop the men looking her way until it was too late.

Pleasepleaseplease, she thought, and again she grew hot with anxiety.

She took another step into the room, legs shaking.

The blackshirt with his back to her groaned, and the other gathered the cards up with the same burst of sneering laughter she had heard from the hallway.

She took a step nearer. She was so close to them now, she dared not breathe, but neither lifted their eyes from the cards.

"What about the man in the first cell? What did he do that he's locked up here?"

Rage waited, curious despite her fear.

"He's a keeper, if you can believe it. Boone said he was found in the provinces snooping around. There's some suggestion he's mixed up with the witch women."

"A keeper working with the witch women!" the other exclaimed. He lifted his head so that he was facing Rage.

She gasped. She couldn't help herself. The blackshirt's eyes widened and focused on her. She hurled some of the witch's dust over the two men, who instantly toppled sideways under the yellow shower.

Still holding her breath, Rage shoved the pouch into her pocket and ran to the wheel. There was a blue arrow on it, pointing up to the roof, and another blue arrow on the wall. If she was right about the wheel controlling access to the cell doors, she must have to turn the wheel arrow to match the arrow on the wall.

She took hold of the wheel and tried to turn it. It was terribly heavy, and she only managed to shift it a little. Struggling, she dragged it another fraction. Unable to hold her breath any longer, she breathed in with a loud gasp.

Nothing happened. The witch's dust must have settled. She put both hands on one side of the wheel and, bracing herself, tugged down as hard as she could. The wheel shifted another fraction, then it simply wouldn't turn anymore.

She heard a sound behind her and was aghast to find the two blackshirts beginning to stir. She tugged frantically at the wheel. In seconds they would be properly awake!

The wheel would not move.

One of the men sat up. He groaned and climbed groggily to his feet, his back turned to her. Rage didn't know what to do. To throw more dust, she would have to get closer, and maybe there was too little left to affect the men. If it didn't work, she would be trapped in the room.

Part of her wanted to run, but she set her teeth together and pulled violently at the wheel. It still wouldn't budge. The second man woke and saw immediately what she was about. "Stop her," he cried in a slurred voice.

The other guard turned unsteadily, but at the same moment a tall man with a bloodied face stepped through the door holding a boot. Rage gaped at him in astonishment.

"Don't think you can trick us," the nearest black-shirt sneered at Rage, then his face changed comically as the newcomer hit him on the head with the boot and he slipped back to the floor. The man did the same thing to the second blackshirt before turning to Rage. "That should keep them quiet for a bit. How did you open my cell?"

Wordlessly, Rage pointed at the wheel. The man took two steps across and turned it the rest of the way with a great heave. "Come on. It won't be long before more blackshirts come."

They dashed out into the hallway to see the fairies limping fearfully out of their cell. Clearly their wings were too weak to use. "Come, little ones," the man said gently, and scooped all three into his arms. Further down the hall, Billy and Elle emerged, and Rage waved them to come.

When he had ascertained that there were no other prisoners, the man bade them follow him and ran lightly down the hall. He descended the stairs two at a time, the fairies clinging to his shoulders and gazing at his face in awe.

Rage followed with Elle and Billy close behind her.

At the bottom, the man opened the door and peered out. "No one. Come on."

They followed him outside, and then they all heard the sound of boots coming along the cobbles.

"This way!" Rage cried, and ran along the street to the ruined building. She meant to lead them through it to the lane, but as soon as they were inside the deserted shell, the man caught her arm and shook his head. He squatted down and held his finger to his lips. After a slight hesitation, Rage and the others did the same. They heard the boots come closer, the sound of the door being opened. Then more steps and a *clank* as the door shut.

The man rose. "There is a back way out of this?"

"There is a hole and it opens to another lane, but I don't know where that leads," Rage said.

As they climbed through the rubble, Rage thought of Mr. Walker and hoped that he had gone back to the river. There was nothing she could do to help him now.

When they were clear of the ruin, the man took the lead again and began to walk very quickly, urging the fairies to climb inside his voluminous jacket. It was all Rage could do to keep up with him. When she began to lag, Billy and Elle each took one of her hands and pulled her along.

The man did not stop until they had left the region of canals and entered the drier territory of Newfork. They came to a sliver of space left between two small buildings. A real tree grew there, though it was gray and sickly-looking. The man stopped under its branches and turned to Rage. "I don't know what you are doing in Fork or how you came to be in that prison, yet I thank you, girl, for setting me and these little ones free."

"I heard one of the blackshirts say that you are a keeper. Is it true?" Rage asked.

"I *was* a keeper," the man said. "Now you might say that the witch women and I have interests in common." He glanced around. "I would like to repay your help, but I have no means, and right now I must get these three and myself across the river before the blackshirts raise the alarm. I would advise you to come with us, for my escape is likely to cause a furor."

"We can't!" Billy cried. "My mother is here in Fork."

"And Goaty and Mr. Walker," Elle said.

A bell began to toll loudly.

The man looked at Rage with regret. "I'm afraid it's too dangerous for any of us to stay out in the open like this. You must go your own way now, or come with me and cross the river."

Rage shook her head. "I can't. We must find our friends."

The man nodded. "Well then, I wish you luck. Maybe we'll meet again someday."

He turned, but Rage caught his arm. "Wait. One of our friends is a true animal. She was hurt, and the black-shirts took her to the conservatorium. Do you know where that is?"

The man looked horrified. "She was taken there? That means she is to be killed and stuffed!"

"No!" Billy screamed. He rushed at the man and shook him. "She's my mother! They can't. They mustn't!"

The man looked at him in pity and wonder. "I don't know how a beast can be your mother, but if you would save her, lad, if she is not already dead, you must go there as fast as you can."

"Where?" Billy demanded, tears streaming down his face.

"The conservatorium is behind the Willow Seat Tower. You will know it when you see it. It is like no other place." He would have said more, but Billy had already dashed away. Rage and Elle ran after him.

"Good luck. . . ." The man's voice faded behind them.

11

Billy ran wildly ahead. All too soon the Willow Seat Tower loomed before them like an accusing finger. Elle growled under her breath at it, and Rage caught hold of Billy before he could rush off again. "We have to go carefully now! We can't help Bear if we're caught."

He gasped, and she saw the effort it cost to calm himself. "All right," he said in a strangled voice.

"That man said the conservatorium was behind the Willow Seat Tower. Let's try walking around it, but let me go first. There is a spell on me that will stop anyone noticing me as long as I see them first and stand very still." Rage hoped it was still working.

They made a wide circle around the tower. Rage felt as if there were eyes peering from the windows. Surely those within must have heard the alarm bell. But there was no sign of any activity, and somehow this was more troubling than if the place had been swarming with blackshirts.

They did a second circuit and still could not see a building that announced itself as the conservatorium. Rage stood still and craned her neck, trying to look past the tower, but this was curiously hard to do. It was as if the building insisted on being looked at. She persevered and, for a moment, caught sight of something looming dark and huge behind it.

Her breath caught in her throat, and whatever she had seen dissolved into the general darkness. Elle began to growl loudly. Rage again looked past the tower, and this time she clearly saw a huge, squat black dome. It was so big that it was impossible they could have missed seeing it, and yet none of them *had* seen it until now. They walked slowly toward it but found themselves lost in a twisting maze of streets that wound and coiled around its base.

Rage went on picturing the dome, even when it vanished from sight. Before long it was visible again and closer than ever. Then the streets began to narrow dramatically. When they finally reached a street that ran to the base of the dome, it was no more than a sliver of an alleyway.

Elle made a little whining sound. "What is it?"

"The conservatorium," Rage answered. She knew Elle had been asking her more than that. But she did not know what to say. The dome was only a building, but she sensed it was also the sick, pulsing heart of all the darkness that inhabited the city. Every instinct bade her flee from it as fast as she could.

Rage noticed uneasily that the distorted architecture she had noticed earlier in buildings around the Willow Seat Tower was far worse here. A dozen different styles of buildings were jumbled together. Minarets and spires and chimney stacks and crenellated openings warred with one another for space. But nothing made sense. Stairs led nowhere; balconies were without guard rails or were fixed upside down onto walls. Windows opened onto walls or doors or other windows. Crooked, half-completed walls listed drunkenly, and paths led to nothing. Things were half completed or finished with impossible and lunatic detail. It was as if a strange frenzy had filled the mind of its designer.

Yet the grotesquerie of the streets, however horrible, did not arouse in Rage the same dread as the black dome.

They stopped and looked at one another.

"Mama is inside that place. I have to go in," Billy said determinedly.

"We will all go in," Elle announced, and Rage was never more glad of her indomitable courage than at that moment.

They walked side by side to begin with, but soon there was room only for two, then one—the alley had reduced itself to no more than a crack. The conservatorium still looked as distant as when they had first seen it.

Rage swung around. The alley behind them appeared wide and inviting. "This is some sort of trick," she said. She felt the crack begin to close on them.

"I can't fit!" Billy shouted.

"We must go back and try another way," Elle said.

Rage shook her head. "No. That's what it wants us to do. There is no other way, and if we try again I think it will find a way to stop us getting even this close."

"But we can't go forward," Elle protested. Then she said in a strange, rigid voice, "I'm trapped! I can't move!"

Inside Rage, the voice of fear urged her to save herself, but she ignored it. No matter how malicious it seemed, the city was made of responsive magic. Even the dome. That meant it could respond to them as well as to the keepers.

It came to her what they must do. "We have to imagine the street opening up and letting us through."

"I don't know how to imagine things," Billy said in a strained voice.

"Just make a picture in your mind of the city letting you through. Imagine the crack opening up," Rage called.

"I . . . I can't!" he cried. "My mind is not big enough for that yet."

"Animals can't imagine things," Elle said in a muffled voice.

"I will do it," Rage said. She concentrated on imagining the city Ania had described: Fork as it had been when the wizard created it, with a wide, graceful street leading up to the dome.

The crack began to close around Rage's shoulders. She could feel the hateful black pressure of the dome as it resisted her vision. The keepers' influence was too deep, too strong. Elle and Billy said nothing, and Rage dared not think of what was happening to them. She had to make the city listen!

I am Rage Winnoway whose name is also Courage! she cried out in her mind. She let her imagination run wild, picturing towers of glass wound with threads of silver and gold and studded with pink pearls; wide, straight streets where there were trees and flowers; graceful rooms filled with air and light and butterflies; a city where antelopes and winged lions wandered freely in and out of buildings filled with human laughter, where bridges sang.

A groaning, as much the sound of crumbling stone as a howl of inhuman anguish, filled Rage's head. She felt the agony of the city so keenly that she had to stop herself from screaming. But she did not stop visualizing the city as it had been, as it could be, as it should be. The city was not evil. It was like someone who had been forced into a bent and crippled position for so long and knew of no other way to be. She offered her vision of the city to free it, and despite the brutal pressure on her arms and shoulders, the imagining became easier. Rage went on dreaming of Fork as it could be, mixing up Mam's carless city with the things Ania had said and with her own ideas. Despite her fear for Elle and Billy, a kind of elation filled her, for surely imagining so hard and so brightly was a kind of magic, too.

There was a loud crack, then the walls on either side of them crumbled and collapsed softly and silently into powdery rubble. Before them, the alleyway was wide and perfectly straight.

"Look!" Elle gasped, and they stared in amazement as blooms as red as blood burst through the piles of shattered stone.

There was no time to wonder at them. Billy scrambled over the debris and was approaching the dome. Rage followed. The door to the black tower was a great heavy slab of what looked like marble. Billy reached for the lever, and the door sprang open at his touch. Behind it was a set of steps going up into darkness. Billy and Elle staggered back, gagging and coughing.

"Whatever is it?" Rage asked.

"Can't you smell?" Elle sounded appalled.

"Something rotten," Billy gasped.

Rage shook her head and entered. As in the blackshirt tower, there was no access to the bottom part of the dome. The steps led to an enormous room that occupied an entire level of the conservatorium. Windows in every wall looked out over Fork. The room was empty and deathly quiet, with wide pillars stretching up to the ceiling. Something about the room, about the muted light, was familiar to Rage. She racked her brain until it came to her.

It reminded her of the Museum of Natural History.

Billy walked to the nearest pillar, and Rage tried to reach him. But she was too late. He gave an anguished cry and started back in horror. Rage was close enough now to see that there was a glassed-in box set into the pillar. A group of tiny, squirrel-like animals, all stuffed, stared blindly and pitifully out into the darkness.

"Mama!" Billy cried, falling to his knees.

Rage thought she heard something. "Wait here with Billy," she whispered to Elle, and crept across the room with a thudding sense of fear. She heard a man's voice, muffled as if through a thick wall.

"Are you sure we should not reconsider?"

Rage could not see any doors, but she heard footsteps. She crept around the pillars, searching until she found a stairwell. The voices grew louder. The speakers were coming up the stairs!

Rage darted behind the nearest pillar just as an old man emerged from the stairwell. He wore a white tunic edged in gold, like the man who had alighted from the litter at the door to the Willow Seat Tower. Maybe this was the High Keeper himself. Studying the man's cold, haughty expression, his small, pouting mouth and glittering black eyes, she could easily imagine him demanding that a man or woman or child be tied to a raft and sent to a horrible death.

The keeper turned and spoke down the stairs: "I see no need to reconsider my decision, Hermani." He had a beautiful, deep voice that compelled attention.

Another old man emerged from the stairwell, carrying a jar in which something dark floated. He wore a plain white tunic. "High One, it is just that we do not know what the beast is yet. That is why I—"

High One! Niadne had referred to the High Keeper of Fork as the High One.

"It is a form of dog."

Rage's heart jumped into her throat. Surely they meant Bear.

"High One, there are aspects of the form that do not seem to fit into our list of canine characteristics. If this is a new species and we conserve it—"

"What is it that you want, Hermani?"

The other man hung his head. "To tell you the truth, High One, I don't like to conserve things that might be saved. The creature is old but—"

"The longer she lives, the more trouble we will have in conserving her well. The coat will dull and become threadbare. The claws will blunt and perhaps fall out, not to mention the teeth. If it is a new species, there is all the more reason to conserve it at its peak. You saw the pelt. It is already considerably scarred."

"Someone has ill-treated the poor beast."

"Witch women," the High Keeper hissed, eyes black and small with hate. "The blackshirts that brought it in said it was with two wild things. I will interrogate them myself."

Rage shuddered at the thought of Elle and Billy in the clutches of the High Keeper.

"High One, the witch women would not ill-treat a true beast any more than they would harm one of their wild things. And why would they send it here, in any case?"

"I don't like to hear you talking this way, Hermani,"

the High Keeper said icily. "You should know by now that the witch women are capable of anything. They are a constant danger to the wizard's Order, and our only hope that he will return to us lies in obedience to his will."

"If he does not return soon, there will be no one to admire our obedience, High One." He waved his arm. "All will be lost when the river reclaims Valley. Surely anything would be better than that. Perhaps if we approached the witch Mother—"

"Silence!" the High Keeper roared, and Hermani shrank from the fury contorting his master's face. But the High Keeper smiled now, the change of expression so complete as to be terrifying.

He is quite mad, Rage thought.

"Do not concern yourself with the river, Hermani," the High Keeper said pleasantly. "Once Wildwood is emptied of blasphemy and witches . . ."

It seemed to Rage that Hermani forced himself to speak, though his voice quivered. "High One, forgive me, but in the last seven days the waters have risen rapidly. Some of the deeper blackshirt tunnels have become saturated and are in danger of collapsing. Even tonight there was a report that a tunnel running to the ferry pier had collapsed. Yet there is no magic in Wildwood for the witch folk to draw on. It cannot be their fault. Something else must be—"

"Enough," the High Keeper thundered. "I am disappointed in you. Let us proceed with this conservation. I am weary. Another five minutes and the beast will no longer be alive for you to—"

Rage had been creeping steadily nearer the two men, and at these cold words a great fury rose up in her heart. She groped in her pocket for the slender pouch of witch's dust and hurled the remainder of it as hard as she could at the two men.

They crumpled soundlessly, just as the blackshirts had done.

"Elle!" Rage cried. "Come and tie these two up and follow me! Billy, hurry before it's too late!"

Not waiting to see if they obeyed, she hurtled down the steps, only to find herself in another huge room with more glass cases in pillars, except there were no windows in the walls, and it was brightly lit. There was a square hole in the floor, which must lead down to yet another level.

Then she saw that there was no need to go further.

Billy cannoned into her.

Incapable of words, Rage pointed to an enormous glass case set against the far wall and lit from above. Bear was inside it, lying on a bed with wheels. A tube from a metal tank fed into the side of the case, and a hissing noise filled the air.

"No!" Billy screamed. He lifted the metal tank with a deep-throated groan and heaved it at the glass case with all of his might. There was a tremendous shattering crash, and then the air filled with a sickly sweet smell. The hissing sound became louder.

"Hold your breath and let's get her out of here!" Rage gasped.

Billy crunched over the broken glass and tried to shove the bed, but Bear's bulk was too much for him to move alone.

"Elle!" Rage screamed.

The Amazon came running down the stairs. "It took me a while to find something to tie—" She paled at the sight of Bear.

Somehow they managed to get the unconscious Bear

to the top of the stairs. Rage saw that Hermani had awakened. He said in a slurred but urgent voice, "You heard the bells before? It means someone has escaped the prisons. Blackshirts will pour through the tunnels into the conservatorium any minute, wanting instructions from the High Keeper."

Ignoring him, Billy peered into Bear's face and patted her loose jaw. She did not respond. Rage laid her head on the old dog's chest with a feeling of dread and heard a heartbeat tap against her cheek. It sounded uneven and too slow, but it was there.

"She's alive!"

Billy burst into tears and kissed Bear's gray-flecked muzzle and forehead.

"You must listen to me," Hermani cried frantically. "There is a chute over by where you came in. Under the pillar with the case of squirrels. The pillar can be pushed aside. It will bring you to a tunnel that lies below the network of blackshirt tunnels. It's your only hope."

"Why would you help us?" Rage demanded.

The keeper looked at his master, who had begun to stir. "Because I would save the beast," he hissed, nodding at Bear. "Go, or it will be too late for all of you."

"They're coming," Elle said. "I smell them."

Rage could hear nothing, but she ran to the gleaming case with the stuffed squirrels and pushed on it. It slid aside with a faint sigh, and there was the promised chute.

"How can we trust that man after what he did to Mama?" Billy demanded.

"We have no choice. Help Bear down the chute, and you two go after her!" Rage commanded.

"What about you?"

"I'm coming, too, of course. Now go!"

Leaving them to drag Bear over to the chute, Rage ran back to the two keepers. The High Keeper's eyes were fluttering. "How do I close the pillar back over the chute?" she demanded of Hermani.

"A lever on the underside of the case. Push it and you will have just enough time to jump through before the pillar moves back into place. Now go! He mustn't know I helped you."

Rage did not waste time on thanks. In seconds she was hurtling down a smooth chute in pitch darkness. At first the speed was terrifying, but then the tunnel leveled out and flattened so that eventually she simply slid to a halt.

Elle and Billy were leaning anxiously over Bear, but they looked up at Rage in puzzlement. She realized that the faint source of light that bathed them all was coming from her. Looking down, she was astonished to find her pocket glowing. Reaching in, she found the hourglass. It was warm to the touch and radiated a bright ruby light. How strange! She held it before her like a beacon and saw that the chute became a proper tunnel that ran away into the distance.

Bear started to retch and cough violently.

"Mama!" Billy turned his attention back to his mother.

The old dog struggled to sit. "Where are we? What has been happening?" she rasped.

"There's no time to explain now," Rage said. "We need to go on if you can." They had to find Goaty and Mr. Walker, and they had to get out of the tunnel in case Hermani had betrayed them. After that, there was really nowhere to go but back over the river to the wild side— if they could get on the ferry.

"What did you do to it?" Billy asked, glancing at the

glowing hourglass as they helped Bear to her feet.

"Nothing," Rage said. "It did that on its own." Was it possible that she had somehow invoked the wizard's magic? Taking the hourglass and holding it high to light their way, she took the lead.

Billy's mind must have been on the same track. "Maybe the hourglass gives wishes if you just think about something. Like the bramble gate tried to make us human after you wished for it. Did you want it to be light?"

"I don't think I thought about light."

"Try wishing for something new," Elle suggested.

Rage doubted it would be that easy, but she said in a loud, formal voice, "Please take us to Goaty!" When nothing happened, she told the others what the firecat had said about the sand representing the wizard's life.

"But it has almost run out," Billy said, looking aghast.

Rage nodded. "I don't think we can do anything to save the wizard, if what the firecat said is true. We can't survive a trip down the River of No Return to find him."

Elle, Billy, and even Bear stared at her. Rage remembered that she hadn't told them about what Ania had shown her. So as they walked she explained all that had befallen her since they had parted in the park of stone trees.

"A waterfall," Billy murmured. "But it must be possible to go down it safely, if the wizard went there."

"He had magical powers to protect him," Elle said.

"If the wizard could use his magical powers, he would have come back to get the hourglass and save himself," Billy said. "That means he went down the river without magic."

"We don't know that. He might have got there some

other way altogether. He might have even used a gate like the one that brought us here," Rage said. "But *we* have only one way to get there, and that would kill us."

"Maybe," Billy said. Then he sighed. "Well, who knows what is true, anyway? The firecat might have lied about the sand showing how much time the wizard has to live. Before, it said the hourglass contained all that the wizard knew."

"It might have lied about everything," Rage said. "But I do believe it wants us to take the hourglass to the wizard. I just wish we knew why."

They walked in silence for a while.

"When I was in that prison cell, I kept wondering why the firecat just didn't magic itself to the wizard with the hourglass, like it magicked itself to us," Elle said presently.

Rage was surprised—usually Elle wasn't interested in thinking about things. But then again, she wasn't usually stuck in jail.

"I was thinking about the firecat, too," Billy said. "I don't think it can magic itself anywhere. I think it only magics an image of itself to us. That's why it won't appear properly and wouldn't unlock your door in the banding house. It can't."

"But if it's not following us physically, how does it know where to send its image?" Rage asked. Then she stared at the glowing hourglass.

Billy nodded. "It has to contain some sort of spell that lets the firecat see us. It knows the hourglass is the one thing you wouldn't lose or give away. You said yourself that it warned you to be careful not to break it."

Rage did not know what to say. Any of their guesses could be right or completely wrong, depending on which part of the firecat's story was true—if any. Rage's thoughts went on turning this way and that, like the tunnel, never reaching any conclusion. When they came round a bend and found the way split into three identical tunnels, she felt it was a perfect symbol of their journey. Every question to do with the wizard and the firecat led only to more questions.

Now that they had stopped, Rage was alarmed to hear how raggedly Bear was breathing. "Let's rest for a bit while we decide which way to go," she said lightly. It was a measure of Bear's exhaustion that she did not even argue. She slumped to the ground, and when Billy lifted her head onto his lap, she did not push him away.

Rage turned to Elle. "What can you smell down the tunnels?"

Elle sniffed the first. "Buildings, people, and metal." She sniffed the second. "Flowers, trees, earth . . ." She frowned. "Animals, too, but their smell is old and faded, as if they were there once but have long gone. I smell . . . sadness."

She turned her attention to the third tunnel. "Water," she said. "And something else . . . I don't know what it is. I've never smelled it before. It makes me want to sneeze."

She turned to Rage expectantly.

"I don't know what to do," Rage admitted. "I thought it was hopeless to try to find the wizard, once I saw the waterfall. But maybe I was wrong about the riddle. Maybe it means something completely different."

"Well, we can't stay in the city," Elle said. "Those blackshirts will be looking everywhere for us."

"Especially since we stole Mama out from under their noses," Billy said. "The High Keeper will want to know how we escaped."

"I think we have to go back over the river and see the witch Mother. Ania says she wants to help us because she wants the wizard found, to save Valley. Maybe she will be able to figure out the riddle on the hourglass. And she might even know something about the firecat."

"So, which tunnel?" Elle asked.

Rage studied the first tunnel. It led to people, so it probably came out somewhere in Newfork, which was the last place they wanted to be just now. The second tunnel? She liked the sound of trees and flowers, but the smell of sadness was daunting. The tunnel probably led to one of the provinces, where there was clearly something wrong. And anyway, there would be lots of keepers there. The third tunnel led to water. That sounded most promising. It might even lead them to one of the tunnels Hermani had mentioned, which had become saturated with water seeping from the encroaching river.

Rage hesitated, worried about Bear. "I think we should take the tunnel that smells of water, but I will go down it alone to see where it leads."

Billy said anxiously, "Don't let's split up again."

Rage bit her lip. "But, Bear—"

"I can walk," Bear said gruffly, struggling to her feet.

12

They had been on the move for half an hour when they came to a grille embedded in the walls of the tunnel, completely blocking their way. Rage stared stupidly at it, knowing they would have no hope of shifting it. Bear was swaying on her feet, eyes cloudy and unfocused.

"We'll have to go back and try one of the other tunnels, but I think we might as well rest here," Rage said. "I've been thinking that if we take long enough, the blackshirts will think we've gone over the river, and they'll give up searching."

"What about Goaty and Mr. Walker?" Elle asked.

"If anyone questions them, they'll simply say they're wild things and they'll be left alone." Rage said this with more confidence than she felt. The blackshirts were bound to be suspicious if they found two wild things wandering about when they had already taken three as prisoners. But they could not go on with Bear in such a state. Given everything, it was sensible to stay where they were for the time being, though she dared not look at the sand in the hourglass.

The old dog lay down with a profound sigh. Billy

took her big, misshapen head onto his lap and ran his fingers over her soft ears. Again she did not reject his caress.

"I wonder what is happening to Goaty," Elle said wistfully, peering through the grate. "He will be afraid if he is all alone."

"I hope he is *not* alone," Rage said. She leaned back against the sloping side of the tunnel, wishing Mam could see Bear and Billy together. It had always upset her that Bear was so cold to Billy. But Mam seemed so far away. It was becoming harder for Rage to imagine being home with her again. Having entered a magical world, she had somehow lost touch with her own world. The longer she was away from it, the less real it seemed. She closed her eyes and slipped into a deep sleep.

A voice was calling her name.

Rage opened her eyes and found she was sitting on the grassy lawn at Winnoway Farm. The dogs were sleeping around her, and she could see Goaty standing on the Johnsons' fence and eating the new buds off the plum trees. She shook her head, thinking Mr. Johnson would go mad when he saw the damage.

"Ra-age!"

Someone was calling, but there was no one in sight.

"Who is it?" she cried, wondering if Mam was calling her from inside the house. Strangely, the dogs remained asleep.

"Help me," the voice called.

It was the same voice that had called her before, out of the streamers of light in the forest.

"How can I help you?" Rage asked.

"Break . . . release . . . before . . . too late . . ."

"I don't know how to break the spell," she cried.

"I already told you. Who are you? Where are you?"
But there was no answer.

Rage woke to find herself sitting in the cold tunnel by the metal grille.

"Rage!" a voice called.

"I must be going mad," she muttered to herself. "First I dream of a voice calling me, and then when I wake up, I can still hear it."

"Rage!"

Rage looked through the grille and was astounded to see a pixie-sized woman wearing a tight-fitting brown catsuit and flat-heeled, high-topped boots. Her hair was a floating cloud of yellow, like spun sugar, and it shimmered in the light of the tiny lantern she carried.

"You must move back so that I can open the grille," she told Rage, waving the lantern with a shooing action.

Billy had been sleeping with his face pushed up against the grille. Wakened by their voices, he opened his eyes and gave a yelp of surprise. "What are you?" he asked.

"I'm Kelpie."

The small stranger lifted her lantern, the sole source of light in the tunnel. Rage glanced anxiously at the hourglass. It was safe where she had left it, but it had gone dull.

"It's a kelpie," Billy told Elle, who had woken, too, and was sniffing through the grille.

"Kelpie is my *name*." The woman giggled. "And you are Billy Thunder."

"How do you know our names?" Rage demanded warily, wondering if the little woman was a wild thing.

"Mr. Walker told me."

"Mr. Walker!" Billy cried in delight. "Then he's safe."

"I will bring you to him as soon as you let me open the grille." Kelpie tapped her tiny fingers impatiently against the metal. Billy woke Bear, and they all moved back down the tunnel. Kelpie knelt and pressed her hand to the ground. There was a grinding noise, and the grille swung open like a gate.

Rage was intrigued. She had supposed Kelpie was a wild thing, yet she was drawing magic from the earth just as Ania had done, and wild things weren't supposed to be able to do that. After they had all come through the grille, it swung back into place with a gritty screech.

"Come," Kelpie said imperiously, dusting off her hands.

"Wait just a minute," Rage said firmly, refusing to be dazzled into acting without thinking. "Before we go anywhere, you'd better tell us how you met Mr. Walker."

"He fell down a shaft and found us."

"And how did *you* find *us*? Mr. Walker didn't know we were coming here," Rage said. "*We* didn't know we were coming here."

"The Mother foresaw it," Kelpie answered. "Now we must hurry. She awaits us with Mr. Walker, in the Place of Shining Waters."

"The witch Mother foresaw us trapped in a drain?"

Kelpie nodded.

Rage did not know what to think. Obviously someone with magical powers might be able to look into the future, but if that was so, why hadn't Ania said that the witch Mother had foreseen *them* meeting?

Rage glanced at the others. Elle and Billy were eager to go, while Bear looked exhausted and ill, but none of them said a thing. They were leaving it to Rage to choose.

Kelpie turned to hurry away down the tunnel, and Rage led the way after her. Though rested, Bear moved slowly. She was still suffering from having breathed in the High Keeper's poisonous gas. Rage hoped she had not suffered any permanent damage. After a time the tunnel began to narrow. Rage's heart sank, but she told herself sternly that her experience outside the conservatorium had made her oversensitive.

"It doesn't get much smaller, does it?" Billy asked Kelpie nervously.

"A bit," she answered cheerfully.

"Why didn't Mr. Walker come with you?" Elle asked.

"The Mother foresaw *me* finding you," Kelpie answered proudly.

This was not really an answer. Rage wondered if the Mother hadn't deliberately kept Mr. Walker with her to ensure that the rest of them came with Kelpie. She had heard nothing bad about the witch women, except from the keepers, and the witch Mother had enabled her to get away from the banding house. But Rage had expected a long, difficult trip back to Wildwood to see the witch Mother. It was unnerving to find that she was here, waiting to see them. And why was she in Fork? If she had come in the hope that Rage had located the wizard, she was about to be bitterly disappointed.

"What about Goaty?" Elle asked, interrupting the flow of Rage's thoughts. "Did the Mother foresee anything about him?"

Kelpie giggled. "Oh, he is waiting for you as well. Mr. Walker told us where to find him. Goaty was very afraid of us at first. He shivered and shook and thought we meant to eat him. 'I must be brave,' he kept saying."

Her imitation of Goaty was so accurate, Rage relaxed. No matter what was going on, at least they would all soon be together again.

Billy and Elle went on questioning the woman, but

she only repeated, in various ways, that all of their questions would be answered by the Mother. Rage had returned the dulled hourglass to her pocket. She ran her fingers over it, wondering again why it had glowed. Had it really answered their need, or was there another reason?

Perhaps the Mother would know.

The way split again, and without hesitation Kelpie chose the left-hand tunnel, which was so low that everyone except Rage and Kelpie was forced to stoop. Bear only just fit. If the way became smaller, she would not be able to go on.

"How much further?" Billy asked worriedly, again voicing Rage's fear.

"I smell something," Elle said.

The tunnel turned a corner and opened out into a vast cavern that seemed to have no walls. The air was filled with an emerald glow, and at first glance Rage thought the cavern held a lake of luminous green water. But as they came closer she saw that there were hundreds of rivulets of shining water flowing around a multitude of small islands. The cavern was a vast subterranean wetland!

Her skin began to prickle as they approached the water. She looked down at her arms and found the hairs were all standing on end, just as they had when she approached the bramble gate.

"The Place of Shining Waters," Kelpie announced reverently, before leading them along a path where the ground was higher and quite dry.

"The witch Mother is here?" Rage asked, for the cavern appeared deserted.

"We must go beyond the hills," Kelpie said, pointing past the shining water to the darker end of the cavern.

Bear was at the end of her strength by the time they

reached the first of the dark hills, which proved to be carpeted in a thick moss. She staggered and then lay down panting, tongue lolling from her mouth.

"She must rest," Billy told Kelpie, and he sat by his mother's head and stroked the fur around her ears tenderly. Rage sank onto the soft moss, too.

Elle wandered over to peer into a streamlet of the glowing green water. Sniffing, she squatted down and cupped her hands.

"Don't drink it!" Rage cried in alarm.

Elle looked over at her in puzzlement. "Why not? It doesn't smell bad."

"I don't think it's bad. I think it's magic, and who knows what it would do if you drank it."

"You are wise to be wary of the waters, Rage Winnoway," came a woman's voice, cold, sharp, and familiar.

Rage looked around and saw the baker's sister, Rue, coming over the hill. She now wore a long, floating dress of russet brown, and her unbound hair hung in a wild and shining tangle to her knees. Woven through it were leaves and flowers, and a plait circled her brow like a crown. She looked younger than she had in the village, but no less severe. With her were two younger women in similar attire, carrying lanterns that gave off a buttery yellow light.

Kelpie went to her with an expression of shy adoration. "Mother," she murmured, and reached out to stroke Rue's hand.

"*You* are the witch Mother?" Rage said in amazement.

Rue smiled, and suddenly she was very beautiful, though her eyes remained stern. "I am."

"Your bands are—" Rage began, but Rue interrupted her gracefully.

"False, of course. But all questions that can be answered will be answered in good time. Now you must come to the place where your friends wait anxiously for your arrival." She looked at Bear with compassionate eyes. "Let the great beast sleep here. These witches will watch over her. Later she will be brought to join us."

"I will stay with her," Billy said.

"No," Rue said. "You can do nothing for her now. The witches will tend her ills, and they will work best if left to their own devices." Such was her serene authority that Billy did not argue. He took a long and longing look at his mother before leaving her side.

Rue caught hold of one of the yellow lanterns and began to walk back over the hill, holding Kelpie's hand. Billy and Elle followed, emanating excitement.

"Is the baker really your brother?" Billy asked the witch woman.

"I am Rue, who is sister to the baker and who cooks and cleans for her keep," the witch woman answered. "Unknown to my brother, I am also a witch who dwells in Wildwood when I can."

"Why are you called Mother?" Elle asked.

"To remind me that I do not rule the witch folk for my own pleasure or gain. Like a mother, I love and I serve and I nurture. Occasionally I scold."

Rage swallowed a lump in her throat.

As they left the wetlands behind, they also left the shining waters, and it became very dark and silent. The rivulets that flowed into the hills were set deep, so that they shed little light. Yet there was enough to see that there were plants growing here and there, bushes and shrubs. Rage did not know how such things could thrive without sunlight and fresh air. It must be the magic in the water. The cave did not smell the least bit musty. If she had not known better, she would have believed she was outside on a dark night.

"How did you know we had stopped back there?" Billy asked.

"There are watchers here who serve me, unseen but seeing all," the witch woman answered. "It was they who summoned me."

They reached the summit of the third and highest hill in the cavern and found themselves looking down into a small, deep valley. A grove of trees grew at the bottom, and light flowed within it, yellow like the lantern light and quite different from the eerie illumination of the magical water. This was obviously their destination, and despite all the strange and wondrous things that had happened to Rage since leaving Winnoway, something about the grove of trees in this cavern deep under the earth thrilled her to the depths of her heart and lifted the black despair that had sunk its claws into her in the dank tunnel. It was true that she was no closer to finding Mam, but she had rescued Billy and Elle from the blackshirts, and they had saved Bear from a horrible death. They were free, and together, and maybe at last they had found someone with the power to help them.

Light was thrown from lanterns suspended from tree branches and from a large bonfire in a small clearing in the grove. There were hundreds of people milling around under the trees. Only when they were closer did Rage see that the crowd consisted not only of witch folk and wild things but also, astonishingly, of gray-clad Fork citizens. Some were little older than Rage. Most looked grave and worried, but a few had wary, suspicious expressions.

There were also natural animals. A leopard with pale blue eyes, several intelligent-looking squirrels, and a number of horses were standing with a handsome male centaur. A monkey with yellow eyes sat on the centaur's back, chewing at its fingers and looking anxious. Another surprise was that some of the witch women, with their long hair and tattered robes, were not women! Apparently men could be witches as well, or at least align themselves with them. In fact, there were representatives in the grove of all the factions in Fork, except for keepers.

Rue went to the center of the clearing, where the fire was lit, and everyone began to draw nearer. She let go of Kelpie's hand and turned to Rage. "There are many things that must be dealt with at this gathering, but first you must greet your old friends." She made a gesture and two sprites came from the trees, leading Mr. Walker and a shyly smiling Goaty, his ringlets plaited with little blue flowers.

"Goaty!" Elle cried, and rushed to hug him so ferociously he gasped.

Rage knelt down and gathered Mr. Walker up, cuddling him for a long, glad moment. "I was so afraid when you didn't come back."

"I couldn't!" Mr. Walker said, twitching his feathery tail in agitation. "That vent led to a pipe, and I couldn't stop myself sliding down it. It went on and on, and I thought I was going to slide forever. But I came out and landed on a pile of soft rags. The Mother—"

"Foresaw that you would drop from a drain and arranged for a soft landing?" Rage finished the sentence for him, sitting back on her heels.

"How did you know?" Mr. Walker demanded.

Rage did not answer because a hush had fallen over the grove. The witch Mother lifted her hand, but before she could utter a word a little man the size of a three-year-old child darted out and took her hand. He bowed with a flourish and kissed her hand extravagantly. Like the fairies he had dragonfly wings protruding from the back of his brown shirt.

"Welcome, Mother," the fairy man said to Rue in a deep, elegant voice that hardly matched his comical face and plump form.

"I *wish* you would not make such a fuss, Puck," the witch Mother said crossly, sounding more like the baker's sister than a leader.

"It is in my nature to revere that which is worthy of reverence," the winged man said, and he bowed again to her. "Was I not made so?" he demanded pertly.

"I fear so," the witch woman said, but now her eyes were amused. "A miscalculation on my part, no doubt."

"I can be irreverent, too, when it is needed," he responded with a sly smile. He snapped his fingers, and two sprites ran forward with a stool for the witch.

Rage stared at the little man in confusion. Puck was a character in a play she had seen with her drama class. Rue must have named him after that character. Something about this idea seemed tremendously important, but there was no time to tease it out.

Now seated, Rue addressed the gathering. "Witch folk, wild things, citizens of Fork, natural beasts, thank you for coming. I know it is dangerous for all of us to meet in this way, and I know that some of you were reluctant to do so. Yet as I said in my message to you, Valley is dying, and we have very little time in which to save it and ourselves."

"Whose fault is that?"

Rage turned around to see a man in gray glaring at Rue.

"What is this place?" another Fork man demanded.

"Why was it necessary for me to be blindfolded to come here?"

"I was in the middle of bathing when your people came for me," a woman complained. "Why was I given no warning?"

"It would have been too dangerous to set a meeting place and time in advance," Rue said calmly. "Someone might easily have spoken out of turn, alerting the black-shirts." She paused but no one spoke. "This is the Place of Shining Waters, and it is the source of all magic in Valley."

Rage was no less astonished than the Fork people. "The wizard gave Valley its magic—" a Fork man began.

"That is true," Rue agreed. "He stood in this very grove and infused the waters in the cavern with pure magic. He knew that it would flow, as water does, up through the land, to succor all things."

"Magic no longer succors Wildwood!" a gray-clad woman said.

"The flow has all but ceased in Wildwood," Rue agreed mildly. "As it has begun to cease in the provinces, and as it will soon cease in Fork."

There were exclamations of disbelief, but there were also nods and cries that it was true, that magic *was* dying in Fork.

"In order to know the truth of what ails Fork, you must know other truths," Rue said in a voice that was suddenly chilly and majestic. "The High Keeper claims that witch folk offended the wizard and made him abandon Valley. This is not true. The wizard wearied of ruling and retreated to his castle and his arcane researches. Then he vanished. I do not know where he went. Witch folk went to dwell in Wildwood after his withdrawal to Deepwood, for we did not desire to live by keeper rules, or Order our lives as they commanded."

There was a mutter of disapproval from the Fork citizens, but Rue ignored it. "We continued to create wild things and to use magic to feed them. But I say to you that the working of magic to free wild things does not remove magic from the land."

"Then why is it that Wildwood lost magic first?" a Fork woman called truculently.

"Because the High Keeper decided it should," Rue answered flatly.

There was a loud rumble of disbelief from the crowd of Fork citizens, who had drawn together into a group. *No doubt to give themselves courage to speak*, Rage thought.

"I *knew* that the High Keeper was bad," Mr. Walker hissed.

"He smelled of badness," Elle agreed.

"*Why* did he stop the magic?" Billy muttered.

"*How* did he stop it, I'd like to know," Mr. Walker said.

"Shh!" Rage hissed, for the centaur had turned to glare at them.

"The High Keeper knows of this cavern," Rue continued, and many of those gathered looked about in alarm. "He knows it is the source of magic in Valley because the knowledge is passed from each High Keeper to his successor. I do not know why the wizard showed this to the first High Keeper. Perhaps in pride, for it was a mighty deed to freeze the moment in time within which Valley exists. Yet it was inevitable that there would come a High Keeper with arrogance enough to try to use the pure magic. The man who is now High Keeper of Fork used the power here to block the flow of magic to Wildwood. He wished to punish witch folk for their disobedience."

"I do not believe this," a man in gray exclaimed. "How do you come to know so much of the High Keeper's doings, you who have always dwelled in Wildwood?"

Rue looked suddenly weary and older. "I have dwelled in Fork. Like many, I was forced here as a girl and unwillingly banded. I made no secret of my unhappiness, and soon agents of the witch folk sought me out. I believed them when they told me that witch folk were not responsible for the harm being done in Valley, and I agreed to help them seek out the source of magic. The witch who was Mother then believed there was some blockage in the flow. She did not dream it had been done deliberately. But she knew there was no point in approaching the High Keeper for help. His hatred of us seemed to grow daily. When I was sixteen, my bands were to be replaced, and the man who was supposed to weld the permanent bands on my wrists gave me false bands. He was an ally of the witch Mother.

"Thereafter, I was secretly trained in the working of magic. Eventually I found this place, and it was here that I first saw the High Keeper dip his hands into the shining waters."

Rue paused, a challenge in her eyes, but no one spoke. "I heard him cackle and shriek like a madman afterward. He ranted his hatred of the witch folk and his horror of the wild things. I heard him command the magic to cease its flow through Wildwood. He vowed he would not reverse his order until all witches and wild things had been wiped from Valley."

She stopped. The anger in her eyes became weariness. "He was a fool not to see what any witch apprentice could have seen. One cannot stop *part* of a flow. When the High Keeper prevented magic flowing through

Wildwood, he began the process that would one day stop the flow of magic in all of Valley."

"You are saying magic is dying here because of an accident?" This from one of the witch women.

"Is it an accident when the wrong done is greater than the wrong intended?" Rue asked. "I do not think so, for wrongness is a flow, too."

"I do not believe the High One did this," a Fork woman shouted. "I did not come here to hear him accused! I—"

"You came to hear how to save Fork and yourself," snapped Rue. "Therefore listen. The High Keeper saw us as evil—"

"Yet it is he who is evil and does evil now." A new voice. The crowd drew back to reveal the speaker. Rage was amazed to see the elderly, white-robed keeper who had assisted the High Keeper in the conservatorium.

"Isn't that—" Elle began, but Billy shushed her as the old man shuffled through the crowd to Rue's side.

"Evil is only another kind of illness, Hermani," Rue said in a surprisingly gentle voice.

"Once the High Keeper was my friend," he said in a quavering voice. "He spoke with such poetry of the need to keep and Order Valley. When Wildwood lost its flow of magic, I agreed to the pogrom against witch folk because I believed you were endangering the true beasts in our care. I believed it was your fault that they had to be kept in provinces, for why else would magic have died in Wildwood? But then the High Keeper began to band children and to forbid travel. He set curfews in the city and allowed the blackshirts to punish anyone who disobeyed him or spoke out against his methods. Fork became dark. Yet I held my tongue, for I truly thought all would be healed once Wildwood was emptied out."

He paused for breath, his face haggard with grief. "But then the High Keeper began to bring natural beasts in from the provinces. He killed them and had them stuffed, claiming they could be better kept in Order dead than alive." Tears began to run down his wrinkled face. "The conservatorium grew and grew. Only now do I understand that his madness began here."

"His madness began before he used the shining waters," Rue said coldly. "It began with his hunger for power."

"At first I made excuses for him," the old man said in a broken voice. "I told myself that the animals were old or ill. That they had lived good lives. I could not admit to myself what was happening. You see, I have loved him, and to face the truth meant that my whole life had been a lie. But I could not go on seeing the animals die. I began to work with others to secretly remove from the provinces animals in danger of conservation and to transport them back over the river to Deepwood." He bent his head forward and wept in earnest. Rage felt her own eyes fill with compassion at his terrible despair.

"Do not torture yourself," Rue said, and now there was pity in her face.

At a signal, a sprite brought another stool, but the stricken keeper turned to face those assembled. "I came to this meeting because the High Keeper is mad, and I can ignore it no longer. Magic is dying in Fork, and all keepers know it. I believe the Mother speaks the truth when she says it is the High Keeper's doing. If there is hope for Valley now, it lies with the Mother and her kind."

Rue laid her hand on his shoulder, and he sat. Then

she examined the pale faces of the Fork citizens. "Many of you came here seeking someone to blame. If we can save Valley, then it will be worth understanding how this came to pass. Only then can we ensure that it will not happen again. But now we have very little time in which to act."

"How long, Mother?" a witch man asked.

"We have perhaps six months before the flow of magic is weakened so much that Valley will slide back into time."

13

"What can we do?" the centaur demanded.

"Can't we use the power in the waters here to make magic flow through Valley again?" a gray-clad woman called.

"Have you heard nothing?" Rue asked. "The magic must flow to us through the land before it can be drawn upon. Anyone attempting to reverse what the High Keeper did by using the shining waters will also be driven mad, and even so will fail. Only a wizard is strong enough to work magic against magic. Only the wizard who created this land we call Valley can save it."

"But you have already said that you do not know where the wizard went," someone pointed out bitterly.

"I said that *I* do not know where he went," Rue said softly, yet a hush fell. "There is one here among us who does know, and on that one rests our only hope." Slowly the witch woman's eyes came to rest on Rage. "Will you speak of your quest, child?"

Rage felt everyone turn to stare at her. She had never been the center of so much attention. Standing on rubbery legs, she was infinitely grateful when Billy and the others stood with her. Even Goaty stood.

"I . . . I am Rage Winnoway," she began.

"Speak up!" someone called impatiently.

She licked her lips. "I am Rage Winnoway, and these are my friends. I came from my world to Valley through a magic gateway. I wanted to see the wizard, but when I got here I learned he had vanished. I was given a riddle to solve that would lead me to him."

"Say the riddle," Rue commanded.

"'Bring me to the shore of the Endless Sea, step through the door that will open for thee.'"

There was a burst of derisive laughter. "There is no such place as the Endless Sea," someone cried.

"Oh, but there is," the Mother said, her eyes holding Rage's.

Rage opened her mouth to say that the riddle had been engraved on the bottom of the hourglass given to her by the firecat, but to her astonishment she could not speak. She tried again. Nothing came from her mouth. There *was* some sort of magic stopping her! No doubt this was the firecat's doing.

"Who gave you this riddle?" Rue asked.

"I . . . I can't say," Rage said, and was relieved to find she had not been silenced altogether.

Billy gave her an odd look and opened his mouth, but nothing came out. He could not speak of the firecat, either.

"Then we will not press you," Rue said. "But you have solved the riddle, have you not?"

"I thought I had," Rage said, and despair welled in her anew. "I thought that since all rivers flow to the sea, then maybe a magical river would flow to a magical sea."

"The Endless Sea," Hermani murmured.

"I thought it would be possible just to get a boat and go down the river—until I saw it."

"You would not make this journey for the sake of your mother?" Rue asked.

"I would gladly, for her sake and for the sake of Valley," Rage said, feeling the weight of all those eyes on her. "But it wouldn't be any use. No one could travel down the River of No Return and *live*."

"It is not fitting to ask a child to undertake such a dangerous journey," Hermani said with quiet dignity. "I will attempt it. Perhaps some of the rivermen who have been working to save the true beasts can accompany me."

A man stepped forward, and Rage was not too surprised to see that it was the ferry captain. "Aye, we will aid you, keeper. It would be a quest worthy of a bard song and a nobler end than dying in a flood of water, if it comes to that."

"A noble end indeed," Rue said with some asperity. "But it is not heroic deeds for bard songs that we need. I tell you bluntly that you will not attempt this journey. You would fail. Death is the destination of any here who would attempt to reach the end of the River of No Return."

There was a silence, and faces fell.

"You brought us here to tell us of our doom?" Hermani asked.

Instead of answering him, the witch woman turned to Rage. "Child you are, Rage Winnoway, yet more than that, too. I did not speak idly before when I said that upon you rests our only hope."

Rage stared at her. "But . . . you just agreed that no one could survive the journey."

"I said no one here. Look." On Rue's palm lay a pink-gold locket.

"Mam's locket," Rage murmured, glancing over at the ferryman.

"It is very old, and strong with images of many kinds of love and sorrow. Perfect as a focusing object. I saw the accident that hurt your mother, child. But know that her illness, this sleep, was not caused by that accident. It is the result of a deeper, longer affliction."

Rage stared silently at the witch woman. The witch woman must be mistaken. Mam was certainly asleep because of the terrible head injuries inflicted on her in the accident.

Rue continued. "I saw you and your quest here. I had thought the Endless Sea a myth, but then I dug deeper. Finally, in an old tome, I found mention of it as a true thing. It was not difficult to discern that you believed the wizard had gone to the Endless Sea. But I could not guess how you meant to get there."

"Why didn't you send someone to ask me, or come yourself?" Rage asked.

"We witch folk have learned to move slowly and carefully in all things, but especially where magic is concerned," Rue said. "For all I knew, your journey was wound about with delicate enchantments, which my interference would undo. I sent my people word to give you what help they could and to tell you that my desire was yours: to find the wizard and let him know that Valley needs him. I thought that if you reached the wizard, you would surely tell him this."

"Why did you bring us here now?"

"Before you appeared, I had come to believe that no single group in Valley would be able to come up with a way to save us," Rue said. "That it would take all of us to find an answer, and this gathering was long planned to that end. But once I reached Fork and learned from Ania of your shock upon seeing the River of No Return, I knew what I had hoped. Only then did I perform a difficult and costly working of magic, using that trinket as a focus. It was during this working that I saw Mr. Walker fall into the drain near one of our secret places, and you and your other companions trapped behind a grille in the lower tunnel system that leads to this cavern.

"I made arrangements for Mr. Walker to be met, and I sent Kelpie to find you and bring you here. It was Mr. Walker who told us of Goaty waiting for you by the river, and so I had him brought here, too." Rue's voice cracked. She made a motion that brought one of the sprites with a cup of water.

"I don't understand why you say that *I* can survive the journey when no one else could," Rage said.

"I performed the magical working to ask if there was any way in which Rage Winnoway could survive a journey down the River of No Return."

"What did you learn?" Billy asked eagerly.

"I learned what I had sensed all along," Rue said. She turned to look at those gathered. "Only in unity can we save Valley." There were confused looks and muttered questions and exclamations that eventually dwindled to silence. "My vision told me that Rage Winnoway and her companions had the best chance of negotiating the river and finding the wizard, but that *we* must provide for her a vessel that will endure the journey."

"But how?" a Fork man asked. "No boat could survive the waterfall."

"I do not speak of any ordinary boat," Rue said. "I

mean we must create a magical vessel. Such a thing can be provided only at great cost."

"What cost can be too great for the saving of Valley?" Hermani cried.

"Time," Rue said flatly. "It will cost time. These vessels can only be created from magic, but this working will do what we witches have long been accused of doing—it will drain magic from Valley, to the extent that the six months or so we have left will be reduced to a few days."

There was an aghast silence.

"You ask us to sacrifice the little magic now flowing in Valley to bring this girl and her companions safely down to the Endless Sea?" the ferryman asked. "Why not send only her? There will be less of a drain for a vessel for one than for six."

"The chances of Rage Winnoway fulfilling her quest will decrease if all of her companions do not travel with her. I do not know why, but that is what I saw. To know more would cost more than I will pay," the witch answered evenly. "Also, I do not know how long the journey to the Endless Sea will take, nor if Rage Winnoway will find the wizard. I know only that she *may* succeed where no other would."

"Why her?" someone called. "She is a stranger to Valley."

"This I tried to learn, but my vision was obscured in ways I do not understand. I saw only that there is some link between Rage Winnoway and the wizard, which increases her chance of finding him."

There was a loud buzz of troubled talk. Rage knew that the link was the hourglass she carried, but of course she was unable to say so.

"We have no choice," said Puck. "We will certainly die in six months if we do nothing. If we help her, we might die in a few days, but we might also save ourselves. We would be fools to choose six certain months of life over the possibility of living full lives."

"Yet we may find our own solution in six long months, and remember, the witch woman has not said that the girl and her friends *will* reach the wizard, only that they have the best chance of reaching him," a Fork man argued, sounding troubled.

"Maybe the wizard knows of all that besets us and will return at the last moment," Hermani suggested.

"We must quickly make a decision about whether or not we will aid Rage Winnoway, else there will not be magic enough to do it without destroying Valley," Rue said. "I will give you one hour to talk, and then we will see what has been agreed upon."

"There is no point in us talking. We have never been able to agree on anything." Hermani sighed. "I say the witch Mother will decide for us."

There were cries of "yes" and "no," mixed with groans of uncertainty. Rage had no idea what to say. She wasn't even sure how she felt, because a queer numbness seemed to have stolen through her senses. The only thing she knew was that if there was a hope of her finding the wizard—the merest bit of hope—she would go.

Rue said nothing until all the shouts and murmurs faded. "Even if you wish it, I will not decide for you," she announced. "I am Mother, yet you are not children. You must take responsibility for yourselves. Again I say, go and talk among yourselves. Seek for an answer together. In one hour I will hear what you have decided."

She turned without waiting for a response and

walked briskly away into the trees. After a moment of bewilderment, in which no one seemed to know quite what to do, the crowd broke up and began walking this way and that or sat in groups. A buzz of talk arose and became steadily louder.

"They will have to give us the vessels," Elle said, her eyes gleaming with excitement.

"They don't have any choice," Billy agreed.

"But that man was right. The witch Mother only said we would have the *best chance* of surviving the journey," Mr. Walker protested. "She didn't say we *would* survive it."

"She didn't even ask if we agreed to go," Goaty said timorously.

"She didn't have to," Elle said. "If we stay, we'll only have six months to live, like everyone else. This way we have a chance at life. And besides, Rage must get to her mam."

"I'm scared," Goaty whispered.

"It will be a great adventure," Elle said, clasping his shoulders.

Billy had a peculiar look on his face. Rage asked him what he was thinking. "I was wondering how Mama is," he said, seeming to read her mind. Rage felt a stab of guilt, and he saw that, too. His expression changed. "It's not your fault Mama is exhausted, Rage. I'm not sorry we came."

"You're not?" Rage asked in disbelief.

"If we had not come, Mama would be the same as she was before. She lets me come close to her now, and sometimes she tells me things. Last night she said she dreamed of me when she was inside that killing box in the conservatorium. She dreamed that I was calling her. . . ."

Elle leaned over to them. "I've just been thinking. If they refuse to magic a boat, I will use the six months to visit Wildwood and see the winged lions again. Then Goaty and I will go to the mountain province."

Goaty gave her a look of adoration.

"I would go to the castle in Deepwood," Mr. Walker said dreamily. "Perhaps there is a magic mirror there. I have always wanted to look into one."

"I would like to see the outermost villages," Billy said.

He looked expectantly at Rage, but before she could speak, Kelpie appeared. "The Mother has asked me to bring you to her."

They followed her through witch folk and gray-clad humans, wild things and true beasts, all talking earnestly and shaking their heads or pounding hands or paws or hoofs, and into the dense trees, which smelled of pine needles and sap. Silence descended around them, and the only sounds were of twigs snapping under their feet and their own breath.

Through the greenish black darkness Rage saw an ancient, thick-waisted tree with great serpentine roots coiling in and out of the ground. A chattering streamlet of the magic water ran close by, bathing the gnarled arms of the tree in a bright emerald glow. Beneath it sat Rue, with Puck and several sprites. The leopard lay dozing at her side, the nervous monkey curled between its paws. Rage was startled to see that in the midst of this exotic tableau, the witch woman was sipping tea out of a flowered teacup.

"Sit, and be welcome," Rue said.

"Do you know what they will decide?" Rage asked.

"I do not, nor will I seek to know what a little patience will give me."

"I taught you patience," Puck said, and leered winsomely at her.

Rue smiled and stroked his shaggy hair. "I have learned much from you and your kindred, little one." She looked at Rage again, her eyes gentler than before. "I am sorry I snapped at you, but the price a witch pays to foresee each glimpse of the future is the loss of that much of his or her own life. So you see, it is not done lightly. Now eat, for that is why I invited you to join me."

She pointed to a picnic cloth laid with buttered scones in a silver tin and more teacups, a plate piled with thick sandwiches, and another with rock buns and little iced cakes with cherries on the top. "You need not fear that it will bind you or enslave you, as so many stories claim of magicked food." She addressed these words to Mr. Walker, who had drawn back in alarm.

Her words rekindled a question that had occurred to Rage when she first heard Puck's name. "How do you know so much about fairy tales and plays from my world?"

Rue quirked an eyebrow at her. "I know nothing of the stories from your world. I spoke only of stories here. Perhaps the same stories are told in all worlds," she said lightly. "Or maybe the wizard learned them from your world and taught them to the first people he brought here. My ancestors."

"There are no wizards or magic in my world," Rage said.

"Our wizard must have been in your world for some time if he created a magical gateway there," Rue said as a sprite poured more tea from a flowered teapot. "And perhaps there are others of his kind in your world. After all, wizards are only people who have discovered how to draw on the power that flows between all matter."

Rage tried to ask about the firecat, but again she was unable to say a word. She gave up and asked, "Why do you think the wizard left Valley?"

Rue shrugged. "I do not think he was evil. If he knew what had happened here, I have no doubt that he would return." She gestured to the food again. "Now, eat!"

Elle and the others did not have to be asked twice. In no time the picnic had been consumed down to the last crumb. Rage managed only to nibble at it politely. It seemed to her that hours had already passed, and all she could think of was that the decision made would decide whether or not she would see her mother again. She refused to contemplate that they would not survive the journey. Rue would not let them go unless there was a good chance they would succeed.

As if she felt Rage's thoughts, the witch woman looked up. Then she said, "I would ask something of you. I sensed that there had been images inside the locket. May I see them?"

Rage groped in her pocket until she found the two tiny photographs, and she handed them to Rue.

"This is the boy for whom your mother grieved so deeply," Rue murmured, looking at one.

"That is my uncle," Rage said, leaning closer. "It was taken a long time ago. He went away and never came back." She wanted to ask if the witch could see where he was and what he was doing, but having learned the cost of looking into the future, she knew she could not.

The witch examined the other photograph with a strange expression. "This is your grandmother?" Rage nodded. "I thought so. This woman is connected to the wizard."

"But—but that's not possible," Rage stammered.

"I sensed it before I saw this image. But now I am

positive," Rue said. "Perhaps they met when he was in your world."

Rage tried to explain that the photograph of Grandmother Reny had been in the same pocket as the wizard's hourglass, but again she was unable to utter the words. She tried to take the hourglass from her pocket but could not. The effort made her so hot she began to sweat.

"I do not know why I cannot see the connection clearly." The witch sighed as she gave the photographs back.

"Someone comes," Puck announced, and Rage looked up to see the renegade keeper they had met in the blackshirt prison. Accompanying him were a sprite, a timber wolf with an enormous ruff of silvery fur at his throat, and a witch bearing a lantern.

"Thaddeus," Rue said, and her sharp face was softened by a new warmth. She stood and embraced the man. "It has been too long."

"Too long indeed. I have not seen you since you were a girl fighting Order in Fork. I never knew you had become the Mother to whom I sent my secret messages. The fairies I brought here told me. Do you know, it was you who originally made me begin to wonder about the provinces? All your endless questions. I was just now on my way to Wildwood, having escaped the blackshirts, when I met a witch who told me that the long-planned meeting was to take place. I hastened here with her, thinking I would speak of what I had seen in the provinces, but I am told you have a more important voice than mine to testify to what is being done to the natural beasts."

"No less than Hermani. I did not dare hope he would

be brave enough to come to this meeting."

"He is not a coward. He found himself in an agonizing position, having to kill natural beasts for the High Keeper."

"He continued to support the High Keeper though he knew him to be evil," Rue said coldly.

"He was not evil in the beginning," Thaddeus said.

"Few are, but his nature was clearly flawed. It was madness to name him High Keeper."

"Peace, dear one," Thaddeus responded gently, and he kissed her palm. "He was brilliant and full of zealotry and bright ideals. He made us feel that we were doing something worthwhile and beautiful in keeping Order. Something necessary and honorable."

"How some people do love to control the worlds they live in," Rue said with sudden bitterness. "Ever does it lead to repression and pain."

Thaddeus shook his head. "Rue, at the time he seemed the answer to our lost sense of purpose."

"It is a pity you could not simply live," she said coolly.

He sighed. "People can change. Even keepers. Am I not proof of that? But tell me, how is your brother?"

"Sweet-hearted and stubborn as ever. He would be glad to see you. Come and eat. You have missed the meeting but not the picnic." All at once the plates were piled with food again, only there was more of it, and even a cake with cream and strawberries.

"A magic tablecloth!" Mr. Walker sighed ecstatically, and reverently took another iced cake.

"I am pleased to see you have come to safe hands," the man said to Rage. He looked back at Rue. "Is it true what they have been telling me? This child and her companions are our only hope of reaching the wizard?"

"What you have been told is true, but let us leave speaking of these things. I am weary with speculating most of all."

"I don't understand about the animals in the provinces," Billy said. "The ferryman said there was sickness among them."

The renegade keeper gave him a sorrowful look. "It is true, but it is not magic's fading that hurts them. It is nothing more than that they are natural beasts and do not thrive while penned away from one another, protected, sterilized, and controlled. It has been so since the provinces were created, I am afraid. It was thought they would adjust in time. But natural animals must be wild, and things grew steadily worse. They breed badly and do not thrive in captivity. This was why the High Keeper's practices found favor."

"I don't understand why the High Keeper just went on pretending it was the witches' fault that magic was fading in Fork. He must have known that wiping out witches and wild things wouldn't save Valley," Billy said.

"I don't think he was capable of reason by the time Fork began to be affected," Rue said. "You heard Hermani. In the beginning the High Keeper was no more than a zealot. Once he drank the shining waters, I doubt he was able to see beyond his hatred for those who opposed him."

Rage wanted to ask where the keepers had come from and why they had been given charge of natural animals in the first place, but Rue stood. "They are ready. Let us return to the clearing."

Rage's heart thumped as she followed in the Mother's wake. If the folk of Valley voted not to help her find the wizard, she would never see Mam again. But if they voted to help them, then she and the others faced a terrifying journey into the unknown. And what if they got to the Endless Sea and the wizard was not there?

There was silence as the Mother walked to the center of the clearing to stand by the fire. "You have made your decision. Is it unanimous?"

A chorus of voices confirmed that it was.

"Who shall speak for you?" she asked.

"I will," the centaur said in his deep, thrumming voice. He stepped forward. "It has been agreed that Rage Winnoway and her companions shall be given the means to travel down the River of No Return in search of the wizard."

14

A group of wild things and witches appeared, carrying what looked like three enormous soap bubbles. Rage stared at them in disbelief. Surely these were not the invulnerable vessels whose creation had reduced the life span of Valley to mere days!

Rue ordered that the bubbles be set down by the cavern wall. Everyone gathered to examine them.

"This is what the magic produced?" Thaddeus asked worriedly.

"It is," Rue said. "I asked for a mode of travel that would survive the journey and keep those within safe."

"Perhaps there was not enough magic," Hermani murmured.

"There was enough. But Valley has only two days remaining."

Rage looked around at the people of Valley, understanding that it had taken great courage to agree to help them. She and the animals were about to undertake a possibly fatal journey, but in a way all of Valley would share the danger. Their sole hope was for her to find the wizard and convince him to return to

Valley. And it had to happen within two days.

Rage ran her hand over the surface of the nearest bubble. It gave beneath her fingers, and she quailed inwardly at the thought of facing the savage River of No Return in such a flimsy vessel. Beside her, Goaty was as pale as his ringlets and trembling visibly. She could not think of a thing to say to comfort him.

Elle went to him and put her arm around his shoulders, looking as fearless as ever. She whispered something in his ear and, surprisingly, he ceased shivering and gave her a shy smile.

"They don't look very strong," Mr. Walker muttered.

"No more are they," Rue said tartly. "The raft boats are strongly made, but they are smashed to pieces. The secret of the river is that one cannot fight and master it, for it is too powerful. One must accept its strength and bend to it. One must face all of its magnificent power with humility. These bubbles are the humblest of crafts, and they will carry you safely with the flow of the river. There is magic in their making that will allow them to bear your weight and keep upright. You will have to ride two apiece."

Looking at the transparent spheres, Rage thought of how fragile they were to carry such a weight of hopes. Yet Rue's words made sense: one could not oppose violence with violence. Rage had only to remember Grandfather. He had fought the sorrow of losing his brother with a harshness that had only driven his son and daughter away.

The tops of the bubbles were lifted away. Rage watched as Elle, Mr. Walker, and Billy tried them out. Bear watched Billy, her expression impossible to read. After some rearranging, it was decided that Goaty and Elle would go in one bubble, Mr. Walker and Bear in another, and Billy and Rage in the last. Rage got in when the others were settled. The bubble felt hard and slippery, like a glass in soapy water.

"Will you magic the bubbles to the river from here?" Elle asked Rue when they had climbed out to say goodbye.

"There is no need," Rue told her. "The river passes on the other side of this wall of stone. I will open the wall with magic."

"Won't water pour into the cavern?" Mr. Walker asked anxiously.

"Will it be dark under the river?" Goaty asked in a tremulous voice.

"What if the bubbles hit something?" Billy asked, moving closer to Rage.

"You will see," the witch said. She looked at Rage. "Are you ready?"

Rage swallowed a lump of fear lodged in her throat. "I'm ready," she said.

"Then I will open the way." The witch knelt and pressed one hand to the earth.

Rage heard a loud ripping sound as the stone wall opened in a wide seam and out of it came a deafening roar. The lanterns flared, and all at once she could see the river thundering by, cloudy with froth and debris. But it was not flowing horizontally. It was flowing downward.

It took some seconds for Rage to realize the water was falling rather than flowing. Then she understood. They were looking out onto the underside of the water-fall.

The witch woman came to stand beside her, and the wind from the falling water blew her hair into a dark halo as she turned. "Thank you," Rage said.

"It is I who thank you, Rage Winnoway," Rue responded serenely, and that was all.

Rage had half expected a speech. "I will do my best to find the wizard and make him listen," she promised, wishing that she had been able to speak of the hourglass and the firecat. "I will tell him everything that I have seen and heard."

"Let us hope it does not take long," Rue said. "Make yourselves ready."

Rage and Billy settled themselves as best they could in a shape with no bottom or sides, and Rue motioned for the top to be replaced. As it sealed seamlessly with the rest of the bubble all exterior sound was cut off, including the roar of the river.

"I hope there is enough air in this," Billy said to Rage. His voice sounded thin and strange in the enclosed space.

"I wish it were over already." Rage felt half suffocated.

All three bubbles were carried carefully to the brink of the opening. Rage experienced a moment of pure mindless terror as she looked down into the black abyss.

"It will be all right," Billy said. He smiled reassuringly at Rage, and she struggled to match his pretense, seeing that it was another kind of courage.

The bubble containing Mr. Walker and Bear was the first launched. With her heart in her throat, Rage watched Thaddeus and the ferryman push it over the edge. Immediately the water bore the bubble down and out of sight. Billy squeezed her hand so hard it hurt.

Then it was their turn. Their palms were slippery now, but they held on tight. Rage looked back at the Mother, and their eyes met for a second before there was a lurching sensation. Then they were falling, and the river was falling with them and around them.

Rage fought against her fear, knowing that if she gave in to panic, she would go mad. She wanted to stand up straight and stretch out her arms and legs and breathe freely. She wanted to scream.

Suddenly there was a great thud and they were under the water with bubbles and debris.

And darkness.

Now they were swept forward. The bubble stayed upright, but they were thrown violently from side to side. Finally, Billy put his arms around Rage. They pressed together, bracing their feet against the bubble to stop themselves being battered.

Rage discovered that she was no longer afraid. It was as if she had felt all the fear she was capable of feeling. A numb dullness stole over her and, incredibly, she began to fall asleep. She tried to stay awake, but her eyelids felt as if they were weighed down with lumps of steel.

"Billy," she muttered, surprised at how loud her voice sounded in the silence of the bubble. Maybe she was getting sleepy because the air in the bubble was being used up.

"Sleep," Billy said, kissing her forehead. "I'll hold on to you. I'm not tired."

She knew he was lying, but she did not have the strength to resist his kindness. And so, in all that flooding darkness, she slept. Her last waking thought was that perhaps it was the river that was endless, and not the sea.

Rage dreamed that she was on a roller coaster. Billy was with her, in his human form, and she could smell popcorn and hot chips and hear the sound of music and the screams of people behind her.

Then she heard her name being called.

"Ra-age!"

"Who is it?" she asked, and suddenly she was standing on the ground and there was no sound but the wind, and nothing but a dark rise in front of her. It took her a moment to recognize the hill above Winnoway. It was night, and the stars were so bright they might have been pressing themselves toward her.

Rage should have been frightened, but she wasn't.

"What do you want?" she called. Looking around, trying to see who had cried out, she saw a falling star.

"Help . . . ," the voice called. It was quite loud, but there was a violent crackling that made it almost impossible to hear. "Break . . ."

It was the voice she had heard in the forest, urging her to break the spell that held it prisoner. "Who are you?" she called.

"Break . . . ," the voice begged.

"I don't know how," Rage cried.

The dream shattered into pieces around her, and she fell through it into another.

Now she was walking through a strange house. A strong wind blew. Her cotton nightie flapped and fluttered against her bare skin. There was no furniture in the rooms and nothing on the walls. The floor was made of some kind of pale, knotty wood with a bluish tinge, and the walls were all white. There were no doors, only open doorways. There was no glass in the windows, but long white curtains coiled and flagged wildly in the wind. One of them brushed Rage's cheek. It felt like someone's fingers touching her face.

She heard her mother's voice. "Mam?" she whispered eagerly.

"Rage!" Mam called, and somehow the wind was in her

voice. "Sammy?" She sounded like a little girl. "Sammy?"

Now Rage was standing on the deck of a ship. The sound of the sea filled the air. Again it was night. A full moon hung among the glittering stars. A man was staring up at it. Rage saw that it was the man with the black, shaggy hair whom she had seen in the jungle. He was not wearing dark glasses now, and she was amazed to see that his eyes were the same color as hers. Winnoway eyes. She reached out to touch him. He started and looked her way, but it was clear that he did not see her.

He reached into his pocket and took out a letter. He stared at it for so long that Rage became curious. She peeped over his arm and was stunned to see her own address written there in a scrawled and childish hand.

The ship hit something, and Rage was thrown hard to the deck. She lay there with her eyes closed, finding it curiously hard to open them or to move. She knew she was lying still, but at the same time she felt as if she were rolling over and over.

Is the ship sinking? she wondered, dazed.

Someone shook her arm, and the world behind her eyelids grew red and bright, the air warm.

"Rage!"

It was Billy calling her. Rage forced herself to open her eyes. She was sitting on a white beach, facing a perfect blue sky. An endless blue ocean unrolled heavy and gleaming onto the shore before turning into froth that was so white it glowed as it sank hissing into the hot sand.

"The Endless Sea," she murmured.

"It's an endless beach as well," Billy said. "There's nothing in either direction but sand and more sand."

Rage turned and saw the graceful undulation of sand

dunes. The beach all around them glittered with shards of broken glass.

"The bubbles exploded just before we hit the shore," Billy explained. "Mama and Mr. Walker saw us land, but Elle and Goaty haven't come yet."

Rage noticed that Bear was sitting behind them, licking her paws. Mr. Walker was standing by her, staring out to sea with a dazed look on his face.

They heard a call, and she turned and saw two dark specks approaching. "It's Elle and Goaty!" Billy said in relief.

"What now?" Mr. Walker asked when they had all got over hugging one another and exclaiming about their incredible journey. Even Bear suffered being hugged by them all, and Rage was astonished to see her sit down and rest her head on Billy's lap of her own accord. He stroked her brow with reverent tenderness.

"We will wait," Rage said, taking the hourglass from her pocket. There was a single grain left. It fell very slowly, even as they watched.

"If this means the wizard's life is nearly over, he'd better hurry up," Mr. Walker said.

"Wasn't it strange how we couldn't talk about the firecat or the hourglass to the witch Mother," Elle said. "The firecat must have cast a spell on us."

"I guess it didn't want anyone to know about it or the hourglass," Rage said. "Maybe it was scared the witch Mother would take it from us."

"How much time do you suppose it took us to get here?" Mr. Walker asked Billy.

"No more than a few hours, but maybe Valley time is different from time here," he answered.

"Like in Narnia," Mr. Walker said eagerly. "You might be away for only a little while, but when you return, any amount of time might have passed. Even years." His face fell as he heard what he was saying.

"It might work the other way," Billy said. "Years might pass here, but only a few minutes there."

"Or maybe no time at all," Rage said. "Remember how the witch Mother told us that the wizard took Valley out of time?"

"We have to do something!" Elle declared. "Shouldn't we search for the wizard?"

The air popped and buzzed. A bright orange creature shimmered into existence on the sand nearby.

It gave off such an intense, hot light that Rage was forced to step back. Squinting against the brightness, she saw the flaring eyes and sharp teeth of the firecat.

"No need for worrying. Firecat being here." The smoky voice of the creature insinuated itself into the bright air.

Rage realized she had been half expecting it to appear. "Where is the wizard?" she demanded.

"Only a little more doing before finding him," the firecat promised.

"We are not doing anything else or going anywhere until you answer some questions," Rage snapped, fed up. "You've lied to us and you've kept things from us, and then you cast a spell so we couldn't even talk about you. Why did you choose us to bring the hourglass here, and what is it for, really?"

"Ragewinnoway wanting to talk or wanting to find wizard?" the firecat asked with silky malice. "Time running out for sleeping mother."

"All right," Rage said stiffly. "Where is he?"

"Stand," the firecat said, a note of triumph in its voice. "Take hourglass. Speak these words: 'Night gate! Appear!'"

Rage obeyed. The hourglass glittered in the sunlight as she spoke the words. They echoed oddly in the air, as if they were being repeated again and again, by many different people.

A slab of pure darkness appeared.

Rage moved back, then stopped. The lines engraved on the hourglass said to step through a door on the shore of the Endless Sea. This darkness was a door. The hair on her arms prickled just as it had by the bramble gate.

"Ragewinnoway must go through night gate," the firecat commanded.

"It doesn't smell like the bramble gate," Elle said, sniffing at it.

"It doesn't smell of anything," Mr. Walker said.

"Ragewinnoway must take the hourglass through night gate *now*," the firecat insisted.

Rage didn't trust the firecat one bit, but what else was there to do? She hadn't come so far just to turn away from the final step of her quest.

"Where will it take me?" she asked.

"To wizard!" the firecat shrilled in fury. "If not going now, then never going."

"I don't like this," Mr. Walker muttered. "Why is it so eager for you to go?"

"It's a liar, and it stinks of lies," Bear growled.

"I don't have any choice, Bear," Rage whispered. "I'm scared, but I have to go."

"Now or never," the firecat hissed. There was a desperation in its voice that told Rage this really was the last moment in which she could act.

"I am Rage Winnoway whose name is also Courage," she said, and stepped toward the door.

"No," Billy cried, grasping her arm and pulling her back. "I'll go first."

"Let *me*," Elle insisted, pushing them both aside.

A violent crackling sound filled the air. Then an explosion threw them all to the ground.

The firecat screamed: *"No!"*

"What happened?" Billy asked groggily.

"A trick! I knew it was a trick!" The firecat's voice sizzled with fury.

"Mama!" Billy howled, and Rage knew that Bear had gone through the gate while they were arguing.

"Where is she?" Rage demanded angrily of the firecat. "Where did you send Bear?"

"Gone!" it hissed venomously. "Gone forever into the black and the nothingness. Gone!"

Then there was another explosion. Rage flew sideways, as if a giant hand had slapped her. She fell into darkness.

15

"Rage . . ." It was the voice that kept asking her to break the spell that bound it.

"I don't know how to help you," Rage muttered. Something heavy was pressing down on her. Something monstrous and unbearable.

She felt a hand on her cheek, and a prickling tingle ran through her body.

She opened her eyes to find a man staring down at her. He was very thin and rather old, with faded amber eyes. He wore jeans and a white T-shirt, and his gray hair was pulled back into a ponytail. Around him the night sky bloomed with stars.

"You . . . you are the wizard, aren't you?" she said. "It was *your* voice that I kept hearing in my dreams."

"I could only make contact when you were asleep, because of the trap spell I was under. But I gave what magical help I could on your journey."

"What help?"

He gave a slight smile. "Light when you needed it in the tunnels under Fork, mental manipulation of black-shirts at the pier, a little direction in the city when you were seeking your friends in the blackshirt prison. And I was able to make you hard to see on several occasions."

"That was you?" Rage said slowly. "But how did you know . . . where . . ." She stopped, remembering all the times the hourglass had grown inexplicably hot. The fire-cat had told her the truth when it claimed that all the wizard knew lay within the hourglass.

"*You* were trapped in the hourglass!" she groaned. And that, of course, explained why Ania's spell had backfired.

"All riddles look simple with hindsight," the wizard said. "I was trapped within that form until the sand ran out, or until it was broken."

Rage sat up and saw that although they were still on the beach, there was no sign of the others.

"I am afraid I have much to answer for," the wizard went on. "I apologize for the things that you have endured since using the bramble gate. I should not have left it there. Yet if you had not used it, Valley and all of its life would be lost."

"Why did you put the bramble gate there?" Rage asked. "And how did you come to be trapped in the hourglass?"

He held up his hands. "Dear girl, I cannot answer a thousand questions at once. It will take time."

"Time!" Rage gasped. "I forgot. There is no time! Sir, the keepers, the river . . . they only have two days, and maybe most of that has already—"

The wizard shook his head and held a finger against his lips until she fell silent. "Have no fear. I will return to Valley in time to save it from destruction. Remember that I know all that you know, Rage Winnoway. Was I not a secret companion on your journey? I know exactly what the sharp-voiced Mother of the witch folk wanted said to me. And I know what the High Keeper has become. I know the stories told of me by Niadne in the banding house, and by the baker in the village. If you could only know how it felt to be unable to speak or act. Never have I felt so helpless!"

"Did you really make Valley?"

The wizard shook his head. "Rue had it most accurately when she said I took Valley from time. The original valley exists in your world, but I seized the moment of its existence *before* it was flooded, and I turned it into a land with its own inner time."

"I don't understand."

"Valley is like that lagoon you swam in by the river," the wizard explained. "It was once part of the flow, but now it exists apart from it."

Rage nodded slowly, thinking she understood, though it was very complicated. She remembered another question she wanted to ask. "Did you really bring women to Valley to serve the keepers?"

The wizard laughed out loud. "Of course not. Look at Rue and Ania. Do they seem obedient and willing to serve?"

"Then why do the keepers—"

The wizard shook his head. "The keepers! You know, when I brought their ancestors to Valley, they were young idealists, weary of a world in which nature was squandered. I bid them take better care of it, but they quickly moved from loving and nurturing to keeping and Ordering." He shook his head. "I did not want to repress the keepers and control them. I thought that they would work it out for themselves, given time."

"Then you didn't tell them to keep Order?" Rage asked, wanting to be clear.

"Of course not! I brought humans to Valley because

I wanted to share my love of it. But the zealots among those I brought to Valley felt useless. All that energy and hunger to be doing something. First they bothered me endlessly. The pettiness of their questions and complaints! The idiocy of their ideas of improving Valley! I felt I would go mad. Generation after generation of them were the same."

"You must be very old," Rage murmured, her mind reeling at all she had been told. To think she had not even believed that magic existed!

The wizard sighed. "Those who dwell in Valley age according to Valley time. I have always spent time outside, and so I seem immortal to the Valley folk."

"I still don't understand why you made Valley into a land if it wasn't for the keepers," Rage said.

"I froze Valley to preserve it. I could not bear to think of it buried under thousands of tons of water. Lost forever to sunlight and greenness. All that natural beauty drowned for no better reason than the rules of economics and politics."

"But you made Fork," Rage said, thinking that any city buried land.

He nodded. "I did, so that the rest of Valley would remain in its natural state. Yet I sought to make a city that lived and shaped itself to nature and life. Oddly, Fork might be the most wondrous thing I have ever made. When I was in your pocket inside the hourglass, I saw that it is not only a city that reflects life but one that is truly sentient. It lives, just as Valley lives. It has been so long since I was in Fork that I had not seen this. I will restore it to light and life. The streets will be green again, and the bridges will sing."

"What will you do with the keepers?"

"I do not know," the wizard admitted. "I see no point in punishing them or locking them up. Some of them might be capable of changing, but some . . . Perhaps I will return them to the world from which their ancestors came. But I must be careful. I do not want to overreact."

"Will you stay in Valley?"

The wizard sighed. "I wish I could swear that I would, but I know my own nature. In time, curiosity and my studies will lure me elsewhere. But I will leave it better able to fend for itself. The time has come for me to atone for the things I have neglected or abandoned."

"Nothing you do will bring back the animals that the High Keeper killed," Rage said, suddenly disliking the wizard. "It won't bring back the wild things that died in the blackshirt prison or the people who were sent down the River of No Return on the death boats."

The wizard sagged before her eyes, and something began to nag at Rage. Something to do with the absence of the animals. Where *were* Billy and the others?

"Don't force your memory," the wizard advised, his eyes watchful. "When the trap spell broke and released me, you took the full weight of the shock because you were carrying the hourglass. You have been unconscious for hours. It is almost dawn."

"Where are the others?"

"Sleeping in the dunes. They were exhausted, and I said I would sit with you. It was windy down here, but I shielded you with magic. It was best not to move you."

Rage had the sensation that something heavy was lying against her forehead. "Where is the firecat?"

"It vanished as soon as it saw I was free. It was afraid of what I would do, of course. But it will return eventually. It won't be able to stay away from me."

"Then it was the firecat that trapped you inside the hourglass?" Rage's head had begun to ache. She rubbed at her temples to ease the pain.

"I am afraid I trapped myself," the wizard said. "I was so eager to be rid of the firecat that it was able to trick me."

"You are not its master?"

"Better to say I am its creator." The wizard sighed. "I was interested in what the witch women were doing in creating wild things. I wondered what would result from the creation of a thing out of pure magic. I was less experienced then, and too foolish to be aware that the things I was experimenting with were dangerous. The firecat is a thing that has no soul. It has no compassion or goodness. You see, I gave none of myself into its making."

"How did it . . ."

"Trick me? I wished to be rid of it, for it had caused endless trouble and mischief over the years."

"What did you do?" Rage prompted.

"I was determined to trick the firecat into unmaking itself. It could use magic, but the deepest workings eluded it. I told it that it could master magic if it gained a soul, and I invented a quest for a soul—the very quest you have undertaken and whose directions were in-scribed on the hourglass. But the firecat did not trust me. It demanded that I bind myself into the hourglass that it was to carry to the shore of the Endless Sea. Like a fool I did so, thinking it would not matter, for soon I would be free of the hourglass and the wretched firecat. I never imagined it would force you to undertake the quest I had set it!"

"Why did it choose me?"

The wizard hesitated. Emotions fled over his face: fear, guilt, sorrow. Finally resignation settled there. "It seems you will have the whole story from me. Well, perhaps it is time."

Rage's head started to ache again, and she lifted her hand to her brow.

The wizard looked concerned. "This should wait. . . ."

Rage was sick of being put off. "Does it have something to do with Grandmother Reny? Rue said there was a connection between you and her. Did you meet her when you were in my world? Did she fall in love with you, and then you left her? Is that why she married Grandfather Adam and then was so unhappy that she faded away?"

The wizard looked as if she had punched him in the stomach. He sat down right where he was standing. "Oh, child! Every word you say is a knife to my heart," he gasped.

Rage was astonished and embarrassed to see a tear roll down his grizzled cheek. "I—I'm sorry," she stammered.

"No. It is I who am sorry. Although I speak of atonement, and mean it, some things cannot be healed. Sometimes it is too late." He paused and wiped his eyes and cheeks with a crumpled handkerchief.

Rage did not speak. She did not know what to say.

"You ask if your grandmother Reny loved me. She did, but only as a friend. It was Adam she loved." He looked into Rage's eyes. "My brother, Adam. I am your great-uncle Peter."

"But how can you be Grandfather's brother?" Rage demanded. "You're a wizard!"

"I discovered magic as a child. Most wizards and

witches begin before they are adults. It seems adults are incapable of making the mental leaps that magic demands. I did not plan to leave my world, but when the government diverted the river to flood the valley . . ."

Rage gasped, suddenly understanding. "*Valley* is the land that used to be part of Winnoway!"

"It is a moment from the life of that valley. The last moment," he added sadly.

Rage frowned. "But Valley is much bigger than the flooded land back home."

He nodded. "I used magic to make Valley bigger within than without."

Rage stared at him in awe. Then she frowned, her excitement fading. "Why didn't you ever go back to Winnoway to see Grandfather Adam?"

The wizard's face fell into lines of grief. "We were so close as boys. He used to follow me everywhere." He shook his head. "I didn't know that my going would mean so much. I always meant to contact him. That was why I left the bramble gate open. I even created the magic mirror so that I could see him, but I never used it."

"You didn't care that he loved you," Rage accused, angrier than she had ever been in her life.

"You are a child," the wizard said, drawing back. "You don't understand."

This was a wizard with terrifying powers, but Rage was reckless with fury. "I'm not old and I can't work magic or create it, but I understand better than you do that when you hurt someone who loves you, it doesn't end there, because love is a flow, too. How come you know so much about magic but you don't know *that*? What use is magic if you can't care about people who love you?"

The wizard looked pale and shaken. "You are right,"

he whispered. "I loved my brother, but I loved my research more."

Rage's head was pounding now, and she was beginning to feel sick. "How can you ever make up for all the harm you've caused?"

"I can't," the wizard said. "My brother died of grief while I was trapped inside the hourglass. I saw it in my magic mirror, even as the firecat held me trapped in the hourglass and scried for you."

"Me?" Rage was taken aback. "The firecat was looking for me?"

"For someone that I would care about. Family. It knew the mirror connected me to my past. It sought my brother out first, but he was close to death. The firecat sought your mother next, but by the time it figured out how to activate the bramble gate, she was . . . well, as she is now. Your uncle Samuel, of course, had gone away."

"Why did you put the night gate *here*?" Rage asked.

"I had to magic a gateway that I could key to nothingness. The firecat was to come to the shore of the Endless Sea and command the night gate to appear. Then it was to leave the hourglass behind and go through it if it desired a soul. The glass would break, I would be freed, but the firecat would cease to exist."

"It was right to mistrust you," Rage said, disliking the wizard more and more. But some terrible awareness was growing in the back of her mind, pushing aside her anger and disgust.

"I told myself that lying to a soulless creature filled with malice and mischief did not truly count as a lie," the wizard said.

Rage felt a great wave of sorrow engulf her as her memory returned of the moments before the explosion. "Bear! *Bear* went into the night gate!" she cried.

The wizard nodded, his pale eyes seeming to glow.

"This is all your fault!" Rage cried. "You are a hateful, selfish man! You are worse than the High Keeper!"

"Yes," he said in a low, sad voice.

Rage could not bear to think of him as her great-uncle. "Bring her back!" she screamed at him. "Use your magic!"

"No magic can return your friend. She went out of time when she entered the night gate. She is beyond time."

"No!" Rage wept, but she had heard the truth in the wizard's voice. They had saved Bear from the river and from the conservation tank of the High Keeper only for her to die anyway.

"It may help you to remember that Bear chose to take a risk so that no one else would have to," the wizard said gently.

Rage stood up and turned her back on him. That was when she saw Billy, sitting alone at the top of a dune. His outline in the dark blue sky was unmistakable.

She went slowly up and sat by him. He said nothing. He did not look at her. Rage put both of her arms around him and held him as tightly as she could. "Oh, Billy. My poor Billy," she whispered, pressing her face into his neck.

He gave a great, wrenching sob and buried his head in his hands. Rage wept for him and for poor, sad Bear, whose life had been so full of pain and hardship. They cried until they were both exhausted, then they sat close together, holding hands as they had in the bubble.

One by one the stars vanished until the sky was a perfect sheet of darkest blue, growing lighter at the edges. It was almost dawn.

"You know, I felt that she . . . she was coming to be able to care for me," Billy said at last in a husky voice. "Coming to Valley healed her."

"*You* healed her," Rage said. "You just went on loving her and caring for her, no matter how cold and hard she was to you. These last couple of days she watched you all the time, as if she was hungry for the sight of you."

He laughed softly. The sound of it was so sad that Rage felt her eyes fill again. Letting the tears trickle unchecked down her cheeks, she felt strangely empty. She thought of something the wizard had said. "You know, she went through that door to stop you from going."

"Us," Billy said gently. "She went for all of us."

Rage brushed at some more tears. From the corner of her eye, she saw Elle and Goaty cuddled together with Mr. Walker in a dip in the sand. The sight of them asleep together squeezed her heart, for she loved them all so. As if they felt the intensity of her gaze, they began to stir, and then they were trudging across the shadowy sand to join her and Billy.

"Are you all right?" Elle asked. It wasn't clear which of them she meant, for she looked at them both with concern. Her eyes were red, too.

Billy said nothing.

"I'm sorry," Mr. Walker said, his big, soft ears and tail drooping down. He patted Billy's hand, then climbed into Rage's lap.

Elle sat down on the other side of Billy. "She always growled at me, but I can't imagine never being able to smell her again."

"I could never forget her smell," Billy said hoarsely, and Rage felt her heart must break.

Goaty said in a low, miserable voice, "She was so brave. Maybe if I had known her better, she could have taught me to be brave, too."

"I don't think anyone really knew Mama," Billy murmured. "Not even me, though I tried so hard. She showed such a little bit of herself, but I always felt that inside her was some vast, wonderful country just waiting for the sun to discover it."

That made them all silent for a long time.

"She was good," Goaty said at last. "I was never so good."

A few faint smears of dull orange on the horizon and then the sky was afire with color. They watched the sun rise without speaking, and the beauty of it, reflected in the silver skin of the sea, was so great as to hurt Rage. This was only the first of many sunrises that Bear would not see.

"I want to see it again," Billy said suddenly. He stood up. The new sun painted him golden red all over, and his hair hung over his forehead like a lick of pure bronze.

Rage got up, too. "See what?"

"The gate she went through." Billy pointed.

Rage had not noticed it earlier because they were facing the side of it. The wizard was further along the beach, sitting and staring out to sea. He turned as they approached the night gate, so at the same instant they all saw that the blackness in it had changed.

It was now filled with stars.

"What happened?" Rage whispered. It was as though they were looking at a gateway that truly led to night.

The wizard had come to stand by them, staring into the gate with a look of astounded awe. "I don't know how this could be, but it has become a world gate."

"A what?" Elle asked.

"A world gate. A gateway that can be used to travel from one place to another."

"Then Bear . . . ," Billy began with heartbreaking hope, but the wizard shook his head.

"I'm sorry, son. When Bear went through it, it was a night gate. A way to nothing." He frowned. "Somehow, her going in has made it a world gate. I have no idea how or why. It shouldn't happen. It *couldn't* happen unless . . ."

"What?" Billy asked.

The wizard shrugged. "Unless she was actually dying at the moment she entered the gateway."

Rage stared at the wizard, but she was not seeing him. She was hearing Bear pant and gasp in the tunnels under Fork, hearing the vet say she should be given an easy time, hearing Goaty say blood had come out of her mouth after they had pulled her from the River of No Return.

"She was sick," Elle said slowly. "I could smell it on her."

"She was so tired," Billy said. "She smelled tired all the time."

The wizard turned back to the door. "It has to be what happened. The night gate became a world gate because her soul magic went into it."

All of them stared into the gateway.

"Maybe the sun did come to that country inside Mama after all," Billy said, and though he was crying, he was smiling, too.

Rage thought of her own mother, waiting to be wakened.

"We want to go home," Rage told the wizard bluntly. She could not bring herself to plead with him or think about the fact that they were related. It had never mattered to him before, and it was too late for it to matter now.

"I can send you," he replied gravely.

"Will you give me magic to wake Mam?"

"No," the wizard said gently. "You see, there is no such thing as waking magic."

Rage stared at him, so devastated that she would have fallen if Billy wasn't close behind her.

The wizard only smiled sadly. "You are wise for your age, Rage Winnoway, and you have great courage, but you do not know everything."

"I don't understand," Rage said.

"Rage, your spirit shines more brightly than you can ever know. What Adam and Samuel did to Mary is what I did to my brother. They made her believe that she is not worthy of being loved. They made her feel she is unnecessary."

Rage made a strangled sound that was partly a moan and partly a cry of protest. "She is necessary to *me*! Doesn't she care about that?"

"She cares deeply for you. But she does not think you need her. She thinks her loss won't hurt you."

Rage wanted to cry at the thought that her mother would just go to sleep and leave her all alone, just as her mother's brother had done to her. One part of Rage grew cold and even angry at Mam, because a mother ought to love her daughter more than a brother. But Mam hadn't chosen to be sick. Rage thought about how Billy had just gone on loving Bear, no matter how she acted. That was real courage.

She took a deep, shaky breath and then pushed all of the coldness and the sadness out of her heart. "I am Rage Winnoway whose name is also Courage," she told the startled-looking wizard. "Send me home."

16

"I cannot summon up a world gate to send you home from here," the wizard said. "We must return to Valley and to the castle first. It will take some days, but you can—"

"No," Rage said, suddenly certain that there was no time to lose. "Can't I go through the night gate? You said it had become a gateway that would take you from one place to another."

The wizard looked troubled. "It is a world gate, but I don't know where you would end up if you went through it. You see, most gates are made by, and are therefore ruled by, the wizards who command their obedience. But this gateway . . . well, it made itself and it rules itself. *It* will decide where to send you, if anywhere."

Rage looked into the star-filled gate and smiled. "I'm not afraid. I don't believe Bear would ever hurt us."

"But it's not Bear," the wizard said. "You mustn't think that."

Billy said, "I'm not afraid, either."

"I am," Goaty said in a humble voice. "It's a terrible

thing, I know. But I can't help being a coward."

Elle said quickly, "It's not cowardly to be afraid. Sometimes it is wise." She looked at them all and said proudly, "I have named him, and you must not call him Goaty anymore."

Rage remembered her whispering into Goaty's ear just before they entered the bubbles in the Place of Shining Waters. "What is your name?" she asked him.

Goaty gave Elle a smile of shy pride. "I am Gilbert."

"Gilbert," Billy echoed. "That's a good, strong name."

"It was the name of one of my litter brothers," Elle said.

"I do not think any of you should go through this gate," the wizard broke in. "It is too unpredictable."

"I have to go," Rage said, but she looked at Goaty, who would not meet her eyes.

"Perhaps Gilbert would prefer to come back to Valley with me, rather than going through the night gate to his own world and resuming an animal life," the wizard offered.

Rage thought that there were many times in life when you had to make hurtful choices. But sometimes there was no other way to do what was right. *That* was why they had taken Billy from Bear when he was tiny. It had hurt all of them, but it had been the right thing to do.

She turned to the animals. "I have to go back, but I think all of you should go and live in Valley."

"No!" Billy said.

"Listen," Rage insisted. "You know what it's like in our world, being owned by humans and ordered and kept by them. Remember how your family gave you away, Mr. Walker?" He nodded. "And Elle, remember how they were going to kill you, the very day Mam took you from the pound?" Elle nodded, too. "And Billy, think how my grandfather treated Bear."

The wizard shifted and seemed about to speak, but then he shook his head and remained silent.

"But we belong with you," Billy said stubbornly. "We're in no danger. You'd never give us away or hurt us."

"*I* wouldn't," Rage said. "But I might not have any choice. I'm just a child, and I don't have much more say than an animal in our world. They are likely to take you all away from me because it will be a long time before Mam can come home from the hospital. I'll probably have to go into a home."

The animals stared at her soberly.

"But if your mother doesn't wake," Mr. Walker said softly, "you'll be all alone."

"I *will* wake her," Rage vowed. "But I wish I could go back there knowing that you are in Valley—all of you—living in the castle, picnicking with Kelpie and the other wild things, exploring the provinces."

"We will never see you again," Mr. Walker said in a small voice.

Rage swallowed hard. "I'll never forget any of you. Never." She looked at Billy, who had not said a word. His face was white under the brightness of his hair. She turned to the wizard. "Go now to Valley and take them with you."

"If you must go through the night gate, I think you had better go through it before we leave. It might vanish when I go."

"Yes, you go first," Billy urged in a queer, fierce voice. "At least let us see you go."

Rage fought to hold back tears and made herself smile as she took his hands and looked into his dear face.

"I love you, Billy. I love all of you, and I'll think of you every day."

She hugged each of them. Then she turned to the gate, hardly able to see it for her tears. "What now?"

"You must enter the gateway with a clear picture in your mind of where you want to go," the wizard said gravely. "If you are sure."

"I am sure," Rage said, and she was, but again she looked at Billy and felt torn in two by the thought that she would never see him again. He was staring at her so hard, she had to turn away from the pull of his eyes.

Taking a deep breath, she jumped through the night gate, but at the same time she felt something hit her hard in the back.

Then she was among the stars and she was not afraid or sad.

She was just floating.

And all at once she heard a child's voice.

What are you? it asked.

I am a girl, Rage said, or thought or dreamed. *I am Rage Winnoway.*

What is a ragewinnoway?

I am, Rage laughed, and the stars seemed to shiver at the sound.

What is that you just did?

I laughed, Rage said.

I like it. May I remember it?

Yes.

May I remember you?

Yes.

Rage felt something run through her like an enormous electric shock, only there was no pain.

So, the voice said, and now it was older and gruff and

familiar. *So that was what I was before.*

Bear, Rage whispered.

Your mind told me that this was once my name. I am more than I was then. Now I must find a new name. But I would like to give you a gift for your laughter. What do you wish for?

I want to see Mam.

Goodbye, said Bear, or whatever it was that Bear had become.

Then Rage was on the grass beside a sign that read HOPETON GENERAL HOSPITAL.

Something hit the ground beside her with a great gasping thud, and she looked around to see Billy Thunder. He gave a bark of joy and flung himself on her, licking her wildly, whimpering and wagging his tail with delight.

"Oh, Billy!" Rage cried, remembering the thump in her back and understanding suddenly that he had never intended to let her go alone.

She buried her face in his silky coat and breathed in the doggy smell of him. "Oh, I'm so glad to see you, and so sad!" She looked into his eyes, thinking of all that brightness and curiosity that had grown in him, now lost. "Do you remember everything that happened? I wonder."

Billy gave a single bark and stared at her very hard.

Her skin prickled, for his eyes looked cleverer than before. "Do you understand what I'm saying?"

He barked again, and she hugged him. Somehow, she knew, he had not lost his new ability to think. Perhaps that had been a gift from his mother. After all, he, too, had come through the night gate, and Bear must have recognized him. But he would never be able to tell her what his mother had said to him.

Billy wriggled free of her arms and barked, then pawed at the sign urgently.

"Mam!" Rage gasped. "Of course. Come on." She started to run toward the main entrance, but Billy whined and growled and tugged at the hem of her coat. "What is it?"

Billy barked again and sniffed loudly, then went a few steps in the other direction and looked back at her.

"You know where she is? You can smell her?"

He raced off.

"Wait!" Rage cried, and ran after him as he made his way around the side of the hospital to a second building. He stopped and sniffed at a door, then ran a bit and sniffed at another doorway.

"Are you sure you will be able to find her?" she asked doubtfully. He seemed to be sniffing for a long time. He looked back and growled, then barked again. He trotted to a nearby window and looked at her expectantly.

"In there?" Rage asked. He whined before sinking into a crouch and lowering his head onto his paws beside a door that said NO ENTRY. STAFF ONLY. Rage slipped through it and found herself in a shiny white hall. There was a desk in an alcove, and behind it sat a nurse. Rage's heart sank. The nurse looked exactly like Mrs. Somersby! Fortunately, she was concentrating very hard on what-ever report she was filling in. Rage began to creep along the hall toward the desk, step by careful, silent step, wishing she had some of the witch's dust.

She froze when the phone on the desk rang, but the nurse took the receiver without looking up. "Somersby. Yes?"

Rage had to force her legs to move.

"*Whose* brother?" the nurse demanded of the phone. Rage was shaking so hard that it was a wonder she could walk at all, but she was almost past the desk.

"I've never heard of such a thing," the nurse said in disapproving tones. "How do they know he's who he says?" A pause. "Incredible! And they believe that?"

Rage was in the first doorway now, but all of the beds in the room were empty. She walked to the next door quickly, now out of sight of the nurse. There were two strange men and two empty beds. She went along to the third door.

"No, she hasn't woken. . . ."

Rage hesitated, suddenly certain the nurse was talking about Mam.

"No, the doctor was here this afternoon, and he said there is very little chance of her waking now. Her vital signs have dropped, and I think it's only a matter of time. Have they found the child yet?"

Rage refused to let herself lose heart, because hope was another kind of courage. She looked into the third room. There was a young woman with bandaged eyes in one bed, and Mam, head bandaged, in the other, exactly as pale and still as Rage had dreamed.

Her heart gave a great lurch of love and terror as she approached the bed. Next to Mam, a big square machine on wheels emitted a steady beep. Wires ran from the machine to the bed and were taped to the inside of her thin wrist.

Rage took her hand and shook it very gently. "Mam?" she whispered.

Still there was no response. Outside a dog barked once. Billy.

Rage blinked back tears. "Mam, please wake. I love you. Billy and I need you. So much has happened. . . ." She wasn't making sense now. Tears were getting all mixed up with the words she wanted to say.

She won't wake, the firecat's voice sneered in her mind.

"What on earth is going on in here?"

Nurse Somersby stood in the doorway, hands on hips. "What do you think you are doing in here? I know who you are, Miss Rebecca Jane Winnoway! Look at you. How can you have got into such a state!" The nurse strode across the room, took Rage's arm, and began to pull her to the door.

"Mam!" Rage cried, pulling uselessly against the viselike grip. Outside, Billy began to bark wildly.

"What is happening here?" A doctor appeared in the doorway. "Nurse, if you can't keep control, I'm afraid—"

"This child is a runaway, and her mother is the comatose patient in bed twelve. I'll just take her out and call the welfare people."

Rage wrenched her arm free and ran back to the bed. "Mam, I know it hurt you when your brother left. I know sadness has been poisoning you for a long time. But he didn't leave you. Grandfather drove him away. Oh, Mam, if you don't wake, it'll be like you're leaving me, too!"

"You don't seem to understand that this sort of thing is likely to harm your mother!" the nurse scolded, dragging Rage away from the bed. "There are rules here. A good girl would obey them."

Rage grew very calm. She realized that the nurse, like Niadne, believed that rules were there to be obeyed, never questioned. There was no way to argue with anyone who thought like that.

She looked at the doctor. He had talked about keeping control, but his eyes were kind. "Sir, I need to be with my mother. I don't think a rule that stops me from seeing her can be a good rule."

His brows lifted. "You are impertinent."

"Is it impertinent to question a rule that seems wrong to me?"

The doctor blinked, taken aback. "Well, I suppose I see your point, but the rules here are made for the safety of our patients. All of this shouting and struggling . . ."

"I'm sorry about that," Rage said sincerely. "I was upset. But I will be very quiet if you just let me sit with her. You won't even know I'm there."

The doctor's mouth twitched. "Yes, perhaps just for a little while."

Rage resisted the urge to hug him. "Thank you, sir," she said softly.

"Doctor, really, I must object," the nurse began.

He shook his head at her. "I think the rules can be bent on this occasion. After all . . ." He didn't finish his sentence as he ushered the nurse out, but Rage knew what he meant. *After all, the patient is dying.*

Rage went to the bed and took Mam's hand again. It felt small and cold. She sat by the bed and began to tell her in a soft voice all that had happened since she had left Winnoway.

She had just got to the part of the story where Goaty was telling her that Billy and Elle had been caught by the blackshirts when the nurse came in. With her was a police officer and a woman in a dark suit who was one of the child-welfare agents who had come to see Mr. and Mrs. Johnson.

She looked down at Mam, who had not moved or fluttered an eyelash.

"Come, Rebecca," the welfare agent said, gently but firmly. "It is time to go now."

Rage wanted to shriek at her that she wouldn't go, that she had to stay with Mam. But she made herself speak softly. "Please, mightn't I stay with her? They say she's dying."

The adults looked shocked, as if by naming death she had said a swear word.

"I really think—" the police officer began, but the doctor entered.

"*Now* what is going on here?" he asked in an annoyed voice.

"Doctor, the police have come for the girl. I called them. I told you she was a runaway," the nurse said.

The doctor gave her a cool look. "I am sure you were only doing your duty, Nurse Somersby. You may leave now."

The nurse paled and hurried out, and the doctor turned to Rage. "Child, I am afraid you will have to go with the officer."

Rage saw there was no point in arguing, because there were rules he had to obey, too, and more rules that the police officer and the child-welfare woman had to obey. She told herself that if she went with them meekly, maybe they would let her come back on another day. But even as the police officer's hand settled on her shoulder, she had the deep, sad feeling that tomorrow might be too late.

"Officer?" the doctor called.

The policeman turned. "Doctor, I'm afraid the law—"

"Officer, in this hospital, I am the law. Let the girl go." His voice was a whiplash of authority, and the officer released Rage.

"Come here, child," he called, and Rage obeyed.

"You see this?" He pointed to the little television screen on the machine beside the bed. "This shows us how your mother is doing. Not long ago, things looked very grim. But right now I think you've pulled her some way back from wherever she has been all these weeks, because this little line is doing what we want it to. Now, why don't you sit down and try to pull her the rest of the way back."

He drew up a chair. Rage sat in it and took Mam's hand again. She thought the dark, curly eyelashes trembled on her cheeks.

"Speak to her. Let her hear your voice," the doctor said calmly.

"Mam?" Rage said softly, hope opening in her heart like a flower. "Mam, I love you. Please come back to me. I need you."

This time the eyelids definitely fluttered. Then Mam opened her eyes and looked straight at Rage. "My darling, I . . . I was having the strangest dream. You were in it, and Billy Thunder. You were searching for someone. . . ." Her eyes fell closed again.

Rage looked at the doctor apprehensively, but he only patted her hand in reassurance. "She's sleeping now. A proper, natural, healing sleep, and I promise you, this is a sleep she will wake from."

"It's a queer thing. The same day you ran off, that goat of ours disappeared," Mrs. Johnson said.

"It's as if he knew I'd finally called the butcher to come and get him," Mr. Johnson grunted. "Well, I suppose him and those other dogs will turn up eventually."

Rage looked at Billy, and his ears twitched—his version of a nudge in the ribs. She hid a laugh in her mug of milk and ate up the last mouthful of pie.

"Have some more, Rage dear," Mrs. Johnson said. "I've baked another one for tomorrow night, when your uncle Samuel gets here. I wonder what he'll look like after all these years. Last time I saw him he was a teenager, but he'll be a grown man now. Just fancy him coming back out of the blue like this."

"Funny, him turning up right now after all these years of nothing," Mr. Johnson grunted, blowing on his coffee. "He didn't know anything about the accident until I told him. He was calling from some strange country I've never even heard of. Said he'd been doing research and was of a mind to call. Hmph. Wonder what put it in his mind."

Rage drank her milk and thought she knew exactly what her uncle would look like. He would be tall and tanned. His hair would be as black as Mam's: the sort of hair that would never lie down and be still. He would wear dark glasses over his amber eyes.

Read about the continuing adventures of Rage,
Billy Thunder, Mr. Walker, Elle, and Goaty in
book two of the Gateway Trilogy:

WINTER DOOR

ISOBELLE CARMODY

is the eldest of eight children. Her father died in a car crash when she was young, and she grew up telling stories to her seven brothers and sisters while her mother worked at night. She began the first book in the award-winning Obernewtyn Chronicles when she was fourteen, and she won both the prestigious Children's Book Council of Australia Book of the Year Award and the coveted Children's Peace Literature Award for her fourth novel, *The Gathering*. She has also won numerous awards for her short stories. *Night Gate* is her fifteenth book. Isobelle lives with her daughter, Adelaide, and partner, Jan, a Czech poet and musician. They divide their time between homes on the Great Ocean Road in Australia and in Prague, Czech Republic.

ACKNOWLEDGMENTS

My sincere thanks to Mallory Loehr, who was a meticulous and tender editor and the perfect companion on my journey back to Valley. Thanks also to Kristin Hall and all of the others at Random House, for making my time there so special. And thanks to Bear, Goaty, Billy, and my brave little Mr. Walker, for love and inspiration.